Bedtime Temptation

Lucy should have been safe, snug underneath the covers, alone in her bed. But she was far from safe.

She was alone with the overbearingly arrogant, fearfully iron-willed Lord Geoffrey St. Athan. He smiled at her, a warm smile, unlike any he'd ever bestowed on her before, and she felt herself melting in its glow. Then he caught her hand, turning her roughly to face him. His blue eyes were dark and intense, promising no quarter. But she didn't try to pull her hand away. She wanted him to do with her as he would. A faint smile played upon his lips then, and his hand tightened over hers as they faced each other. She smiled and raised her lips to his. His kiss was arousing as he caressed her through her gown. . . .

It was a dream of course. But even as her conscience recoiled, Lucy found that she did not want it to stop. And it did not . . . not then . . . and not even when she awoke. . . .

Lucy's Christmas Angel

Sandra Heath

A SIGNET BOOK

SIGNET
Published by the Penguin Group
Penguin Books USA Inc., 375 Hudson Street,
New York, New York 10014, U.S.A.
Penguin Books Ltd, 27 Wrights Lane,
London W8 5TZ, England
Penguin Books Australia Ltd, Ringwood,
Victoria, Australia
Penguin Books Canada Ltd, 10 Alcorn Avenue,
Toronto, Ontario, Canada M4V 3B2
Penguin Books (N.Z.) Ltd, 182–190 Wairau Road,
Auckland 10, New Zealand

Penguin Books Ltd, Registered Offices:
Harmondsworth, Middlesex, England

First published by Signet, an imprint of Dutton Signet,
a division of Penguin Books USA Inc.

First Printing, November, 1995
10 9 8 7 6 5 4 3 2 1

For Marcia Carlsten

One

Exactly six months before Christmas 1816, little Emily Trevallion had a wonderful dream. There was a contented smile on her lips as she lay in her grand bed at Trevallion Park, the family estate near Windsor, for in her sleep she was far, far away from this world.

A brilliant white light shone before her as she ascended a glittering staircase. She could hear a heavenly chorus, and knew she wasn't alone. A host of shimmering figures appeared beside her, beckoning her gently toward a beautiful light at the top of the staircase. They were singing one of her favorite Christmas carols, "Hark! The Herald-Angels Sing."

She wasn't frightened, for she was among those who loved her. Someone took her hand. It was her beloved father, so handsome and dashing, with his ash-blond Trevallion hair and loving green eyes, but he was an angel now, winged and golden, like the illustration on the front of her Bible.

Tears stung her closed eyes. "Papa?" she whispered.

The light was irresistible now, and she was glowing with it, floating like gossamer, free of all feeling except joy. She saw others she'd loved and lost, relatives and friends who were very much alive in this glorious other world. A great gladness began to fill her, for her mother was waiting beyond the gleaming gates that now appeared ahead. Soon she'd be with her parents forever. . . .

But then the joy was sharply arrested, for the gates didn't open. Her mother, golden and winged too, stretched a tender hand toward her. "Oh, Emily, my precious babe, you've come too soon. It isn't time yet."

Emily caught the dear fingers and held them to her cheek. "Please, Mama . . ."

"It's too soon," her mother said again.

Fresh tears sprang to Emily's eyes as she looked up imploringly at her father. "Let me stay, Papa," she begged.

"You must go back, my sweeting, But you will join us at Christmas," he said tenderly, bending to kiss her hair.

"Do you promise?"

"We promise."

Emily felt herself being pulled inexorably away. She was falling, and the brilliant light was spinning away into a velvety darkness. The staircase began to fade, and the heavenly voices echoed and grew indistinct. "Hark . . . hark . . . hark . . ."

"Miss Emily? Miss Emily, are you all right?" Someone was shaking her.

Emily's eyes flew open and she gasped as another light flickered in the darkness. A candle! She stared up into the anxious face of her maid, Nettie, who always slept in the adjoining room.

"Are you all right, Miss Emily?" Nettie asked again, the silver cross around her neck shining in the uncertain light. Her trim figure was concealed by her voluminous white nightgown, and her tawny hair hung in two long plaits from beneath her night bonnet.

The dream's loving tendrils still coiled around the little girl, and she smiled. "Yes, I'm quite all right, Nettie."

"You were crying in your sleep. Was it a nightmare?"

Emily shook her head. "No, it was wonderful. Nettie, I'm going to be with Mama and Papa at Christmas."

The maid's lips parted. "Oh, please don't say such things, Miss Emily!"

"Why not? I was with them for a while tonight, Nettie. They told me I'd join them this Christmas, and I do so want to."

"It was only a dream," Nettie said uneasily, for tonight there was something very strange about her little charge.

"No, it was real, Nettie. I—I heard angels singing, and I think I was one too. Mama held my hand," Emily said softy, reaching up to touch the cross at the maid's throat. Suddenly her little fingers began to glow softly, but as she took her hand away again, the glow disappeared.

Shaken, Nettie drew back. "I—I think I should awaken Mr. Edwin . . ."

"Grandfather? But why? I'm all right, truly I am, and he isn't at all well at the moment. Besides, I'll sleep now." Emily snuggled down in the bed and closed her eyes again.

Nettie gazed down at the long lashes resting against the child's rosy cheeks, and her ash-blond curls spilling over the lace-edged pillow. Miss Emily was a Trevallion through and through, and one of the greatest heiresses in England. The maid hovered, still unsure whether or not to tell Mr. Edwin about what had just happened, but then decided the child was right. His heart was weak, and being told something like this might prove too much for him.

Protecting the candle flame with her hand, Nettie went quietly back into her own room, where she stood by the window for a moment, staring up at the night sky. She believed in angels and heaven, and knew that tonight something very special had happened to Miss Emily. But please don't let it have been a premonition, for it would be so sad if such a dear little girl were soon to be no more. And as surely as night followed day, Edwin's poorly heart would break if he lost her, and he'd soon follow her to the grave.

That would mean Miss Emily's uncle Robert inheriting everything. He wasn't her real uncle, for he was Mr. Edwin's stepson. His name was actually Robert Waverly, but he called himself Trevallion—not, Nettie was sure, out of love for his stepfather, but because he hoped for financial reward. There weren't any more Trevallions after Miss Emily and her grandfather, because she was the only child of Mr. Edwin's eldest son, Richard, and the second son, Nicholas, hadn't had children at all. With Emily gone, Robert would be the closest thing the old man would have to an heir.

Nettie lowered her eyes. No one liked Robert, who was scheming and spiteful, and didn't do anything unless he'd calculated it right down to the last farthing. Everyone knew he hadn't married yet because he hoped to become the Trevallion heir. The brides he could aspire to now were as nothing to the grand matches that would come his way if he were to become master of one of England's most enviable fortunes.

October of that same year was particularly beautiful, but as Robert Waverly Trevallion looked from the bedroom window of his mistress's Kensington house, he had no interest in London's autumn splendor. With his hazel eyes and wavy dark hair, graying a little at the temples, he was considered quite good-looking, albeit in a rather hard way, but at the moment his gaze was sour and his thin lips twisted cruelly as he considered what stood between him and the family fortune. Why should a ten-year-old girl and a feeble old man bar his way to riches?

His mistress stretched lazily on the bed behind him. Dorothea Weybridge was very beautiful, with a voluptuous figure, pale skin, long chestnut hair, and soft brown eyes. She was a woman with a past, and had ceased to be respectable at the age of fifteen, when she'd discovered how very generous the opposite sex could be in return for her favors. The daughter of a Cheltenham jeweler, she'd been sufficiently well spoken and educated to get by in high circles, and soon found a wealthy protector to take her to London.

Her disreputable elder brother, James, had preceded her to the capital. He was a charming but untrustworthy adventurer, always on the periphery of society, but never quite part of it. Just like her. They'd both been cast off by their father, who couldn't bear the shame of having a scoundrel for a son and a whore for a daughter.

In the years since leaving Cheltenham, Dorothea had been both kept woman and one of the sought-after demireps in a sophisticated establishment in St. James's known as the Devil's Den. Outwardly a gaming house, the Den was known in upper-class male circles as a nunnery with a supply of very stylish nuns, and it was here that she'd met Robert Trevallion.

But Dorothea was over thirty now, and conscious that hers was the sort of beauty that would soon begin to fade. Suddenly the respectability she'd once scorned had become desirable again. She no longer wished to be part of the demimonde, acceptable to gentlemen but not to ladies, and in Robert she saw a chance to achieve that aim. He might not be heir to the family fortune, but when his doddering old stepfather had the grace to die . . . She knew Robert eventually wanted a wealthy wife, but still she schemed with all the fierce determination of the survivor she was.

No man had ever had a more inventive or sensuous mistress. There wasn't a male fantasy she wouldn't enact, an erotic wile she wouldn't use, or a limit to the lengths she'd go in order to make herself indispensable. She knew no other woman could ever pleasure him as constantly or excitingly as she did, and once he realized it too . . .

She was always alert to his moods, and today knew he had something on his mind. She studied him as he stood naked by the lace curtains that kept prying eyes out, and at last she knelt up in the bed, her straight chestnut hair cascading over her pink-tipped breasts as she smiled at him. "What is it, my love? What's wrong?"

"Nothing," he murmured. Something in the street had aroused his interest. A small girl on a dappled gray pony was being instructed by her riding master, but no amount of tuition would ever make a horsewoman of her. She bumped up and down on the sidesaddle, her little face white with fear, and Robert watched until the pair turned the corner at the end of the road.

Dorothea's brows drew together. Nothing on his mind? What a

lie. "I'm not a fool, Robert. You came here today to make love, but I'd hardly describe you as ardent."

He turned, his glance flickering over her. "Are you saying I've done you less than justice?" he inquired coolly.

She knew the warning signs. "No," she replied quickly, slipping from the bed and coming to put her arms around his waist from behind. She rested her head against his shoulder. "Tell me what's bothering you," she urged softly.

"Being excluded from the Trevallion inheritance is what's bothering me," he replied. "Edwin Trevallion calls me his son, and treats me like a son in every way but the one that matters. If it weren't for dear little Emily, I'm sure I'd gain everything I desire, but as it is . . ." He didn't finish.

"Robert, you have to accept that she's the heir."

He was silent for a moment, and then gave a chilling smile. "That's where you're wrong, for I don't *have* to accept anything."

"What do you mean?"

He turned to take her face roughly in his hands. "Why are you my mistress?" he demanded suddenly.

"Because I love you," she replied quickly.

"Don't lie, my sweet, for the truth is less flattering. Like me, you have an eye to the main chance. You're a whore who wishes to leave whoredom behind, and when you look at me you see someone close to the Trevallion fortune. Except that until now, that's all I've been—*close* to it." He released her.

"I'm with you because I love you," she lied.

He looked outside again, thinking of the small girl and the riding lesson. "I intend to do something to rectify my situation," he murmured.

"Rectify? What do you mean?"

He gave a mirthless laugh. "I'm tired of having to rely upon old Edwin's largesse all the time. Damn it, I don't even own the Berkeley Square house I live in—it's his. I've done everything in my power to take the place of his two dead sons, but it's still dear Emily who'll get everything. So my sweet little stepniece has to be helped to her maker."

Dorothea's eyes widened. "Helped to her . . . ? Murder? Is that what you're saying?" she asked faintly.

"An ugly word, but appropriate."

Her mouth ran dry.

Robert went on. "And with Emily out of the way, Edwin will have to make me his heir. After that, with his age, and the grief of losing Emily, no one will question it if he's found dead in his bed one morning."

She went cold. He was serious!

He smiled. "I tell you this, Dorothea; come Christmas I mean to hold the Trevallion purse strings."

Dorothea began to tremble. "Please say you don't really mean all this, Robert," she whispered.

"I mean every word, and what's more, you and your brother are going to help me."

"James? But—"

"But what, my dear? You aren't too much of a lady, and he's certainly not too much of a gentleman!" Robert laughed, and suddenly put knowing hands on her breasts, teasing her nipples between his fingers. "What's your price, my dear? A little band of gold to convert harlot into lady in the space of a church service? What if I were to offer you that, Dorothea? Would you still shrink from the thought of murder? Or would you prefer to return to the Devil's Den?"

The Devil's Den? When he was offering marriage? Suddenly she had no scruples, but before agreeing to help him, she needed reassurance. "How serious are you about marriage, Robert?" she asked levelly.

"Completely serious. Help me get rid of Emily Trevallion, and I'll make you my wife as soon as my doting fool of a stepfather follows her to the hereafter."

It was a dangerous proposition, but one she wasn't able to resist. Excitement surged through her, and as he continued to caress her, the excitement became sexual. "I'll do whatever you ask," she said huskily, closing her eyes as he stroked her hard nipples.

He smiled. "How adorably venal you are, to be sure," he murmured.

"Make love to me again, Robert," she said, pressing closer, linking her arms around his neck, and raising her parted lips to his mouth.

He kissed her with a hunger that had been absent earlier. Aroused as much by his decision to eliminate those who stood in his way as by the surge of eroticism sweeping through his mistress, he swept her up into his strong arms and carried her back to the bed, where their wicked pact was sealed with a savage passion that almost overwhelmed them both.

Two

Two weeks later, before breakfast on a bitterly cold morning early in November, when the garden in the center of Mayfair's Berkeley Square was indistinct in a cloak of freezing mist, a groom led a thoroughbred gelding and a plump pony around from the mews lane to the door of the Trevallion town residence.

The animals' breath stood out in white clouds as they stamped and shifted restively. The door of the house opened, and Robert emerged with Emily. He was splendid in an olive riding coat and gray breeches, with a black top hat tugged low over his forehead.

His diminutive niece wore a new amber riding habit, and her green Trevallion eyes widened anxiously as she saw the pony selected for her. "Do I have to ride such a big one, Uncle Robert?" she asked uneasily.

"Big? Sorrel isn't big," Robert replied jovially. The role of fond uncle didn't rest easily with him, but he'd been playing it well since inviting the child to stay. He glanced down at her, cursing Edwin's elder son for ever siring her, and thanking God that Nicholas, the second son and onetime black sheep, hadn't contributed anything to the next generation of Trevallions.

Emily wasn't reassured about the pony. "I—I'm not a very good rider, Uncle Robert. Can't I stay at home?"

"Sorrel's as steady as a rock, and I'll be there to take care of you. Besides, every young lady should be seen showing off her equestrian skills in Rotten Row before breakfast. It's the thing, you know."

"But I don't have any equestrian skills. Grandfather never expects me to ride now; he knows how useless I am."

"Then just think how delighted he'll be when I return you to him an accomplished *équestrienne*." Robert's tone remained amiable, and before she could say another word, he swung her onto the saddle.

She blinked back frightened tears as Sorrel danced around. Trevallion Park and Grandfather suddenly seemed much more than twenty miles away on the other side of Windsor. She didn't like Uncle Robert; there was something false about him, as if behind his smiles he'd rather strike her than be nice.

Robert mounted the gelding and forced a smile. "Cheer up, in a few minutes we'll have the freedom of London's lungs to enjoy."

"Yes, Uncle Robert."

His smile became fixed. Dear God, how on earth had a dedicated horseman like Richard Trevallion spawned such a mouse? But then the smile warmed again, for if Emily were anything other than a mouse, this plan might not be so inordinately easy. It only remained for Dorothea and her brother to play their parts, and within an hour dear little Em would be no more.

He urged the gelding away over the cobbles, and after a moment the groom gave Sorrel's rump an encouraging whack to make him follow. The pony's hooves clattered, and Emily clung to the pommel, hoping the ride would soon be over.

They crossed Park Lane toward the great green expanse of Hyde Park, which stretched for a mile past the Serpentine as far as Kensington Palace. But everything was indefinite in the mist as Robert led Emily through Grosvenor Gate, past the Gloucester Riding House, and then across the frosty grass to Rotten Row, where numerous riders already paraded to and fro, undeterred by the low temperature.

Emily didn't like the park this morning. There was something dismal and almost haunted about the ghostly trees, and it was so bitterly cold that her gloved hands were frozen. Sorrel pricked his ears mischievously as he began to canter, and she was sure he sensed her fear.

Dorothea was nervous as she waited on horseback by an elm tree close to the ice-covered Serpentine. She wore royal blue, and her chestnut hair was swept up beneath a beaver riding hat. At a casual glance she appeared composed enough, but her courage was beginning to fail. She'd been terrified of water since nearly drowning as a child, and that terror was with her now. It was as if the Serpentine's dark depths were lurking menacingly beneath the ice. Oh, where were Robert and Emily?

Suddenly they emerged from the mist, and as rehearsed, she urged her horse over to them. "Why, Mr. Trevallion, what an unexpected surprise," she declared brightly.

They reined in, and Robert doffed his hat politely. "Mrs. Makepeace, isn't it?"

Dorothea gave a tinkle of laughter as she proceeded with the diversion. "La, sir, don't you remember? We met at Devonshire House last week."

Emily had never liked people with brittle laughs, and this woman had one that seemed it might splinter at any moment. The child studied her curiously, thinking her as false as Uncle Robert.

Robert smiled at Dorothea. "Actually, I believe it was at Holland House," he said, his brown eyes glittering with anticipation.

"So it was. Well, I trust I find you well?"

"Yes, madam, and—" Suddenly he affected great dismay as he pretended to notice something wrong with his mount. "Plague take it, I believe my horse is lame!" he declared, dismounting and moving around the gelding to examine the leg closest to Emily. Then he surreptitiously removed his neckcloth pin.

Dorothea distracted Emily. "You must be Mr. Trevallion's niece, Emily," she declared patronizingly.

"Yes, I am." Emily drew back from the disturbing brightness in the other's shining brown eyes. She didn't like this Mrs. Makepeace at all.

Unseen by anyone except Dorothea, Robert jabbed the pin into Sorrel's hind quarters. Emily screamed as the pony reared and bolted. Dorothea was primed as to what to do next. Pretending to be overcome at the sudden danger to the child, she slid from the saddle and fell on the icy ground as if in a faint.

Robert contrived to be stunned by the swiftness of everything, and cast around desperately for help. It was to hand, of course, in the handsome form of Dorothea's elegant brother, James, who rode up, dressed in a dashing Guards officer uniform to which he had no right.

Robert was the picture of agitation. "For pity's sake, go after my niece, sir! My horse is lame, and this lady requires my assistance!"

"Your servant, sir!" James cried, spurring his horse after Sorrel.

There was a stir all around the misty park as other riders began to realize what was happening. Even the carriages in Rotten Row came to a halt.

Emily was terrified as she clung to the pony's mane. She'd lost her stirrup, her little velvet hat had fallen off, and her ash-blond hair blew wildly about her shoulders. Tears blinded her and sobs choked her throat. Stop, Sorrel, please . . .

James timed his pursuit with precision. He could have caught the pony many yards before he did, but that wouldn't have done at all. The tree where Dorothea had waited was just ahead, and Sorrel would have galloped right past it if, at the last moment,

James hadn't urged his mount alongside and snatched the pony's reins. He made it seem his balance was affected, and swayed in the saddle, dragging sharply on the reins. Sorrel swerved violently, and Emily was catapulted forcibly into the tree trunk. There were screams from onlookers as the little girl fell like a rag doll and lay motionless on the frost-whitened ground.

But then, unobserved by anyone, something miraculous happened, for although Emily's earthly body lay on the grass of Hyde Park, her spirit floated invisibly up into the branches of the tree that had freed it. The beautiful staircase stretched up toward heaven again, and the bright light was drawing her toward the wonderful gates at the top. She could hear the angels singing sweetly, but they were distant this time, and there were no ghostly figures to accompany her. She wanted to climb the staircase, but her earthly body was tugging her back, and she knew it still wasn't time.

Then her father suddenly spoke, although she couldn't see him. "You're needed to help Lucy, Emily. Go back, for Lucy's sake."

Lucy? Emily didn't know anyone called Lucy. She wanted to ask her father what he meant, but the staircase was dissolving and the angelic singing growing faint. She looked back toward the ground, and saw herself lying there, with anxious people hurrying from all directions to help.

Her gaze went to James, who didn't linger at the scene, but rode swiftly away across the park, and she saw Dorothea hastily remounting to ride off in the opposite direction. Why didn't they stay to see if she was all right? But then her attention was drawn to Robert's fine display of anguish. The concerned crowd pressed around as he knelt distractedly by the crumpled little figure. The moment he touched her, Emily felt herself being pulled sharply down, and suddenly she was in her body again. Her lungs filled, and she began to breathe again, although she couldn't move, see, or say anything. There was no pain, but she could feel his touch and hear everything, and her mind was conscious, even if her other senses had deserted her.

Robert's dismay was huge as he heard her inhale. Somehow she'd survived the fall! For a moment his mind went blank, but almost immediately he gave a glad sob. "She's alive! My niece is alive!" It was an acting *tour de force* that convinced totally.

An elderly lady pushed anxiously forward. "I have my carriage, sir, and gladly place it at your disposal."

Robert seized the offer. "I'm grateful for your kindness, madam. If she could be conveyed to my residence in Berkeley

Square . . . ?" He gathered Emily into his arms, and carried her swiftly to the hooded landau.

For the benefit of the lady, he continued to choke back heartrending sobs as he placed the little girl gently on the blue velvet seat, and as the carriage drew carefully away, no one could possibly have dreamed he was anything less than a grief-stricken uncle. With the lady watching, he held Emily's limp little hand in his, and even managed to squeeze tears from his eyes.

Emily was still aware of everything. She could smell lavender on the upholstery, feel the vehicle's swaying motion, and hear the cries of the flower girl by Grosvenor Gate. Hers was a strange half-world. She desperately wanted to float out of her body and return to the brilliant light, but remembered her father's words. She was needed for Lucy. Except she didn't know who Lucy was.

The landau halted in Berkeley Square, and Robert scrambled out to hurry into the house. A startled footman came running, and Robert pointed at the carriage. "There's been a terrible accident, and Miss Emily is badly hurt! Send someone for Sir Joshua Carey of St. James's Square!"

The elderly lady dabbed a lace-edged handkerchief to her eyes as he carried the child into the house. The world would surely be a finer place if all were as good and loving as he, she thought.

Emily's head dangled as Robert carried her upstairs to her room. Her long hair caught on his sleeve, and when he glanced down he saw that her little face was deathly. He took heart. Surely her life could only be hanging by a thread?

But when Sir Joshua arrived, he dashed Robert's hopes for her immediate demise. After a lengthy and very thorough examination, the physician, whose hooked nose and black clothes made him resemble a tall crow, said he feared her injuries were fatal, but he could not predict how long it would be before she drew her last breath.

Robert stared at him. "Do you mean it might take days?"

"Maybe even weeks. Injuries such as these can only lead to death, but there is no way of saying when that moment will come. She may even regain consciousness, although I don't hold out much hope of that, and anyway, consciousness will not make any difference, for she still cannot survive."

The physician closed his bag. "Your father—er, stepfather—is one of my patients, and I happen to know how very fond he is of his granddaughter. While I realize the devastating effect this might have upon a man in his poor health, I still feel he should be sent for. As I said a moment ago, there is no way of knowing how long the child might linger. It might be weeks, but it could be only hours. He should be with her."

"I have already decided upon that course, Sir Joshua."

"Well, there's nothing more I can do for the moment, but I'll call regularly. If anything should happen, you have only to send for me."

"I will, Sir Joshua."

The physician inclined his head and left.

Alone with Emily, Robert moved closer to the bedside. A cold smile played upon his lips. "Well, sweet little Emily, you're proving uncommon difficult to dispatch. Who else but a Trevallion could still draw breath after striking that tree as you did? Maybe Weybridge bungled it, but I don't intend to. I'm about to make absolutely certain you breathe no more." He began to ease a pillow from under her head.

Awful realization coursed invisibly through Emily. She lay motionless, but her thoughts were in turmoil. The accident wasn't an accident after all; Uncle Robert had tried to kill her! Oh, someone help me, please! I can't die yet, I must save Lucy!

As if in answer to the silent prayer, the door opened suddenly and Nettie came tearfully in, halting in dismay on seeing him. "Oh, begging your pardon, sir, I didn't know you were here," she said.

He pretended to smooth the pillows, and then drew hastily back from the bed.

Nettie explained. "I—I've come to sit with Miss Emily, sir."

"Sit with her?"

"Why, yes, sir. Sir Joshua said she mustn't be left alone, for there is a small chance she may regain consciousness."

"Yes, of course. By all means sit with her, er . . . ?"

"Nettie, sir."

His gaze returned to the bed. "See you look after my niece, Nettie."

"I will, sir."

He went out and closed the door behind him, then he paused to close his eyes. Another second or so and he'd have been caught in the act! Well, it was a salutary lesson. In future, he'd make certain his was never the actual hand to perform any evil deed. Others would do it for him.

Three

It was dark when Edwin Trevallion's traveling carriage halted swiftly in Berkeley Square. Thick mist curled and coiled around the glowing carriage lamps as the coachman flung open the door for the elderly passenger to climb stiffly down.

Edwin was well wrapped against the cold, with a shawl over the shoulders of his greatcoat, and his face was pale with anxiety as he accepted the walking stick the coachman held out to him. Then, with unsteady steps, he made his way to the house, where a footman swiftly opened the door.

The chandelier light from within shone brightly into the old man's worried eyes. "How is my granddaughter?" he asked as he entered.

"I fear there's no change, sir." The footman closed the door on the night chill, and then assisted Edwin with his outdoor garments.

A fire crackled in the hall hearth, and the dancing flames cast leaping shadows over the cream walls and black-and-white tiled floor. Edwin's stick tapped as he went to the staircase, but as he began to ascend, Robert appeared at the top, anxious to present himself in as favorable a light as possible.

"There was nothing I could do to prevent what happened, Father," he said in a broken voice.

"I'm sure there wasn't, my boy, so please don't think I blame you." Edwin continued to ascend, his gnarled hand sliding painfully up the shining handrail as he forced his arthritic limbs to obey his indomitable will until he'd reached the top. "What exactly did Sir Joshua say? Is the prognosis really as stark as your message implied?"

Robert fought back tears. "There's no hope for her, Father. I fear it's only a matter of time. Maybe hours, possibly weeks."

Edwin gripped the handrail. "I-I'll go to her," he murmured.

Robert started to follow, but his stepfather shook his head. "I wish to be alone with her, my boy. I'm sure you'll understand."

"Yes, of course."

As the door closed behind the old man, Robert's lips curled un-
pleasantly. *Yes, I understand. I'm not a real Trevallion, and must
be excluded at such a sad time. Well, soon I mean to be the only
one left, and everything that is Trevallion will be mine!* Turning
on his heel, he went to the drawing room, where he poured himself a large measure of cognac.

Nettie had fallen asleep in the chair by the fire, and didn't stir
as the grief-stricken old man propped his walking stick against
the coverlet before sitting on the edge of the bed. The room was
candlelit, and the fire had burned low. It was warm and still, with
all outside sounds muffled by the thick damson velvet curtains at
the windows.

Edwin took Emily's hand. "Oh, my dearest child, my dearest,
dearest child . . ."

She felt his touch and heard his voice, but couldn't respond.
She wanted to tell him how much she loved him, and that as soon
as she'd somehow helped someone called Lucy, she'd go to her
parents beyond a bright light in the sky, where she'd be very
happy. But most of all she wanted to warn him about his stepson.
He should be told that Robert's tears were as false as his smiles,
but she was helpless.

Edwin sat there for half an hour, holding her hand and weeping
silently, but then his walking stick clattered to the floor and Nettie
awoke with a start.

She saw him, and got up quickly. "Oh, begging your pardon,
sir, I didn't know you were here." She hastened to retrieve the
walking stick.

"I saw no need to awaken you," he replied, taking out a large
handkerchief and wiping his eyes.

"Shall I leave you, sir?"

"No, that will not be necessary. I-I don't think I can bear to sit
here any longer, not just at the moment."

She gave him the stick as he eased himself achingly to his feet.
He gazed down at Emily's ashen little face. "I can't believe fate
has been so cruel as to strike her down like this," he said softly.

"Nor I, sir," Nettie replied, her own eyes filling with tears. "She
was such a dear little mite. I-I mean, she *is* such a dear little
mite . . ."

"I can see she's in good hands," he observed, giving the maid a
grateful smile.

"I'm very fond of her, sir, and you can rest assured I'll not leave her side until . . . until . . ." Nettie couldn't finish.

Edwin nodded, and said no more as he turned to leave the room. He paused in the doorway to glance back, but then went out. Composing himself, he went to the drawing room, for he had something important to tell Robert, something that was now of much greater significance than it had been. He didn't know how his stepson would take it, for to be sure the news was to his disadvantage. But Robert was a good boy.

Robert was lounging back on a blue brocade sofa, and rose hastily to his feet as his stepfather entered. "Is-is there any change?" he asked quickly.

"No, I fear not." Edwin lowered himself into a fireside chair, then leaned his gray head back wearily. "Pour me a cognac, my boy."

"A cognac? But—"

"I know Carey has forbidden it, but I need it right now."

Robert did as he was told, and then paused with his hand on the decanter stopper. "Emily may not be my blood niece, but she's very dear to me, Father, and I feel responsible because I not only invited her here, but insisted she go riding with me in Hyde Park. I-I had some notion of turning her into an accomplished horsewoman."

"Must I say again that I do not hold you to blame? Robert, I *know* how fond you are of her, and I don't wish you to sink beneath a weight of guilt over what was, after all, a tragic accident."

Robert brought him the cognac. "This may not be the time to mention it, but I, er, suppose this alters everything," he said carefully.

"Everything? Ah, yes, the inheritance."

Robert's eyes glittered as he went to replenish his own glass, and then resume his seat. "I pray you hold me in sufficient regard to make me your heir," he said in a tone of humble devotion.

Edwin drew a long breath. "Robert, I will always have high regard for you, but you cannot be my heir."

Robert was taken unawares. "I-I beg your pardon?"

"You cannot be heir, my boy, for there is someone else with more claim than you. I've been awaiting final confirmation of her existence, and it arrived today, an hour before your message about poor little Emily."

Robert struggled to sound composed. "Confirmation of *whose* existence? I-I don't understand."

"Do you remember my old friend, Lady Amelia Stafford?"

"Yes, isn't she in Bath?" What in God's name did that interfering old biddy have to do with anything? To hide the sudden trembling of his hand, Robert swirled his glass and took a large mouthful of the fiery liquid.

His father shook his head. "Not any more. She's in Switzerland, where she's taken a villa on the shores of Lake Geneva, and three months ago she sent a very intriguing letter. It seems that on leaving Bath, she employed a new companion, a Miss Lucy Trevallion."

Robert's lips parted. "*Trevallion?*" he repeated.

Edwin nodded. "Nicholas's daughter."

Robert's fingers tightened around his glass. The black sheep had had a lamb? "How can you be sure she's who she says she is?" he demanded.

"She has her parents' marriage certificate. Amelia enclosed it with her letter. She's twenty-four years old, and was born in Bath. It seems Nicholas eloped with a young Scottish heiress, who was cut off without a penny for her pains. But they were truly in love, and Nicholas mended his reprobate ways to reside modestly in Bath until he and his adored wife were killed in a carriage overturn three years ago. Lucy was left penniless, and was forced to seek a position as companion, which is the usual lot of gentlewomen in her unfortunate financial situation. Her mother's family continued to wash its hands of her, and it seems Nicholas never mentioned his background, so she didn't know she had paternal relatives, but during conversation one day, Amelia realized who she must be. You see, Amelia knew Nicholas in the days before his, er, disgrace."

Edwin broke off for a moment. He always found it difficult to speak of the son who one terrible Christmas shocked the family by being dishonorably cashiered from his regiment for cowardice and insubordination. There had been no yuletide joy that year, no seasonal thanksgiving or gaiety, just the darkest gloom and devastation.

Such shame would have been hard enough to endure on its own, but Nicholas compounded his sins by flinging himself into a life of hard drinking and gambling, and nothing made him see the error of his ways. As a last resort, he'd been threatened with disinheritance unless he changed, but things continued as before. The threat was carried out, and father and son hadn't seen each other from that day. Nicholas's name had long since been cleared by the army, but he'd never resumed his commission, and he'd certainly never contacted his father, who had gladly reversed the disinheritance. Edwin had never been able to forgive himself for doubting his son, and Nicholas's death had robbed him of any chance to put right the wrong.

The long silence was too much for Robert. "Please go on, Father," he prompted.

"Forgive me, my boy, I-I was just remembering Nicholas. Now, where was I? Ah, yes. Well, there's no doubt at all that Lucy Trevallion is my granddaughter."

Robert was stricken to the core. He was no nearer his goal than before!

Edwin glanced at him. "I don't need to remind you there's no male entail on the Trevallion estate, or that I'd reinstated Nicholas in my will. Lucy is my flesh and blood, Robert, and although I love you dearly, that is something you can never be. I once made a grave error by casting out the son in whom I should have had more faith, and now I have the opportunity to make some amends for the wrong I did him. I mean to bring Lucy home, and see she receives all I denied her father. As soon as I received Amelia's letter and saw the marriage certificate, I wrote back entreating Lucy to return to England. I will dispatch a suitable chaperone to escort her safely on what is, after all, too long and arduous a journey for a young woman to make alone. I'm given to understand that at this time of year it can take up to three weeks, possibly longer. Anyway, this morning word arrived that my prayers have been answered, and Lucy only awaits whomever I send to accompany her."

Robert's mind was racing. "Do you have a chaperone in mind?" he asked.

"I mean to approach reputable sources as quickly as possible, and will pay well. You see, I wish Lucy to be with me for Christmas. It was at Christmas all those years ago that I failed her father, so it is more than fitting that I should welcome his daughter at the same time."

Robert gave a smooth smile. "I understand, Father, and I agree with your sentiments. What's more, I can save you the trouble of having to search for chaperones, as I happen to know two eminently suitable persons, a gentleman and his sister. They're very respectable, but have fallen on difficult times, their late father having lost everything through unwise speculation. They are trustworthy and kind, and a remunerative undertaking such as this would be most acceptable to them, perhaps even a godsend."

"Who are they?"

"Mr. James Weybridge, and his sister, Dorothea."

"And how do you know them?"

"James was a member of my club, and I've kept in touch with him since he was forced into reduced circumstances." Robert lied efficiently, for he already saw a way of eliminating this new Trevallion heiress. "I've dined with both James and his sister at their Kensington home on several occasions, and can vouch for their integrity and virtue. I know they'll gladly act as Lucy's chaperones, and that you will be able to rest easy, knowing she is in such good hands."

"You certainly sing their praises. Send for them as soon as possible, for it would gladden my old heart if Lucy could be here with us in time for Christmas." Edwin's eyes filled with fresh tears. "The Lord giveth, and the Lord taketh away," he murmured sorrowfully, his thoughts returning to Emily.

His son's eyes were bright with determination. The Lord taketh away? No, taking away was now Robert Trevallion's preserve, not the Lord's! Dear Lucy wasn't going to reach journey's end, of that there was no question. And wicked Uncle Robert would be safely here in London, far away from all suspicion! It would be left to Dorothea and James to see that an "accident" befell her somewhere between Switzerland and the English Channel. If anything went wrong, and the accident were discovered to be a criminal act, there'd be nothing to connect Robert Waverly Trevallion with the vile crime. His hands would be lily-white.

Edwin looked fondly at his stepson. "I must say I'm proud of you, my boy, for there's not many a man would react so honorably to news such as this. I will not forget your generosity of heart, of that you may be sure. Lucy may inherit the greater part of the family fortune, but I will see you receive a suitable portion, you have my word on that."

Robert smiled. "Thank you, Father."

Edwin drained his glass. "I-I think I'll return to Emily's bedside now. I was a little overcome before, but I feel stronger now, and she needs me."

He struggled to his feet again, and Robert hurried solicitously to assist him. Edwin patted his shoulder. "You're a comfort to me, Robert, no true father could be more proud than I am of you."

Somehow Robert contrived to give the old man a loving smile, but the moment the door closed behind Edwin, the smile turned ugly with malice. "May you rot in hell, Father! Nicholas's brat will *never* inherit what's mine!"

Four

When Dorothea and James came to be interviewed two days later, Robert was in Emily's room, where he'd spent many hours acting the grieving uncle. He'd become expert in the role, but he didn't fool Nettie. The maid knew he wasn't interested in the child, but was far more concerned with the sudden appearance of Lucy Trevallion. Everyone below stairs felt that the last thing a man of his ambition wanted was another stepniece to stand between him and the fortune.

Robert watched the maid's neat figure as she knelt to tend the fire, but just as he pondered how good it would be to take that firm behind in his hands, he heard Dorothea and James being shown to the drawing room. The maid's charms abruptly ceased to matter. "You may have an hour off now, Nettie. Take a dish of tea in the kitchen."

She stared at him. "An hour, sir?"

"That's what I said."

"But . . ." Her glance flew toward Emily.

"You needn't worry about my niece, for I will stay with her."

She had no choice. "Yes, sir." Bobbing a curtsy, she withdrew.

Robert looked toward the bed. The child was safe enough from him now, for she clearly grew weaker by the day. It was a slow process, but relentless, and he only had to wait. His reason for wanting the maid out of the way now was to have the room free for a last word with Dorothea and James before they left. He didn't doubt they'd be engaged as Lucy's chaperones, which meant they'd have to set off for Switzerland without delay if they were to stand any chance of bringing the new heiress home in time for Christmas. He meant to make sure they were in no doubt about how much hung upon their success. They must be reminded that Lucy Trevallion's survival meant an empty purse for James and an empty ring finger for Dorothea.

*   *   *

In the drawing room, Dorothea could not have looked more sweetly respectable. She wore a gray dimity spencer over a white woolen gown, and there was a small plume in her maroon silk hat. The clothes weren't the work of her fashionable couturiere, but had been especially purchased for the occasion, because it wouldn't do for Edwin to see anything from the rather extravagant wardrobe she'd coaxed out of Robert. Today she was supposed to be the embodiment of the unfortunate lady fallen on hard times, and she'd succeeded very well.

James was equally correctly attired, having wisely discarded his purloined Guards uniform in favor of an unremarkable brown coat and fawn trousers. He was the perfect gentleman of reduced circumstances, as well as the loving attentive brother.

Edwin smiled at them both. "Please be seated," he invited.

James ushered Dorothea to a chair, but instead of sitting as well, he took up a discreet position at her shoulder.

"My son recommends you for the responsibility of escorting my granddaughter from the Villa Belmont, near Vevey on Lake Geneva," Edwin said.

James nodded. "My sister and I are eager for the undertaking, sir."

"It is a long and difficult journey of at least three weeks' duration, and must be completed in both directions by Christmas, which may prove too much for Miss Weybridge." Edwin looked kindly at Dorothea. "Are you up to such rigors, my dear?"

"Oh, yes, sir," Dorothea replied, "for when the task is such a happy one, how can one fail to find the fortitude required? Were my strength to flag, I would only have to think of your new granddaughter being with you at a time of joy like Christmas, and my courage and determination would be renewed ten times over."

"What charming sentiments, my dear," Edwin said approvingly, his mind already made up. "Very well, I gladly engage you both."

They smiled virtuously.

Edwin went on. "I believe my son has already explained the terms, and trust they are acceptable to you?"

James nodded. "Most acceptable, sir."

"And you're certain you'll be able to leave immediately?"

"We will, sir."

"I wish you to bring my granddaughter here to Berkeley Square, not to Trevallion Park. I mean to spend the rest of the winter in town."

"As you wish, Mr. Trevallion," James replied. "We can leave

tomorrow, for we've, er, anticipated a little. As soon as Robert informed me of your wishes, I took the chance you'd engage us, so our packing is almost complete, and a suitably large traveling carriage has been hired."

Edwin smiled. "I find such initiative most enlightening, sir. It proves you to be just the sort of person I would wish to have custody of my granddaughter. I will send immediate authorization to Coutts' Bank, so that you and Miss Weybridge may withdraw the agreed amount of traveling expenses as soon as possible. The balance will be yours when you return with Lucy." He rose slowly to his feet and extended a hand to James. "I wish you Godspeed, sir."

"We'll bring her safely to you, Mr. Trevallion," James promised righteously. "This will be a happy Christmas after all—well, as happy as possible under the circumstances."

At the oblique reference to Emily's tragic situation, Dorothea dabbed a handkerchief to her eyes and gave a choked sob. James placed a comforting arm around her shoulders. "Don't cry, Sis, for our task is to replace sorrow with joy," he murmured, ushering her to the door.

They withdrew, but as they were about to go down the stairs, Robert suddenly appeared in the doorway of Emily's room. Putting his finger to his lips, he beckoned them inside, and then closed the door.

"We can talk safely in here; the maid has been told to stay away for an hour. I take it you've been successful?"

Dorothea nodded. "The old fool thinks us charming and agreeable. We're to leave as soon as possible."

Lying forgotten on the bed, Emily recognized the voice. It was the woman called Mrs. Makepeace, and from the way she spoke, she was clearly Uncle Robert's accomplice!

James laughed, and the little girl realized Dorothea wasn't the only newcomer in the room. "How do I look today, Robert?" he asked. "I almost chose to be a naval captain, or even a Guards officer again, but thought better of it. I trust I'm restrained enough?"

A Guards officer again? Emily became frightened. The man who'd made Sorrel swerve! He must be another accomplice!

Robert didn't answer James, and Dorothea glanced toward Emily's bed. "One down, one to go," she murmured callously. All trace of conscience had gone. Now she'd come this far, she was wholly committed to carrying out Robert's evil wishes.

"One down, *two* to go," Robert corrected. "There's my dear old stepfather, don't forget. Still, once he's obliged by making me his heir, I'm afraid his heart is certain to, er, fail after the loss of two granddaughters within weeks of each other."

Emily was shaken. *Two* granddaughters? What was he talking about? And what did he mean about Grandfather's heart? Was Grandfather in danger too?

Robert's glance sharpened toward James. "You make certain of it this time. There can't be any bungling. I want Lucy Trevallion dead, is that clearly understood? Because if she survives and I don't inherit, you'll get nothing."

Lucy! This was the first time anyone had mentioned the name in Emily's hearing. A torrent of emotion passed invisibly through the little girl.

James responded to Robert's warning. "Your new stepniece will be dispatched somewhere en route, of that you may be sure. She'll be dead long before we board the Brighton packet at Dieppe."

Robert's gaze swung to Dorothea. "Just remember that if you want that wedding ring, this whole business must be accomplished to perfection."

"You may rely on us both, Robert," she said softly, stepping up to link her arms around his neck and kiss his mouth. She pressed close, molding her body sensuously to his as her little tongue flicked between his lips. She took her time, and then gradually drew away. "Just a reminder of what you'll be missing while I'm away," she said softly.

The door opened suddenly and Nettie returned. She halted in surprise on seeing Dorothea and James. "Oh, forgive me, I . . ." She lowered her eyes quickly and bobbed a belated curtsy.

James cleared his throat. "Well, I suppose we had better leave, Robert. We've much to do if we're to set off within a day or so." He ushered Dorothea to the door, and Nettie stepped aside as they passed.

Robert accompanied them from the room, and Nettie thankfully closed the door behind them. Then she went to the bed to take Emily's hand.

"There now, little one, I'm back now."

Emily struggled to move her lips, but it was impossible. She could feel Nettie's hand and hear her voice, but couldn't do anything. And she needed to do so much! She was supposed to help Lucy, but was trapped here in this bed!

So great was her secret turmoil that a single tear welled from beneath her lashes and wended its sad way down her pale cheek. Nettie saw it and brushed it gently away.

"Poor little mite," she murmured sadly.

Edwin stood by the drawing room window, watching as Robert saw Dorothea and James off. As the hackney coach conveyed Lucy's chaperones away, a light breeze scurried playfully through the carpet of fallen leaves in the square, tumbling them around for a moment or so and then dying away again.

He turned from the window and sat in an armchair, leaning his head wearily back and closing his eyes. The fire was warm, and the room quiet. In a few minutes he'd fallen asleep. He dreamed of last Christmas, when he'd walked with Emily to pick holly at Trevallion Park. There was a light sprinkling of snow underfoot, Emily's cheeks were pink, and her eyes danced with happiness as she skipped at his side. He held her little hand, and it felt warm and real. Everything seemed real, even the hint of woodsmoke drifting in the air from the gamekeeper's cottage.

The holly trees were bright with berries, and Emily laughed as he stretched up with his walking stick to bend a branch low enough for her to pick. Edwin smiled in his sleep, for it had been a day to cherish forever. But when she'd gathered an armful and turned to face him, she said something he knew she hadn't said at the time.

"I'm going to be very happy, Grandfather, so you mustn't worry about me."

"Why should I worry, my dear?" he asked in amusement.

"Because I won't be here next Christmas, I'll have gone to Mama and Papa."

His smile faded. "Please don't say that, Emily."

Emily went on. "You'll have Lucy, though, for I'll watch over her and keep her safe from harm."

His brows drew together in puzzlement. "How do you know about Lucy, my dear?"

"I just do, and I want you to know I'll protect her."

"Protect her? From what?"

"From—"

The dream was shattered as the drawing room door opened suddenly and Robert came in. Edwin started awake, and for a moment was so confused he didn't know where he was. All memory of the dream slid away into the recesses of his mind.

He smiled at his stepson. "I'm so glad you recommended Mr.

Weybridge and his sister, for I found them very much to my liking."

"I knew you would," Robert replied with a facile smile.

"I'm more than content they'll take every care of Lucy, and I'm quite certain she'll be with us for Christmas."

Robert's smile didn't waver. "Let us pray for that," he murmured.

Five

Later the same morning, hundreds of miles away on the shore of Lake Geneva, Lucy Trevallion left the little summerhouse in the grounds of the Villa Belmont. She walked slowly along the path that followed the water's edge for a short distance to the tiny private harbor, before it wound up through the grounds to the house. Lady Amelia Stafford's Swiss residence wasn't large by English standards, but was exquisitely situated among vineyards on the lower slopes of the alps that formed the lake's northern boundary, between the towns of Vevey and Montreux. It wasn't without reason that Lady Amelia had chosen to live here, for the climate was almost Mediterranean. The summer months were hot and sunny, if liberally interspersed with heavy rain, and since the end of the war the previous year, British society had flocked here to indulge in this latest place of *ton.*

The blue water stretched serenely into the haze of the cold November sun, and to the south and east the soaring peaks of the Savoy were thickly capped with snow. To the west, as yet untouched by the real grip of winter, were the green, less lofty heights of the Jura mountain frontier between Switzerland and France.

The long autumn had been unexpectedly mild, and there was a crisp carpet of bronze and scarlet leaves beneath Lucy's feet. At twenty-four, she was pale and slender, with the green eyes and ash-blond hair of the Trevallions. She wore a lavender velvet cloak over a pink woolen gown, and her long, thick curls were pinned up beneath a white-ribboned gypsy hat. Daintiness was her mark, rather than beauty, but when she smiled, she was arrestingly attractive.

Reading and embroidery were her two great pleasures, and she'd just spent an hour in the summerhouse indulging in the former. At the moment she was engrossed in Rousseau's *La Nouvelle Héloïse,* a story of passionate love set in this very part of Switzerland, and the embroidered bookmark peeping from the pages showed her to be halfway through. She'd made the bookmark herself, and was in the process of making another for Lady Amelia's cook, who was much smitten with the local pastor and wished to give him a suitable Christmas gift. Nothing could have been more suitable for a clergyman than the delightful design of angels, lilies, and holy stars that was now almost completed.

Lucy approached the elegant balustraded steps that led up from the circular, stone-enclosed harbor to the lawns. The Villa Belmont was square, and built of gray brick, with its upper story surrounded by a balcony. Green shutters flanked the windows that enjoyed a matchless view south over the lake. It was a place of flowers in the summer, but now the acacia leaves were scarlet as they fell softly to the ground, the roses had ceased to bloom, and the beds of mauve and yellow pansies had faded. But it was still lovely, and Lucy felt a little sad to think she wouldn't be here when everything burst into bloom again next spring.

She paused by the steps to the lawn. The lake lapped gently in the harbor, where two boats rocked at their moorings. Far out on the lake there were lateen-sailed fishing craft, and a larger vessel taking casks of Vevey wine to Geneva, twenty miles away at the other end of the lake. As she gazed across the shimmering water, it was all so soothing and comforting that she found her dramatically changed circumstances almost too incredible to be true.

With a sigh she sat on the steps, resting her book on her lap and her chin in her hands. Part of her shrank from the new London life that now stretched before her, for she'd been happy with Lady Amelia, who was a good mistress, but the other part wished to be united with the family she never knew she had. Her father had never said anything about his background. All she knew was that in his hot-headed youth something had led to a bitter parting.

Now she'd been summoned by the man from whom her father had so irretrievably separated, and she was afraid. But Lady Amelia spoke very warmly of Edwin Trevallion as an old and valued friend, and Lucy was sure her employer wouldn't deliberately mislead her. Besides, there was no doubt from Edwin's letters that he'd long felt a genuine and deep regret over the quarrel with his second son. Lucy sighed again. She knew she must go to England, to at least meet this unknown family. What were they like, her grandfather, her uncle, and her little cousin Emily?

Footsteps approached through the fallen leaves on the lawns behind her, and she turned quickly, her heart sinking as she saw Geoffrey, Earl of St. Athan, coming toward the harbor. He was Lady Amelia's nephew, and the one good reason why Lucy thought England might after all prove infinitely more agreeable than the Villa Belmont! Life had been quiet and amiable until his arrival at the beginning of the month. He was on his way to Italy, but had decided to stay a while with his doting aunt. As far as Lucy was concerned, Lord St. Athan had no redeeming features. Oh, he was tall, dark, breathtakingly handsome, supremely elegant, and in his eligible prime at thirty-two, but he was also frosty, sarcastic, quick to take offense, and made it abundantly clear he didn't approve of the informality existing between his aunt and her employee. She didn't know what her supposed crime was, only that he'd taken one look at her and disliked her on the spot. Nothing could have been more cold or superior than the way he inclined his head without saying anything in response to his aunt's introduction. Even Lady Amelia had been taken aback by such unwarranted hauteur.

To look at him now in his corbeau-colored coat and cream breeches, with his top hat worn at a rakishly casual angle and his cane swinging idly in a gloved hand, one might have thought him the most dashing and engaging of men. But he certainly wasn't. It was his highly starched neckcloth and solitaire diamond pin that gave the game away, for he was an unbearably stiff as the former, and as hard and bright as the latter!

There was no doubt Lady Amelia was angry with him for treating so badly a young woman who'd turned out to be one of the wealthy Trevallions, but her displeasure made no difference, for he didn't change his ways. Something about Lucy Trevallion grated upon him like a fingernail upon glass, and that was that.

Lucy returned her attention to the lake, thinking it had probably never occurred to him that the object of his dislike thought *he* was base, ill-mannered, and a discredit to his poor aunt. Oh, how excellent it would be to tell him a few home truths, if only to see the fury in his blue eyes.

He reached the top of the steps behind her, and began to slowly descend. For a moment she thought he intended to ignore her entirely, but instead he gave the curtest of greetings.

"Miss Trevallion?"

"Lord St. Athan?"

"My, er, aunt informs me you wish to visit the Castle of Chillon." He nodded southwest along the lake toward Montreux, about four miles away, where the beautiful, atmospheric fortress jutted out into the water.

It was the most civil thing he'd ever said to her, and Lucy couldn't hide her surprise. "Why, yes, that is so, but—"

He interrupted. "I intend to sail there now. Would you care to join me?"

She stared at him. "I-I beg your pardon?"

"I believe I spoke clearly enough, Miss Trevallion. Do you wish to see the castle? If you do, you're welcome to accompany me."

She met his eyes, very tempted to tell him what he could do with the castle, turret by turret. Unfortunately, she longed to see over the famous prison-fortress, and this might be her only opportunity. But to go there with *Lord St. Athan* . . . ?

"I await your response, Miss Trevallion."

"I'd like to take you up on your offer, my lord, except . . ."

"Yes?"

It was on the tip of her tongue to say she didn't think they'd survive the close proximity of a small boat without one tipping the other into the icy water, but it wasn't her place to speak to Lady Amelia's nephew like that, even if he did richly deserve it. "Oh, nothing," she replied.

His blue eyes rested briefly on her, then he stepped down to the stone quay and turned to extend his hand. Reluctantly she accepted, and, with her book clutched tight, allowed him to assist her into the larger of the two boats. She'd forgotten to wear gloves that morning, and so was fleetingly conscious of the warmth of his hand through the skin-tight leather of his.

Placing the book at her side, she made herself as comfortable as she could on the little seat at the bow, and he cast off the mooring rope and then stepped on board as well, using one of the oars to push the craft away from the quay. The tiny harbor was fringed with willows, and trailing fronds brushed his shoulders as he maneuvered the boat through the narrow entrance to the lake, then he hoisted the gleaming white sail.

As the wind caught the canvas and the vessel sprang forward, Lucy gazed back at the villa and thought she saw Lady Amelia standing on the balcony. She waved, but there was no response.

Geoffrey glanced at her. "If you imagine my aunt's myopia

permits her to see more than the sail, you're very much mistaken."

"Can you be sure of that?" she replied, a little more sharply than she intended.

His eyes swung back to her. "Reasonably sure."

"But with an element of doubt, therefore she *might* have seen, and that's what matters."

"To whom? You, or my aunt?"

"To me, sir, for I know I waved and she might have seen, which is preferable to her having observed that I *didn't* wave."

"A neat riposte, but based upon the surmise that my aunt cares one jot whether or not you waved."

Lucy's resentment stirred. "Yes, Lord St. Athan, but when one considers the kindly nature of the lady concerned, one must conclude she will take pleasure in so friendly a thing as a wave. One only waves to those whom one likes and respects, and I feel both of those things toward Lady Amelia."

To her surprise, a faint glimmer of wry humor passed through his eyes. "And you certainly wouldn't wave to me, would you?"

She gave in to her dislike. "Only for the infinite delight of saying farewell," she murmured.

He inclined his head, and then returned his attention to the boat as it skimmed over the water.

Glad their acrimonious exchanges were temporarily at an end, she turned to look ahead at the castle, which shone red-roofed against a background of pine-clad slopes and distant white peaks. Chillon was steeped in tales of man's cruelty to man, but although it was grim and menacing, it was also incredibly beautiful, its reflection shining in the dark blue waters from which it rose as if from the depths. Beyond it, basking in the November sun, was the little town of Montreux.

As the boat sailed into the lee of the fortress, Geoffrey hauled down the sail and rowed to the tree-clad shore, where he leapt onto the grass to make the mooring rope fast to a low branch. Then he held out a hand to assist Lucy.

She left her book on the seat and got up, but then hesitated, for there was water between the boat and the shore.

He raised an eyebrow. "Faint heart, Miss Trevallion? Regrettably, one must exchange boat for solid ground if one wishes to examine Chillon."

Slowly she slipped her hand in his, and took as long a step as she could. She almost overbalanced, but he caught her, putting his hands to her waist to keep her steady and then releasing her as quickly as he could.

She was very conscious of the haste of that release, and embarrassed color flooded into her cheeks. Suddenly she wished she'd declined his invitation, but it was too late now, and she had to make the best of it.

They were like strangers as they made their way onto the road from Montreux, and then crossed the wooden bridge into the castle.

Six

The visit to Chillon proved disastrous, and before it was over, Lucy's relations with Geoffrey had deteriorated from poor to downright dreadful. There was nothing upon which they agreed, save their dislike for each other, and the gloomy chateau provided rather too much scope for argument between two people of confirmed but divergent opinions.

It began at the gates, where they were greeted by their guide, an old Swiss corporal who was clearly a little worse for wear, and who repeatedly told them how a month or so earlier he'd conducted the great Lord Byron and Percy Bysshe Shelley over the castle. Lucy would have preferred to dispense with the services of someone who seemed he might at any moment fall headlong down one of the many flights of worn stone steps. But Geoffrey found the man both amusing and knowledgeable, and was more than prepared to steady him whenever necessary.

And thus they made their meandering way over Chillon, examining towers, torture chambers, and subterranean dungeons. It was in the latter that another disagreement commenced, this time concerning the castle's most famous prisoner, the sixteenth-century Swiss patriot, François Bonivard. His unlit dungeon was hewn out of rock and situated below the level of the lake, and the chains and fetters which had held him were still to be found. Another, perhaps even more sad, reminder of his long incarceration was the path his endless pacing had worn in the rocky floor.

Lucy shivered, and Geoffrey noticed. "Are you cold, Miss Trevallion?"

"A little, yes."

Without a word he removed his coat and placed it around her shoulders, then he began to tease his gloves off finger by finger.

"Oh, there's no need—" she began.

"There's every need, Miss Trevallion," he insisted, holding the gloves out to her. "Put them on, please."

Slowly she slipped her hands into them. The warm, soft leather seemed to cling to her skin. It was a far from unpleasant sensation; indeed, it was oddly affecting, as if his hands were holding hers. Hastily she shrugged off such an unwelcome thought.

The guide held up a lighted candle to better show the dungeon. It was an eerie moment, for he was swaying as much as the flame, and as a consequence the light moved strangely over the awful hole. To Lucy, the creeping shadows seemed like ghosts, and suddenly she felt unaccountably nervous.

She looked uneasily at Geoffrey. "I-I don't like it in here, can we please go up into the air again?"

He was disposed to mock her. "Leave Bonivard's stone cage after barely a minute? Surely this evil chamber is the reason for Chillon's fame, certainly one of the reasons you wished to come here in the first place?"

"Maybe so, sir, but a minute is all I need to appreciate the scope of man's inhumanity to man."

"Perhaps it could be argued that if Bonivard hadn't conspired against the Duke of Savoy, he wouldn't have been brought here. Conspiracy inspires cruelty."

His manner stung her. "How practical an observation, sir, if a little lacking in any understanding of patriotism."

His faint smile faded, and his eyes became cool in the candlelight. "And what would you know of my views on patriotism, Miss Trevallion?"

"I'm merely interpreting your comment, sir."

"And doing so incorrectly."

"Is that so? Well, forgive me, my lord, but how else was one to understand what you said? If your sentiment were to have been applied throughout history, we should have laid a red carpet for the Romans and the Normans, and clapped Bonaparte on the back as a jolly fine fellow!"

"What a waspish tongue you have, to be sure," he murmured.

"You are entitled to your opinion, I to mine."

"Opinions are something you possess in overabundance."

Her resentment of him bubbled over. "And ill manners would seem to be your forte, sirrah!"

The corporal continued to teeter, his bemused glance moving from one of them to the other. Then he gave a lopsided grin and nudged Geoffrey, with whom he'd conversed off and on in French since the tour began. *"Milord, cette mademoiselle à besoin d'un bon homme, oui? Elle à trop d'esprit!"* He laughed throatily, satisfied she had no idea what he was saying.

But he was very wrong, for she spoke French very well indeed and knew exactly what he'd said. So she was in need of a good man, was she? And she had too much spirit? Well, she had no intention of allowing *that* to pass, and so in perfect French, she replied. "Well, sir, it's perfectly clear to me that *you* are the one with too much spirit, all of it from a bottle!"

With that, she gathered her skirts and left them.

The corporal's jaw had dropped, but he swiftly recovered, giving Geoffrey a huge wink. *"Dieu! Quelle vipère!"*

Geoffrey sighed. What a viper? Yes, that about summed up his aunt's difficult companion.

Lucy hurried across the bridge to the road, where the Swiss equivalent of London hackney carriages were to be hired. Called charabancs, they weren't carriages at all, but little one-horse carts like Irish jaunting gigs, capable of carrying the driver, with two passengers seated back-to-back behind him. She considered hiring one to take her the four miles back to the villa, but as the thought crossed her mind, Geoffrey spoke behind her.

"No, Miss Trevallion, for not only do you still have my coat and gloves, but I certainly can't permit you to travel alone."

She whirled about, swift color rushing into her cheeks.

He met her eyes. "It's regrettable you can't endure a little light-heartedness."

"I didn't find what was said lighthearted, sirrah; in fact, I found it downright offensive," she replied stiffly, removing his coat and gloves and thrusting them toward him.

He took them. "Then I apologize, but for the moment you're under my protection, and must return to the villa with me."

"I don't have to do as you order, sir."

He donned the coat. "On the contrary, madam, that's precisely what you have to do, and since Chillon has clearly lost its charm for both of us, I suggest we return to my aunt without further delay." Before she knew it, he'd caught her hand to virtually drag her toward the boat.

"Let me go!" she breathed, trying to wrest her hand away.

But he held on tightly. "Behave yourself, Miss Trevallion, or I'll be obliged to use even more force, and, believe me, I'm quite capable."

"Oh, I believe you!"

As they reached the boat, he again caught her off-guard by suddenly swinging her from her feet and into his arms, then stepping into the shallow water and placing her bodily in the boat. Then he undid the rope and jumped in after her, swiftly using an oar to shove off from the shore before she'd had time to compose herself.

Mortified color burned on her cheeks as she did her best to recover her dignity. What a fool she'd been to come here with him. The St. Athan leopard was incapable of changing its spots!

The return voyage was accomplished in mutual silence. She gazed stonily toward the west and the rolling summits of the Jura mountains; he found the snow-capped peaks to the east equally absorbing. It seemed an age before the villa's little harbor mouth appeared ahead, and the boat slid beneath the willows.

She didn't wait for him to make the rope fast and assist her ashore, but got out of the boat on her own. Geoffrey gazed coldly after her as she hurried toward the house. That was the first and last time he ever put himself out for Miss Lucy Trevallion; in future he'd be deaf to any of his aunt's bright ideas! He was almost savage as he finished tying the rope to the mooring hoop. "Be nice to Lucy, Geoffrey," he muttered, mimicking Lady Amelia's voice. "Be nice to her and I'm sure you and she could get along famously! She's such a treasure, so very sweet and kind!" Sweet and kind? The creature had the sweetness of vitriol, and the disposition of a Gorgon! How his aunt could view her as a treasure was beyond him.

He straightened and watched Lucy as she disappeared into the villa. Discovering she was one of the wealthy Trevallions had clearly gone to her head, giving her airs and graces that he found decidedly unbecoming. By God, what a pleasure it would be to tame that unwarranted audacity by rolling her on her back and teaching her the facts of life!

He was appalled at himself. She'd irritated him so much that all the revenge he could think was to dominate her sexually! Great God above, he'd never before met a woman who'd provoked him so much. Not even Constance. He exhaled slowly then, for Constance was the last person he wished to think of.

Glancing down to make certain the boat was properly fast, he noticed the volume of *La Nouvelle Héloïse* lying on the seat. With a sigh, he stepped aboard again to retrieve it, but misjudged his balance so that the boat rocked violently and with a huge splash he fell into the icy water. Coughing and cursing, he hauled himself back into the boat, where he stood dripping and shivering. God damn the woman! She was fast becoming the bane of his life! Snatching up the book, which hadn't suffered so much as a droplet, he stepped onto dry land again and squelched up the steps toward the villa.

Leaving a damp trail behind him, he entered the warm, firelit hall of the house and immediately saw Lucy coming down the staircase. She paused in amazement, and to his fury he saw she had difficulty in hiding her mirth at his drenched appearance. It was too much! He strode to the stairs and thrust the offending volume into her hands.

"Your book, madam!"

"Th-thank you, sir."

"Don't mention it, madam," he replied ungraciously, and then he went stiffly up the stairs.

She wanted to laugh, for in truth he looked more than a little comical, but discretion was called for now. Clasping the book to her breast, she hurried across the hall to the library to find the volume of poems Lady Amelia had just requested.

Geoffrey watched her from the top of the staircase, noting her lithe figure and the almost silver lights in her hair. Suddenly it wasn't Lucy Trevallion he saw, but another young woman with ash-blond hair. Constance. Oh, if ever a woman was misnamed, it was she. Her beauty had captivated him, and her charm and wit had kept him bound. He'd asked her to marry him, only to find he was one of the few fools in London who didn't know she was married already! Her deceit had caused him to break one of his cardinal rules, that of never bedding another man's wife, and for that he could never forgive her. Or Lucy Trevallion, for so resembling her that she became Constance every time he looked at her. His damp hand tightened on the topmost newel post as the library door closed.

His aunt's skirts rustled behind him. "Good heavens, Geoffrey, whatever have you been doing?" she inquired in astonishment, pausing to stare at his dripping clothes. At the age of seventy, Lady Amelia Stafford was still elegant and fashionable, her figure trim in a frilled brown taffeta gown. Her fine gray hair was almost hidden by a lace-edged cup, and there was a warm cashmere shawl around her shoulders.

He turned reluctantly. "Aunt?"

Her blue eyes were quizzical as they met his. "Well, sir? I trust there's a suitable explanation for your appearance?"

"I would have thought it obvious, Aunt. I fell in the lake."

"Indeed? Well, I've seen Lucy since her return, and she made no mention of any such mishap."

He was stiff. "She'd already left. I saw she'd left her damned book in the boat, and—"

"Books may be described as engrossing or tedious, sir, but never damned," she said reprovingly.

"You choose your adjectives, Aunt, and I'll choose mine."

She eyed him. "My, what a sulky bear you are, to be sure. I gather from Lucy that the excursion to Chillon was not all it might have been."

"It was an entirely disagreeable experience," he replied shortly.

Lady Amelia sighed. "I really think you might have made more effort, Geoffrey."

"*I* might have made more effort?" He was incredulous. "Aunt, it may interest you to know that your precious Lucy Trevallion is without a doubt the most obstinate, cantankerous, dogmatic, and willful young woman it has ever been my misfortune to meet."

"Her opinion of you is more or less a match."

"She's only a damned companion!" he snapped angrily.

"And your great-grandmother was an actress, sir, so such snobbery ill becomes you, don't you think?" she pointed out.

He met her gaze and fell silent.

"That's better, sir, for if you have nothing sensible to say, it's better by far to hold your tongue. Besides, it isn't Lucy's character that's upsetting you, is it?"

"Meaning what, exactly?"

"That she's too much like Constance."

"I don't wish to discuss it, Aunt," he replied, beginning to walk past her.

"No, and perhaps that's the trouble," she said after him. "It isn't Lucy's fault that your vanity suffered at Constance's hands, but it's certainly your fault you haven't come to terms with it yet."

He continued to walk as if he hadn't heard, and after a moment Lady Amelia drew her shawl closer a little crossly. "Foolish boy," she muttered, and then adjourned to the grand saloon to await Lucy and the book of poems.

Seven

It was November thirtieth, and at last Dorothea and James were within eighty miles of the Villa Belmont, having taken much longer than planned because they'd both been unwell for a week in Burgundy. Now, on their way to their penultimate halt, at Pontarlier at the foot of the Jura mountains, sudden heavy rain forced them to halt overnight instead at the Franche-Comté town of Ornans, on the banks of the River Loue.

The only accommodation they could find was at a rather uninviting inn called the Black Unicorn. The French postilion they'd hired at Dieppe maneuvered the tired horses into the yard behind the ramshackle building, and James quickly assisted Dorothea down. The afternoon was prematurely dark, and so heavy was the rain that they were obliged to enter the inn through the low-linteled kitchen door at the back.

By the light of a roaring fire, Dorothea immediately noticed four men in dripping cloaks sitting in the chimney corner. They were enjoying bread and soup, and their wide-brimmed hats cast dark shadows over their features, but she could see they were all bearded. Their manner was secretive and vaguely menacing, and when one of them moved, she saw a long-barreled pistol tucked into his belt. She knew the area was notorious for bandits, and felt certain four of them were being harbored by the Black Unicorn. She'd rather drive on through the rain than halt here!

Alarmed, she tugged at James's sleeve, but at that moment the innkeeper hastened over. He was a short, round man, with receding red hair and beads of perspiration on his forehead, and by the way his glance kept moving to the four men, Dorothea knew he wished to keep them from the public gaze.

James was too wet and hungry to be particularly observant as he addressed the innkeeper. "You have rooms?" he inquired in French.

"Certainly, sir."

"We'll take two."

"Sir." The man inclined his head.

"What are you serving for dinner?" James asked then.

"Perch caught here in the river, sir."

"Oh, God, not more fish. What I wouldn't give for a good feast of English roast beef!" James said to Dorothea as the man ushered them from the kitchens into the dining room.

Dorothea glanced uneasily back toward the kitchen door, but then decided not to mention her fears. If the landlord was anxious to keep the men out of sight, it wasn't likely they'd intrude into the dining room.

The perch was unexpectedly good, as was the "yellow" wine, made from the first frost-nipped grapes of autumn, and as James began to feel more relaxed, his thoughts turned to the purpose of their journey. "I wish to God we hadn't been delayed; it's put our itinerary out quite a lot."

"It can't be helped. Besides, what difference does it make when we haven't yet decided how to dispose of Lucy Trevallion?"

"We need a single masterly stroke."

"I've already said we should simply push her overboard from the Brighton packet," Dorothea replied, for her dread of water made this seem the most obvious course.

James gave a derisive laugh. "Be sensible, Sis. She might spend the entire voyage below decks, and even if we somehow contrive to push her overboard, it isn't unknown for people to be able to swim, even women. Then, if the sea should also happen to be a mill pond at the time, not only will she probably be rescued, but she'll point a finger at us!"

Her eyes flashed. "I'm so pleased you find it amusing, but I don't notice you supplying a better alternative."

He became more accommodating. "I know. Look, Sis, there's nothing to be gained by falling out."

"What we need is an ambush by *banditti*," she mused, thinking of the men in the kitchen.

"How droll, for to be sure we'd perish alongside her!"

"Yes, but—" Dorothea broke off, suddenly realizing that the kitchen door had opened slightly. Someone was eavesdropping! Alarm rose through her, and she pointed urgently.

James got up swiftly and crossed to pull the door fully open, but he didn't count upon the height of the man beyond.

Dorothea realized it was the leader of the four "bandits," and she screamed. This was it! They'd come to do away with Lucy Trevallion, but instead would be done away with themselves!

The man grinned broadly, pushing James back to his seat and

then coming to place a muddy boot on their table. He brought with him a smell of leather, horses, and woodsmoke, and still wore his cloak and hat, but there was no mistaking the bright glitter in his eyes.

After taking a mouthful of wine from their bottle, he wiped his mouth with his cloak hem, and then leaned forward to James. "So, Rostbif, you wish someone to be . . . ?" He drew an expressive finger across James's throat.

James swallowed. Personal bravery had never been his strong point, and at that moment if the fellow had demanded Dorothea, he'd have given her up without a struggle.

"I listen to what you say. You wish someone dead. I kill if you wish, but you pay." The man rubbed his fingers and thumb together to indicate a large sum, and then grinned. "We talk, yes?"

It was Dorothea who recovered her wits first. "Yes, we talk," she said suddenly.

The bandit looked swiftly at her, his glance moving to the curve of her breasts. "So, *mademoiselle,* you are the man here, *non?*"

James flushed angrily. "My sister is rash, sir, for we don't know anything about you."

"I am Mansart," the man replied quietly, and in such a way that Dorothea had no doubt he was not only a bandit, but one to be reckoned with.

James cleared his throat. "Very well, Monsieur Mansart, I—"

"Just Mansart," the bandit interrupted.

"Very well, Mansart. You're right, we do wish to do away with someone. A woman." James paused, waiting for this to make a difference, but Mansart only laughed.

"Man, woman, child, it is all the same if the price is right. Who is this woman?"

"Her name is Lucy Trevallion, and she'll be traveling with us when we return this way in about a week's time."

Mansart nodded. "It will be done. Now—the price?"

Dorothea got up suddenly. "I-I'll leave you to discuss the details, James. I'm sure you don't need me." She didn't want to stay a moment longer in Mansart's presence. She recognized in him someone even more conscienceless than Robert, but where Robert's lack of scruple excited her, she found the bandit repellent.

Mansart called after her as she hurried away. "You wish I come to you tonight, *mademoiselle?*" he asked with a knowing grin.

Hot color flooded into her cheeks as the waiting innkeeper conducted her to the nearby ground floor bedchambers allotted to James and her. As soon as she was inside she wedged a chair against the door. The candlelit room was cold because the fire had gone out, and the floorboards squeaked as she went to the window and drew the curtains back to look out.

To her surprise, the window was actually a glazed door that opened onto a roofed balcony. A balcony? But the room was on the ground floor! Puzzled, she opened the door and stepped out into the chilly rain-drenched night, where she was immediately confronted by one of her worst nightmares, for the balcony was only inches above the River Loue, which flowed directly against the inn's foundations! Deep and silent, the water slid almost eerily by, its surface lashed by the heavy rain which had been falling for several hours now.

She drew agitatedly back into the room. Her heart raced with dread, for she felt as if the river were rising inexorably, soon to steal over the balcony and into the room. But then the horrid spell was broken as footsteps approached the door. She turned, her hand creeping anxiously to her throat as the steps halted outside. Who was it? James? Or Mansart?

"Are you there, Sis?"

"James!" She ran to drag the chair aside and admit him.

He glanced uneasily back along the dark passage, and then entered, pushing the chair back beneath the door handle. Then he looked at her pale face.

"What in God's name is the matter?"

"The river . . ." She pointed to the window.

Frowning, he went to look out, and she closed her eyes tightly as he opened the door to step onto the balcony. She heard the rain on the water.

With a low laugh he came back into the room. "We'll take breakfast *al fresco*, eh, Sis?

"I hate you sometimes," she breathed.

"I'm every sister's ideal brother," he replied, flinging himself onto her bed and putting his hands behind his head. "To more important matters. It's all arranged. Mansart and I have agreed on terms and settled on a precise plan."

She began to recover a little. "What's going to happen?"

"A supposed highway robbery. When we're on the return journey, we're to stop at the Silver Apple in Pontarlier, which is where we should have been tonight anyway. We're to inform the landlord there, and he'll send word to Mansart."

"What then?"

"An ambush will be laid at an agreed place between here and Pontarlier, where the road narrows between rocks and the river descends rapids. Apparently, it's quite easy to identify; we'll pass it tomorrow. Mansart will pretend to hold us up, shots will be fired, and dear Lucy will be no more."

Dorothea was uneasy. "It's all very well, but what if Mansart decides to put an end to all of us?"

"A little matter of money. He gets half now, and the rest when Lucy's dead. I've agreed to stay overnight here again to hand it over."

"And you *trust* him?" Dorothea was alarmed. "James, what's to prevent him from still eliminating us both and stealing everything we have?"

"Nothing at all, except that he regards himself as honorable."

She stared at him. "What would he know of honor?" she said dryly.

"About as much as we do," James replied accurately, "but in this instance I think we can trust him. He's nothing if not a man of business. *Courage, ma soeur*, for the day after tomorrow we should be at the Villa Belmont, and a month from now we'll have accomplished everything we came to do. Just think what a Christmas it will be for us this year."

She smiled too. "God rest us merry?"

"Oh, I trust very merry indeed."

Eight

The following morning, as Dorothea and James departed from the Black Unicorn in continuing rain, eighty miles away at the Villa Belmont the weather was fine and sunny. But dealings between Lucy and Geoffrey were anything but fine, and certainly anything but sunny.

The day started badly for Lucy. She was late for breakfast, and was still putting the final pin in her hair as she hurried along the passage in her sage dimity gown. The dining room was situated next to the grand saloon, with a fine view over the lake, and the door stood open, so she heard the conversation at the table. Hearing her name mentioned, she paused.

Lady Amelia was speaking. "All I said was I hope you'll endeavor to be at least vaguely civil to Lucy when she joins us."

"I trust I'll have left the table before then," Geoffrey replied flatly.

"To be honest, so do I," his aunt declared with feeling. "Lucy's kind, warm-hearted, and amiable, but *you* somehow manage to quarrel with her every time you meet!"

"It's taken years of dedication to reach this degree of disagreeability," he said dryly.

"On the contrary, sir, I think it's the result of a natural tendency. Really, Geoffrey, I don't know what's come over you of late." She paused. "Then again, perhaps I do."

Lucy heard him put his coffee cup down with an irritable clatter. "Aunt Amelia, if you're about to harp on about my failed love life—"

"No, I'm not. As it happens I'm more concerned now about certain whispers I heard yesterday in Lausanne."

"Whispers?"

"I'm given to understand that straitened finances are your reason for temporarily quitting England."

There was a long silence before he replied. "Now who on earth said that?"

"It was just some gossip I overheard."

"Inaccurate gossip."

"Then you deny you are in monetary difficulties?"

"Aunt Amelia, I'm not going to dignify your unflattering lack of faith in me by giving you an answer."

Now it was Lady Amelia who fell briefly silent. Lucy heard some more coffee being poured before she spoke again. "You may call it an unflattering lack of faith, I prefer to call it kind concern. You're a trial to me, but you're my only nephew, and if I can help in any way . . . ?"

"I will be sure to turn to you," he said gently.

"Do you promise?"

"Yes, but it's not necessary."

She drew a long breath. "Very well, let us return to the matter of poor Lucy—"

He groaned. "*Must* we?"

She continued without pause. "—whose life here you've managed to make quite intolerable. I'm really most ashamed of you, Geoffrey, for whatever you may use as an excuse, the fact remains that your conduct toward her has been little short of monstrous."

"Damn it all, Aunt, I—"

"Don't blaspheme!"

He drew a long breath. "I apologize."

"I'd prefer it if you apologized to Lucy."

"Why should I? The creature gives as good as she gets."

"I find your attitude childish, and patently transparent," Lady Amelia replied sharply. "I told you what I thought that day you fell in the lake, and the more I witness your conduct, the more firmly I believe I'm right."

"This has nothing to do with Constance."

"No?"

"No!" he snapped.

At the door, Lucy's brows drew together in puzzlement. Who was Constance?

Lady Amelia stirred her coffee. "Then why do you behave so abominably toward Lucy?"

"Aren't I permitted to simply dislike her? Must there be a hidden reason?"

"Now you're being tiresome again, tiresome and blind."

"Blind? What's that supposed to mean?"

Lady Amelia sighed. "That a gentleman who might be in a precarious financial position would be better advised establishing warm relations with a young lady who stands close to the Trevallion fortune, not alienating her beyond all redemption!"

Lucy's lips parted in disbelief. Surely Lady Amelia wasn't thinking of promoting a match between Geoffrey and her? Oh, no, that couldn't possibly be.

Geoffrey found it hard to credit too. "Aunt, are you suggesting I woo the creature?"

"Why not?"

"The reasons are legion."

"Legion? List them, pray."

"There's no point, since only one appears to be material. I refer to the lady's Trevallion connections. Let me point out that however close she is to the fortune, she isn't the fortune itself, her cousin Emily is that. Maybe I should hightail it back to London this instant and lay siege to *her* instead? At ten, she's probably ripe for marriage!"

"Don't be facetious, Geoffrey, it isn't becoming."

"Nor is your rather obvious matchmaking. Aunt Amelia, I know you're very fond of Lucy Trevallion, but please spare *me* the consequences of that fondness. I don't like her, I don't want to be near her, and I'd rather go to debtor's jail than woo her! Have I made myself abundantly clear?"

"Perfectly."

"Good."

Lucy could feel Lady Amelia's cross silence, and after a moment so could Geoffrey. He sighed. "Oh, very well, I concede that I've been every bit the beast you say, so in future I'll do my utmost to be more agreeable toward her. Will that do?"

"It will have to, I suppose. But Geoffrey, it really would please me if you and she were on pleasant terms for the short while she remains here. I don't know how long it will be, but it can't be long. Edwin's last letter was most specific that he wished her to be with him for Christmas, which means that whomever he sends to accompany her back to London must arrive shortly."

"Yes, I suppose so."

"I wonder who will come?"

"Perhaps it will be his son," Geoffrey suggested.

"If you mean Robert Trevallion, the fellow isn't Edwin's son, he's his stepson, and I certainly hope *he* isn't about to come here," his aunt replied with feeling.

"Why's that? Don't tell me he's another sulky bear?"

"No, he's a grasping, scheming bear," she declared.

Lucy's eyes widened a little at the palpable dislike in her employer's voice. Lady Amelia had never spoken derogatorily to her about Robert Trevallion.

Geoffrey gave a brief laugh. "Dear God, I had no idea bears were of such varied character."

"Oh, I may be wrong about him, for I've only met him once, but I certainly didn't take to him. His eyes are a little, er, shifty. One feels he'd skin his own grandmother for sixpence."

"What a charming phrase."

"But appropriate, I'm certain. Oh, you have no idea how much I'll miss Lucy. That's why it's so important to me that you're at the very least civil to her. You do understand, don't you?"

"Yes, of course I do."

"And even if she is only second in line to the Trevallion fortune, she—"

"Aunt!"

"As you wish." Lady Amelia stirred her coffee again, and nothing more was said.

At the door, Lucy was too embarrassed to go in. Gathering her skirts, she hurried quietly away. She went to the kitchens, where the Swiss cook was soon persuaded to give her a glass of fresh milk and some warm bread straight from the oven. Shortly after that she collected her cloak and went down to the summerhouse with her volume of Rousseau, for Lady Amelia had already indicated her services as companion wouldn't be required until a little later.

Lake Geneva was very still and beautiful in the winter morning sun. The alps were very crisp and white against the icy blue sky, and their reflection shimmered in the mirrored surface, where white-sailed fishing boats went about their business with an unhurried calm that was almost soothing. Lucy's gaze was drawn west to the Jura mountains. Soon her grandfather's representative would arrive to see her safely to London; then she'd traverse those heights and leave this idyllic place forever.

Reaching the summerhouse, she sat facing the lake, the book open on her lap, but she couldn't concentrate because her thoughts kept returning to two intriguing points from the overheard conversation. The first was Geoffrey's apparently straitened financial position, the second was Constance. Both were clearly prickly subjects about which he wasn't prepared to talk.

Suddenly a shadow fell across the page, and with a gasp she looked up to see Geoffrey himself standing there. He wore a fur-collared gray greatcoat and a top hat. He removed the hat. "Forgive me, Miss Trevallion, I didn't mean to startle you, it's just that I saw you come here, and since I wish to speak to you, I decided to follow."

Recovering, she eyed him coolly. "You wish to speak to me, sir?"

"Yes. May I join you?"

What was this? Second thoughts concerning her close proximity to a fortune? Or was he carrying out his promise to Lady Amelia? "By all means, my lord."

He joined her on the bench seat. "I've come to try to redeem myself in your eyes, Miss Trevallion."

"Indeed?" Instinct told her he wasn't concerned with his aunt, just with the fortune, but her face gave nothing away.

He ran a gloved hand through his rather unruly dark hair. "This morning my aunt rightly ticked me off for behaving shabbily toward you, and I concede that that has indeed been the case. I offer no excuse, but I do abjectly seek your forgiveness, in the hope that we may start again."

"Is that what you'd really like, sir?" she asked innocently.

He looked into her wide green eyes. "Yes, Miss Trevallion, it is."

"Then it gives me great pleasure to tell you to go to perdition, Lord St. Athan," she said cordially.

He was caught off guard. "I-I beg your pardon?"

"You heard me, sirrah." She rose to her feet, her book clasped neatly before her. "I find you every bit as abhorrent as you clearly find me, and if you were the last man on earth, I wouldn't wish to start again. Redeem yourself? You've sunk too far for that!"

Leaving him to stare after her, she turned on her heel and walked away. She trembled with anger, and not a little triumph. Oh, how *good* that had felt! It was a moment to hug herself with forever more. How *dared* he trim his odious sails like that! Well, he reckoned without the proverbial ear at the door.

She inhaled the chill air sweeping down from the mountains. Suddenly she felt better than she had in weeks, and all because she'd given his supercilious snout the verbal poke it had richly deserved since the moment it arrived. Now she could leave the Villa Belmont knowing she'd acquitted herself more than adequately in this particular little war.

Her glance returned across the lake toward the Jura. What awaited her in faraway London? She shivered a little, for in spite of her small victory over Geoffrey, she felt unaccountably vulnerable and ill-at-ease. A sixth sense warned her that the coming weeks were going to be difficult, perhaps even hazardous.

Nine

Two days later, on the afternoon of December second, Lucy was again in the summerhouse when James and Dorothea's carriage swept in through the villa gates. Lady Amelia received them in the grand saloon, and the moment she heard their sad news about poor little Emily, a maid was dispatched to bring Lucy. Lady Amelia wished to break the sorrowful tidings herself, so the maid was instructed to say only that the chaperones had arrived.

Geoffrey had been enjoying a vigorous ride through the vineyards above the villa, and the newcomers and Lady Amelia were still awaiting Lucy's return when he rode back along the drive. He wore a mulberry riding coat and fawn breeches, and his neckcloth had become a little windblown after several hours in the saddle, but he felt refreshed as he urged his sweating horse toward the villa.

He reined in as he saw Lucy walking back from the summerhouse. The volume of Rousseau was clasped rather nervously in her hands, and he could see the hem of her cinnamon-colored gown peeping beneath her cloak. A stray lock of ash-blond hair bounced from beneath her gypsy hat, and she didn't notice him.

He couldn't help being thankful she'd soon be gone, for try as he would, he couldn't be easy in her company, especially after she'd snubbed him so monumentally two days earlier. Every time he looked at her, he saw Constance, and it was a reminder of the unhappiness he was striving to put behind him. He lowered his eyes then, knowing he was thinking only of himself. Lucy was anxious about the new life awaiting her in London, and his aunt made no secret of her sadness on losing her much loved young companion. What did his private feelings really matter?

As he continued to watch Lucy cross the lawns toward the house, he became suddenly aware of how deliberately she kept her eyes lowered. It wasn't to avoid him, for she didn't know he was there, so why? Curiosity prompted him to announce his presence.

"Good afternoon, Miss Trevallion," he said, riding over to her.

With a gasp she whirled about. "Lord St. Athan!"

He saw how tense she was. "Is something wrong?" he asked, dismounting.

She met his gaze with steady green eyes. "You'll be relieved to know two chaperones have at last arrived to take me back to England."

For the first time he saw the travel-stained carriage in front of the villa. "They've left it a little late to reach London comfortably in time for Christmas," he observed.

"It's still possible."

"Provided the weather holds out."

She nodded.

He studied her. "You hardly seem ecstatic about your imminent departure. What is it? Second thoughts?"

"Oh, don't worry, my lord, I still intend to leave," she replied dryly.

"As it happens, my inquiry was genuinely solicitous."

She glanced at him again. "Forgive me if I find that hard to believe."

He searched her pale face, for although her words were as spirited and prickly as usual, he detected a certain tremble in her voice. "Who are these chaperones?" he asked curiously.

"A Mr. and Miss Weybridge. They're brother and sister. I-I've just received an urgent message from Lady Amelia that they've arrived and I'm to go immediately to the grand saloon. So, if you'll excuse me . . ." She hurried on toward the villa.

Urgent? Immediate? Something was up, he thought, for his aunt wouldn't use such words unless something untoward had occurred. He swung the reins thoughtfully in his hands. Perhaps it would be better if he attended this meeting as well, just to see what was afoot, and to get the gauge of Edwin Trevallion's representatives. Swiftly remounting, he urged the horse to the stables behind the house, and then hastened through the kitchens and up the back stairs, arriving at the door of the grand saloon at the same moment as Lucy.

She hesitated in surprise, her hand still outstretched to the door handle. "My lord?"

"I've decided to see your chaperones for myself."

"To be certain they'll take me swiftly away from here, I suppose?"

"No, to be certain they're suitable."

"I'm sure you'd find *anyone* suitable, my lord, even Old Nick himself," she murmured coolly, opening the door and going in.

James and Dorothea were seated by the fire with Lady Amelia, who looked stylish in a kingfisher wool gown and a frilled muslin cap with ribbons to match the gown. Dorothea was dabbing her eyes with a handkerchief, and Lady Amelia looked shaken about something.

James immediately rose to his feet, toying nervously with his cravat as if it were a little too tightly knotted. He wore a dark blue coat and gray trousers, and his chestnut hair shone in the firelight that countered the dull day outside.

Lady Amelia squeezed Lucy's hands, and then patted the sofa beside her. "Please sit with me, my dear."

Lucy obeyed.

Lady Amelia then took her hands gently. "Oh, Lucy, before I introduce you to your chaperones, I fear I have sad news to impart."

Lucy's heart lurched. "Sad . . . ? Is it my grandfather?"

"No, my dear, I'm afraid it's your cousin Emily. Some weeks ago, just before your chaperones left England, she suffered terrible injuries in a riding accident, and wasn't given any hope of surviving. By now, I'm sorry to say, she has probably passed away. I'm so very sorry."

Geoffrey was startled. So Lucy was to be the Trevallion heir after all!

Lucy didn't realize the implications; all she could think was that she was losing—had lost—the new cousin she'd only recently learned about.

Lady Amelia squeezed her hands comfortingly. "Now, my dear, let me introduce Mr. James Weybridge, and his sister, Miss Dorothea, who are to take care of you on the journey home."

Home? To Lucy, right now London didn't seem at all like home. Involuntarily, her glance flew to Geoffrey, although she didn't know why.

He caught the glance, and saw her wretchedness written large and clear. Against his will, it affected him. Damn it, he cared what happened to her!

As James bowed over Lucy's hand and then inclined his head to Geoffrey, the latter put Lucy from his thoughts to study her male escort for the coming weeks. From the moment he met James's gaze, he felt Mr. Weybridge wasn't quite the gentleman he appeared. Geoffrey had met the type too many times before not to spot a charming adventurer with a thin veneer of respectability. It was there in the smooth smile and the speculative glances turned discreetly upon Lucy. The fellow was clearly a womanizing rogue with an eye to lining his own pockets, and heaven only knew how Edwin Trevallion had chosen him for his present role. Weybridge had known Lucy was the new heiress before he left London, so what was his real purpose? To conduct her safely home to her grandfather? Or to win her for himself? There was no doubt in Geoffrey's mind that even if the former were the case, the latter was bound to be an almost unbearable temptation for such a man.

As for the beautiful sister . . . Geoffrey turned his attention to Dorothea as she sipped her cup of tea and evinced great solicitude toward Lucy. Like James, she wasn't the lady she seemed. Oh, she was very poised and polished, there was suitable restraint in the way her gleaming chestnut hair was pinned up beneath a little brown beaver hat, and nothing could have been more demure and tasteful than her fawn pelisse and cream woolen gown, but . . .

Geoffrey sighed. Why did there seem to be so many "buts" where these two were concerned? He withdrew thoughtfully to the window to observe the little group around the fire. It was clear he was alone in mistrusting the Weybridges, for his aunt seemed charmed by them both, and Lucy was gradually relaxing in their company.

Dorothea suddenly glanced toward him. It was a glance he caught, and to his surprise he saw apprehension in her lovely brown eyes. It was as if they'd met somewhere before, and she was afraid he'd remember. With a start, he suddenly realized they *had* met somewhere, or at least, seen each other somewhere. But where, that was the question? There was something very familiar about that flawless profile and those voluptuous curves, even about the way she tilted her head. If only he could place her . . .

Suddenly his aunt was addressing him. "Is that not so, Geoffrey?"

"Mm?"

"I was saying that I trust everyone's health will stand up well during the return journey."

"Health?" He looked blankly at her.

She became cross. "Mr. and Miss Weybridge were taken ill on their way here, that's why they've arrived so late."

"Oh, I see."

"The unfortunate delay means they'll have to set out on the return journey almost immediately, the day after tomorrow, in fact."

"Er, yes."

Lady Amelia frowned at him. "You aren't paying attention, sirrah," she reproved.

"Actually, I was wondering where Miss Weybridge and I had met before," he said, looking directly at Dorothea.

James's glance flicked uneasily toward his sister. She and St. Athan knew each other?

Dorothea gave a light laugh. "But we haven't met, my lord."

"Are you quite sure?"

"Absolutely."

"But I feel certain we—"

He was interrupted by Lady Amelia. "Geoffrey, if Miss Weybridge says you haven't met, then that is so. I'm sure you must be thinking of someone who merely resembles her."

He inclined his head, and fell silent, but he saw James and Dorothea exchange a nervous glance, and his suspicions deepened. This pair had something to hide, and far from being suitable chaperones, were decidedly suspect. He might wish to see Lucy Trevallion's departure, but not in the care of these two undesirables. But on what grounds could he interfere? It was hardly sufficient to say his instincts told him not to trust the newcomers.

After dwelling on it for a while, he decided his best course was to speak privately with his aunt as soon as he could. His opportunity came about ten minutes later, when Dorothea and James were shown to their rooms, and Lady Amelia despatched Lucy to bring her a warmer shawl.

The moment they were alone, he turned to his aunt. "The Weybridges aren't in the least suitable," he said bluntly.

She was startled. "I beg your pardon?"

"I don't profess to know why Edwin Trevallion chose them to look after Lucy, but I do know dissemblers when I see them."

Lady Amelia looked faint. "Dissemblers? How can you possibly say that?"

"Because Weybridge is clearly a knave, and his sister is—well, heaven alone knows what she might be."

Lady Amelia rose a little shakily to her feet. "Have you any proof to support your statement?"

"No, save the evidence of my own eyes. I've seen Weybridge's type before, the fringe of good society abounds in them, and no matter what she may say to the contrary, I *have* met his sister somewhere before, although I still can't think where, but I'd hazard a guess she's far from being a lady."

"Geoffrey, how can you possibly say such things of two people who've done you no harm at all? And when they're clearly distressed about what's befallen poor little Emily Trevallion. Shame on you, sirrah!"

"Can't you trust my judgment?"

"Trust *you* where Lucy is involved? Since your arrival you've done your utmost to be unpleasant toward her, and I'm sorry to say I regard this latest whim in the same disagreeable light."

"It's not a whim, Aunt, it's a very strong conviction. Believe me, I've never disliked her sufficiently to give her into the custody of two such as these!"

"I find Mr. and Miss Weybridge most amiable, Geoffrey, and unless you can *prove* them to be otherwise, I suggest you hold your tongue. This is my house, do I make myself clear?"

"Aunt—"

"Do I make myself clear?" she interrupted coldly.

He nodded. "You do."

"Then let this be the end of it. Apply your intellect to your own problems, Geoffrey, for to be sure you have them in abundance."

The door opened and Lucy returned with the shawl. Geoffrey strode out, passing her without so much as a glance.

Lady Amelia glared after him, and then her face softened into a smile for her soon-to-be-gone companion. "Thank you, my dear; it's really getting quite cold in here," she said, turning for the new shawl to be placed around her shoulders.

Ten

Lady Amelia had instructed one of the maids to attend Dorothea, so it was some time before James was able to speak to his sister alone about her apparent acquaintance with Geoffrey. He paced restlessly up and down in his room, and then looked from the window. Geoffrey was walking down by the lake, the smoke of his cigar curling up into the icy air. James watched him, wondering where he'd become acquainted with Dorothea. Given her career thus far, it wasn't likely to have been anywhere respectable! Of all the god-awful luck!

James's thoughts broke off as he heard the maid leave Dorothea, whose room was next to his. At last! But as he emerged from his door, he walked straight into Lucy. She was carrying her embroidery box, which fell to the floor. Pins, needles, scissors, and bright silks scattered everywhere, and the Christmas bookmark she was making for the cook fell directly at his feet.

She bent swiftly to retrieve everything, and he apologized profusely. "I'm so sorry, Miss Trevallion."

"That's quite all right, Mr. Weybridge, it was an accident."

He watched her for a moment, taking in the lithe curves of her figure. She was an unexpectedly tasty morsel, he thought approvingly, picturing her completely naked, and imagining her pliant warmth lying beneath him in a feather bed.

He bent to pick up a pin she'd missed, and then glanced at the bookmark, with its beautifully worked religious design. Was the lady devout? The thought aroused his fantasies. She was a nun plagued by carnal appetites! Or a novice who'd be refused the veil because she succumbed to the sins of the flesh!

Lucy looked quizzically at him, for he still held the pin he'd picked up. "Mr. Weybridge?"

He pulled himself together and returned the pin. Then she hurried on to her room.

He gazed after her. The last thing he'd expected was to desire the woman he and his sister had come to destroy. It was base desire, of course, a need to possess and then forget, but it was a strong urge he intended to satisfy. After all, when the lady was no more, who'd ever know she'd been ravished first? Turning, he went to his sister's door.

"Well? What does St. Athan know of you?" he asked as soon as he was safely inside.

"Not a great deal." She went to the window. Geoffrey was still by the shore. "He knows me from the Devil's Den," she said softly.

"Oh, great God above." James felt suddenly sick.

"Don't worry, I doubt if he'll remember any more than he already has."

"Not remember meeting you in a high-class whorehouse?"

"He wasn't there for the female company; he came with friends to enjoy the gaming tables."

"If he didn't bed you, how does he remember you? There must have been more to it."

"Yes, there was." She turned to face him. "As I said, he was with friends, two of whom argued for my favors. There'd have been a fight if St. Athan hadn't separated them. I was different then; I wore my hair short and my face was painted, which is why I doubt if he'll make the connection between then and now."

"But what if he does?"

"It will have to be before we leave the day after tomorrow, and should that happen, I'll treat Lady Amelia to a fit of the shocked maidenly vapors that anyone should accuse me of frequenting a house of ill repute."

James was acid. "Always presuming you can remember how to be maidenly, or shocked." He drew an unhappy breath. "I don't like this turn of events, Sis. St. Athan has an air about him."

"Air?"

"Of someone intent upon getting to the bottom of something. Believe me, I've encountered it before. Just when one thinks one has an advantageous situation comfortably in hand, someone like him comes along to wreck it."

Dorothea looked at him. "All we have to do is hold fast to our story that we're from a respectable family fallen on hard times, and so are reduced to taking positions such as this in order to support ourselves. You are the loving, protective brother, I the vulnerable but exceedingly proper sister."

"I still don't like it."

"There's no backing out now, James. I intend to be Mrs. Robert Trevallion, and if you want the handsome sum he's promised you,

you'll keep on our agreed course. We'll leave here as planned, and Mansart and his men will see that dear little Lucy meets her doom. After that, its the altar for me, and a fat purse for you." She held his eyes.

After a moment he nodded. "All right." He turned to leave, but then paused. "Lucy Trevallion is religiously inclined," he said with a slight laugh.

Dorothea was taken aback by the change of subject. "Of what possible relevance is that?"

"None, I suppose."

Dorothea turned to the window again, and then gave one of her brittle laughs. "Provided religiousness doesn't make her immortal, I couldn't care less if she spends every waking hour on her knees in prayer!"

Without another word he went out, but as he closed the door and stood alone in the deserted passage, there was a cynical glitter in his brown eyes. Lucy's mortality was of more concern to him than his sister imagined. As was the promised plumpness of his purse. Ravishing her was no longer sufficient; he was now of a mind to possess her in the eyes of the law. Why should Robert Trevallion have the fortune? Might it not come to James Weybridge instead? It might, if he played his cards right.

Dinner was a subdued affair. Geoffrey continued to observe, and everything he saw convinced him more and more that the Weybridges were up to no good. He wished he knew what it was, and he certainly wished he could remember where he'd seen Dorothea before, but, mindful of his aunt's wrath, he said nothing more.

Dorothea had dressed rather unwisely that evening. Instead of remembering her own advice about respectability fallen on hard times, she'd elected to wear a beautiful fuchsia silk gown paid for by Robert. In Geoffrey's opinion it was far too bang-up-to-the-mark and expensive for someone supposedly living in reduced circumstances. It was also not quite as demure as the lace tucked into the neckline might make it seem. Without the lace, far too much of the lady's admittedly desirable bosom would have been revealed; indeed, if she bent forward, he was convinced her charms might tumble out entirely. But the lace made the difference, sparing her questionable modesty and satisfying Lady Amelia that all was as it should be.

James came to the rescue whenever Geoffrey's heavy silence became too obvious. He had a store of amusing anecdotes, and dropped names as frequently as an ostler dropped his aitches. He made it seem he was welcome at Carlton House itself, and certainly that he'd been granted vouchers for Almack's, but Geoffrey had never seen him before, which he was certain he would have done if the fellow were genuine. London's exclusive high society wasn't extensive, and if James Weybridge was part of it, Geoffrey would have seen him before. So would Lady Amelia, if she hadn't shunned London for so many years before coming abroad.

From James, Geoffrey's attention moved to Lucy. Her silvery hair was worn in a simple French pleat, with a little frame of curls around her face, and he had to admit that it suited her well. She wore a primrose brocade gown he'd seen many times before. There was nothing startling about its square neckline and long tight sleeves, and nothing costly about the hand-embroidered buckle on the belt beneath her breasts. It had never been the height of fashion, but possessed serviceability in plenty.

Regrettably, she was beginning to warm toward Weybridge. Occasionally there was a soft blush on her cheeks, and she glanced at the fellow from beneath lowered lashes. The blackguard was master of his art, that much had to be conceded. He never smiled too much, or too obviously, he just caught her eye at relevant moments. Oh, yes, James Weybridge was a fortune hunter, and in Lucy Trevallion he'd found a fortune second to none!

By the end of the meal, Geoffrey could stand no more. Rather than adjourn to the grand saloon with the others, he announced his intention to walk by the lake again.

Lady Amelia was astonished. "At this hour? But it's absolutely freezing out there!"

"I'm in need of fresh air." His glance flickered toward James and Dorothea, then without ceremony he left the room.

Lady Amelia tried to smooth over his blunt departure by linking James's arm and ushering him toward the grand saloon. "Mr. Weybridge, I'm sure you'll enjoy one of the fruit brandies in which the Swiss so excel. There's pear, white plum, and kirsch, and they are all quite superb."

"I look forward to them," he replied with a smile as they proceeded into the grand saloon, followed by Dorothea and Lucy.

Geoffrey didn't regret his spur-of-the-moment decision to take a stroll outside. His aunt was right, it was damned cold, but he didn't feel it as he lit one of his favorite Spanish cigars and walked down the lawns toward the lake. He took his time as far as the summerhouse, and then strolled back again, before lighting a second cigar. Damn Lucy Trevallion for intruding upon his existence like this, but most of all, damn Edwin Trevallion for sending two such questionable escorts. Turning, he retraced his path to the summerhouse.

How long he walked to and fro along the shore he didn't know, he only realized suddenly that he was cold after all, and decided to return to the house. But as he neared it, he saw two figures by the brightly lit window of the grand saloon. It was Lucy and James Weybridge. They were looking out at the night and talking, in clear view of Lady Amelia and Dorothea. Then they turned away and were lost from Geoffrey's view, but in the second before they stepped out of sight, he distinctly saw James's arm rest fleetingly at her waist. Geoffrey had been watching closely for just such an unwarranted intimacy. No gentleman would have made so bold, and by giving in to the temptation, James Weybridge had revealed his true colors.

Geoffrey went slowly back into the house. What was he to do about this? His aunt refused to listen, and he had no reason to think Lucy would be any more disposed to pay heed. But he had to try. Somehow or other he had to find a suitable moment to advise her that if she left the Villa Belmont with the Weybridges, she would be very unwise indeed. Possibly even foolhardy.

Eleven

It wasn't to be until sunset the following afternoon, on the very eve of the return journey, that Geoffrey was able to speak to Lucy alone, but before then, far away across Europe in London, Emily's condition suddenly worsened.

Sir Joshua was sent for, and his carriage arrived in one of the thickest and coldest fogs so far that year. It was preceded by a man carrying a smoking flambeau, and the light shone on the shining cobbles as the coachman drew the vehicle to a halt. The physician alighted, pausing only to adjust his top hat before snatching his bag and hastening into the house, where a distraught Edwin was waiting at the top of the stairs.

"Oh, do hurry, sir, for I fear she sinks fast now!"

Emily's room was candlelit, and the curtains tightly drawn against the freezing fog. Nettie's eyes were red from crying as she stood at the foot of the bed, but she wept silently. Robert, however, shed copious and noisy crocodile tears as he held his step-niece's limp little hand. It was his finest hour, a thespian masterpiece; indeed, he was so magnificently anguished that he almost convinced himself!

Locked in her half-world, neither really living, nor yet dead, Emily was relieved when Sir Joshua's arrival meant Robert had to release her hand. Oh, how she loathed the man who'd brought this fate upon her. He'd deliberately schemed to kill her, and yet pretended to be inconsolable with grief. As his physical grasp was broken, however, she suddenly realized she was looking down at the scene around the bed. From the darkness that had engulfed her since the day in Hyde Park, suddenly she was able to see again.

But any joy was fleeting, for she saw Sir Joshua sadly shake his head, and her grandfather hide his face in his hands. Nettie gave in to tears again, and ran weeping from the room, pushing her way through the small gathering of equally heartbroken servants crowding the passage. Robert played his part to the very end, but

Emily could see his shining eyes. There was triumph in that wicked gleam.

She wanted to reach down to her grandfather, who was so overcome he was close to collapse, but she was already being drawn away from the room. She felt something pulling her toward the window, and then out into the swirling fog that enveloped the capital. Faster and faster she went, until suddenly the fog wasn't there any more; instead, there was the shining staircase with the wonderful bright light at the top. Spectral figures surrounded her again, smiling and welcoming, touching with hands that warmed and comforted. Beautiful carol-singing filled the air. A Christmas lullaby. *Lully, lulla, thou tiny child, By by, lully, lullay. . . .*

The shining gates stood open at the top of the staircase! Her parents were waiting, their beloved figures imbued with the heavenly glow that seemed to pervade everything in this marvelous place. But as she flew gladly toward them, they shook their heads again.

"Not yet, my darling babe," her mother said sadly.

Emily was filled with fresh dismay. "Can't I stay with you now?"

Her father put a loving hand to her cheek. "No, my dearest child, for you have a task to complete."

"A-a task?"

"You must save Lucy," her father reminded her.

Lucy! In the emotion of the moment, Emily had quite forgotten the cousin who was in so much danger. "But I don't know what to do." Tears sprang to her eyes, and her lips quivered.

Her mother knelt to put her arms around her. "You must go to Lucy and warn her, my darling."

Emily clung to the beloved mother she'd missed so very much. "I'm frightened, Mama."

"There is no need, for you are an angel now. See, you have little wings, and you shine as we do." Her mother took a strand of Emily's long blond hair, which now seemed to shimmer as if sprinkled with gold dust.

Emily choked back the tears, and struggled to glance back over her shoulders. She *did* have wings! Such beautiful wings, like those of a dove. . . . She looked at her mother again. "Can I really save Lucy?"

"Of course."

"But she's in Switzerland."

"You will go to her there, and once your task is complete, you can come to us forever."

"I-I'll be able to go through the gates?"

"Yes, my sweeting, and you'll be so happy here, for there is only joy in Heaven."

But angel or not, Emily was still a little girl, and more frightened about now than about what was to come. "Can't you come with me to help Lucy?" she ventured in a small voice.

"You must do it alone, my dear, and there is one thing you must remember. Only the first person you encounter will be able to see and speak to you, so you must make certain that that person is Lucy. You must tell her what your uncle has already done, and what he still plans. She must not make the journey to England with the Weybridges."

"But what if she doesn't believe me?"

"My dearest babe, she will believe, for you are an angel now."

Emily's father leaned forward then, putting a gentle hand on his daughter's shoulder. "There is something else you must remember, my darling. Whenever you are near something holy, whether it is a church, a crucifix, a wayside shrine, or anything else, you will begin to glow sufficiently for all to see. This is strictly forbidden by the Lord, unless the circumstances are very urgent indeed, and He has instructed me to tell you."

Emily's eyes widened. "He knows about me?" she whispered.

"Oh, yes, He knows about every angel, even very small ones like you."

Emily swallowed, and then glanced around. A sea of gentle faces gazed kindly at her, and she drew strength from them. She hugged her parents again, and then her father smiled regretfully at her.

"It's time for you to go, Emily."

"But how will I know the way?"

"You will, for you will be guided, and when it's time for you to join us properly, we will come for you."

Her mother hugged her tightly. "Good luck, my darling."

Emily clung to her for as long as she could, and then turned to embrace her father too. But the light began to recede, and once again she was flying through the air. The singing of the Christmas lullaby died away into silence, and suddenly she saw a glorious sunset. Oh, she'd never known a sunset like it; the rays seemed to flame with color, from the palest lemon, to the most fiery and splendid of crimsons.

She flew into the heart of its dazzling magnificence, and the colors seemed to caress her. She felt warm, and knew the light now suffused her whole being. She was like the sunset! A little smile sprang to her lips, and her confidence grew. She would and could help Lucy! Uncle Robert wasn't going to succeed in his wickedness.

The air was suddenly much colder, but her inner warmth was a shield. There were mountains below her now, their snow-capped peaks blood-red as the sun sank toward the horizon. A great expanse of water lay ahead, and she knew it was Lake Geneva. An invisible force drew her toward the part of the shore where the Villa Belmont stood among the vineyards.

She glided down and saw a young woman in a warm winter cloak seated deep in thought on the steps by a tiny harbor. She knew it was Lucy, but just as the little angel was about to make her presence known, a gentleman appeared. Lucy got up swiftly and turned to face him. Dismayed, Emily retreated to wait among the thick willows fringing the harbor.

Neither Lucy nor Geoffrey, the gentleman who'd appeared, was aware they weren't alone; they were too intent upon each other to sense a supernatural presence. Geoffrey had been waiting all day to tell Lucy of his reservations concerning the Weybridges, and he knew as he faced her that it wasn't going to be easy.

Lucy waited for him to speak, for she had no intention of opening the conversation. She thrust her hands deep into her fur-lined muff and raised her chin defiantly. He was the last person she wished to see, or speak to.

He drew a long breath. "Miss Trevallion, I know you and I haven't hit it off at all, but right now I have your interests at heart."

"Indeed?"

"I gravely mistrust the Weybridges."

Emily parted the branches to look down with interest. He mistrusted the Weybridges? Who was he, she wondered.

Lucy was coolly angry with him. "I'm indifferent to your opinions, sir."

Her hauteur brought a flush to his cheeks, but he pressed on. "It's clear they aren't what they purport to be. By that, I mean that James Weybridge isn't a gentleman, and his sister certainly isn't a lady."

"Sir, there's been precious little of the gentleman in your conduct toward me."

"My past conduct has nothing to do with what's on my mind now."

A light passed through her eyes. "Oh, I'm sure of that," she murmured.

"Look, I'm concerned that if you entrust yourself to them for the journey to London—"

She interrupted. "Lord St. Athan, your effrontery beggars belief. Mr. Weybridge and his sister have been all that's kind to me since they arrived."

"Weybridge is too kind by far!" Geoffrey snapped.

"And what do you mean by that?" she demanded.

"That he has fortune hunter written all over him."

Her eyes flashed. "And you don't, I suppose?" she inquired softly.

"I beg your pardon?"

"Lord St. Athan, until now you have shown me nothing but rudeness and contempt, but suddenly you are all concern. I have to wonder why, and the reason is too basely obvious, I fear."

"Is it, indeed? Pray elucidate, for to be sure *I* don't know what you're suggesting."

She met his gaze. "Well, I'm the Trevallion heiress now, am I not?"

He became very cold and still. "If you're suggesting I have a mercenary motive in this, I—"

"That's precisely what I'm suggesting, sirrah!"

"Then go to hell, Miss Trevallion, for to be sure that's where you'll end if you accompany the Weybridges!" He strode furiously away. Damn the woman! She was more mulish than a mule, and more infuriating than . . . than . . . Oh, than he didn't know what!

Lucy was trembling as she turned her back on him to gaze at the harbor again. How *dared* he be so blatantly designing!

Emily hesitated among the willows. Lucy was facing her now, so this must be the perfect moment! But just as the little angel glided from hiding, Geoffrey turned to say something more.

"Miss Trevallion!"

Lucy whirled about. "I don't think we have anything more to say, sir," she replied coldly.

"Whatever you may think, my motives now are—" He broke off to stare past her at the shining winged child floating in the air above the harbor.

Emily returned his gaze in unutterable dismay. Oh, no! The wrong person had seen her!

Shaken, Geoffrey looked swiftly away again. Dear God, he was seeing things! But when he looked once more, the vision was still there.

Lucy was puzzled, for even in the fading light of the sunset she could see how pale he'd gone. "My lord?"

"I, er . . ." Geoffrey continued to stare at Emily, who stared wretchedly back, not knowing what to do.

Lucy turned to follow his gaze, but saw nothing. Her brows drew together and she faced him again. "My lord, I don't know what you're up to now, but I'm in no mood to humor you. If you will not leave, I will."

Geoffrey hardly heard her. If he'd been inebriated, he could almost have understood what he saw, but he was as sober as the proverbial judge! How then could he see a little golden angel hovering in the air above the harbor?

Lucy had had enough. Plunging her hands even further into her muff, she stalked past him. Oh, how glad she was that she was leaving in the morning. Not even for Lady Amelia's sake could she endure another day of him!

Geoffrey caught her arm as she passed. "Miss Trevallion, will you please look over there and tell me what you see?"

She snatched her arm away, but did as he asked, and saw only harbor, lake, and sunset. "I see what one would expect to see, sir."

"You don't see a-a . . . " Oh, God, he couldn't say it! She'd think he'd taken leave of his senses, and perhaps he had!

Lucy eyed him. "I don't see a what, sir?"

"A winged child. A little girl. Damn it, an angel!"

Lucy's eyes flashed then, and she drew sharply away from him. "Enough of this, sirrah! Do you take me for a fool?"

"No, madam, but it's clear you take me for one! Do you honestly imagine I'd stand here and talk of angels if I didn't see one?"

"My Lord St. Athan, you're capable of saying anything, no matter how preposterous," she replied, hurrying away before he could detain her longer.

Geoffrey glanced after her, then at Emily again, and as soon as Lucy was out of earshot, he spoke. "Am I really seeing you?" he asked.

Emily nodded and floated unhappily toward him. "I was supposed to appear to Lucy. Now it's all gone wrong and I don't know what to do! I haven't been an angel for an hour, but I've failed already!"

To his horror her lips quivered, her face crumpled, and she began to sob heartrendingly.

Twelve

Geoffrey was completely confounded. *She* didn't know what to do? Neither did he! He wasn't simply seeing a vision, he was talking to it!

Emily's wretched sobs affected him. He wasn't used to children, and didn't have a clue how to proceed next. He put out a tentative hand, but it passed right through her. He stepped back involuntarily, but then took a grip on himself. What else did he expect of an angel? She was hardly going to be flesh and blood!

Gradually her sobs quietened, and she looked sorrowfully up at him. "I don't know how to be an angel yet, Lord St. Athan. You *are* Lord St. Athan, aren't you? I heard Lucy call you that."

"Yes, that's who I am, and I'm not exactly well up on angels either," he replied dryly.

"I'm Lucy's cousin, Emily Trevallion."

"Emily Trevallion?" he repeated incredulously. The child whose demise would turn Lucy into a great heiress? Correction, the child whose demise already had turned Lucy into a great heiress.

Emily nodded. "You must help me, my lord. You see, I'm Lucy's angel now, and I've been sent to save her, but everything's gone wrong. I was supposed to appear to her first, so she'd be the one who could see and hear me and I'd be able to warn her she's in danger. Instead, I can only talk to you!"

The significance of her words dawned on him. "Danger? What danger?"

"It's Uncle Robert. He killed me, and he means to kill her too."

Geoffrey stared at her. "Robert Trevallion *killed* you?"

"Yes. He wants the inheritance, you see." Emily sat down on the steps, folded her wings, and rested her chin in her hands. "That's why you must help me, Lord St. Athan. You can see and hear me, so you must be the one to tell Lucy what I've said."

"Emily, she loathes the sight of me, and you must have seen

how she reacted when I mentioned you a moment ago! If you think I'm going to be fool enough to attempt to—"

"But you *must* help, Lord St. Athan. If you don't, I'll have failed, and Uncle Robert will have won."

Geoffrey drew a long breath. This wasn't really happening, he told himself. He didn't believe in angels—or ghosts, fairies, goblins, pixies, or anything else! But as he looked down at the little golden figure seated so forlornly on the steps, he knew that angels at least existed.

So he sat down next to her. "I'm not promising anything, but I'm prepared to listen. Tell me about it. What is Robert Trevallion supposed to have done?"

"Oh, there's nothing *supposed* about it, Lord St. Athan, he really did it. Well, not personally, but with the Weybridges' help."

"What have they to do with it?" he asked quickly.

"You're right not to trust them, Lord St. Athan, for they're Uncle Robert's accomplices. They helped him cause my riding accident in Hyde Park." She explained how it happened, and then went on. "Now he's promised James Weybridge a lot of money, and Dorothea marriage, if they get rid of Lucy. And I'm afraid for Grandfather too, if my uncle becomes the next heir."

Geoffrey didn't say anything. So his suspicions about that pair were only too well founded! And it was all at Robert Trevallion's instigation.

Emily looked at him. "I don't know what they plan to do, Lord St. Athan, I only know Lucy's in terrible danger from them."

He remained silent. There was something puzzling him. James Weybridge was a fortune hunter, and clearly had his eye on Lucy, so what was to be gained by killing her? Could it be that James had secretly decided to pursue the entire fortune, not just the portion Robert chose to hand out?

His silence perplexed Emily. "You *must* stop Lucy from going with them. She'll be safe if she stays here with Lady Amelia and you."

Geoffrey exhaled slowly. "Do you really imagine your cousin is going to listen to such a tale? Angels, wicked uncles, plots upon her life? It's outrageous."

"But true."

"Yes—not that she'll think that."

"You have to try."

"You ask the impossible."

"Please!"

It was hard to withstand such anguished imploring. Geoffrey

looked toward the fading rays of the sunset. The Jura was touched with crimson, and reflections reached across the smooth surface of the lake.

Emily tried a different tack. "Lord St. Athan, if something were to happen to Lucy, and you'd done nothing, how would you feel?"

He gave in. "All right, I'll try, but it won't do any good. She won't even hear me out."

"I'm sure you can be very persuasive, Lord St. Athan."

"Not in this instance."

Emily got up. "We'll go to her now!" she declared firmly.

Geoffrey shrugged resignedly. "As you wish, but don't expect miracles." Miracles? The irony of using such a word wasn't lost upon him.

Meanwhile, James had waylaid Lucy. He'd observed her meeting with Geoffrey, and made it his business to "accidentally" encounter her on the staircase as she returned.

She was deep in thought, still fuming about what she saw as Geoffrey's incredible gall. How *dared* he pretend to be concerned about her! And as for all that nonsense about angels . . . !

James spoke suddenly from the top of the stairs. "Why, Miss Trevallion, how very stalwart to walk in these temperatures."

She halted with a start. "Mr. Weybridge! I didn't know you were there."

"I trust I haven't alarmed you?" James gave her one of his most amiable and sincere smiles.

She smiled too. "No, of course not."

"Is it your custom to walk at sunset?"

"Occasionally. I had things to think about."

"Yes, of course you have." He came down toward her. "I'm only sorry Dorothea and I have been the bearers of such sad tidings. I didn't know Emily, but I understand she was a very dear child."

"It's so very strange to learn one has a cousin, only to have her snatched away before we've met."

"You still have your uncle, and your grandfather, of course."

"Yes." Lucy managed a smile.

"I'm sure Lady Amelia will miss you, but her loss will be London's gain," he said gallantly.

"You flatter me, I think, sir."

"Are you looking forward to London?"

"I-I don't really know. I still feel a little bewildered by it all."

"Forgive me if what I'm about to say is a little presumptuous, but I can't help observing that you and Lord St. Athan are hardly, er, on friendly terms."

The change of subject took her a little unawares. "Lord St. Athan?"

"I *am* being presumptuous. I crave your pardon," he said quickly.

"No, for you're quite right. Lord St. Athan and I do not see eye to eye on anything; in fact, I think him the most obnoxious man I've ever met."

"To be honest, I view him in the same light. He has a most, er, unfortunate way with him, and quite upset Dorothea when he insisted they'd met somewhere before."

Lucy nodded. "Lord St. Athan is disagreeable in the extreme."

"May I escort you to your room?" He offered her his arm, and they ascended the staircase. He took his leave at her door. "Until dinner, Miss Trevallion."

"Until then, sir."

He drew her hand to his lips, and held her gaze warmly for a moment.

A blush crept over her cheeks, and she went quickly into her room.

He smiled a little as the door closed behind her.

Lady Amelia's maid hurried down the staircase as Geoffrey and Emily ascended. He halted in immediate dismay, fearing the angel *must* be visible, in spite of assurances to the contrary. How could the maid not see something so incandescent with light?

But the maid paused only to bob him a swift curtsy before hurrying on, and Emily smiled at him." It's all right; no one else apart from you will ever be able to see me."

"So it seems," he murmured, going on up and then along the passage to Lucy's door. There he paused before knocking. All this was going to achieve was a monumental snub, and probably another oblique suggestion that it was somehow part of his designs upon her damned fortune!

Emily looked reproachfully at him. "You said you'd help me, Lord St. Athan."

Oh, to hell with it. He knocked firmly. "Miss Trevallion, may I have a word with you?"

For a moment nothing happened, but then Lucy reluctantly opened the door. "My lord?" Her green eyes were both wary and suspicious.

He decided to plow straight in, albeit with a blunt shear. "I've, er, come to advise you not to set out on this journey tomorrow."

She was immediately angry. "*Advise* me! I don't want your advice, sirrah!" She began to close the door again, but he pushed his foot swiftly in the way.

"Miss Trevallion, it's vital that you listen. The little girl, the angel, I mentioned earlier is your cousin Emily."

She drew back in shocked disgust. "How *dare* you use poor little Emily like this! I don't know what you hope to gain, but let me assure you it won't succeed!"

He kept his foot in the door. "I don't have anything to gain, Miss Trevallion, except your safety."

"Please go away, sir."

"Miss Trevallion, you *must* pay heed!"

Her voice quivered with outrage. "Please take your foot from my door, sirrah."

Having gotten this far, he felt he had to persist. "Everything I say is the truth, Miss Trevallion. You'll be in danger if you set out on this journey, and Emily has come to save you. Robert Trevallion is after the inheritance for himself, and the Weybridges are his agents. They mean you harm! You can't see her, but Emily is next to me right now."

"Go away this instant!" Lucy cried. "If you persist, sir, I'll call for Lady Amelia!"

Realizing he might as well knock his head on the wall, he resignedly removed his foot The door was immediately slammed in his face.

A nerve flickered angrily at his temple as he glanced down at Emily. "There, what did I tell you?"

"But she's in danger, and we must save her, my lord."

"*We* aren't obliged to do anything," he corrected. "I regret ever opening my fool mouth, and certainly don't intend to repeat the exercise."

"You surely won't desert me now, Lord St. Athan?" Emily's angelic eyes were huge and imploring.

"Look, there's absolutely nothing I can do. Whatever I say to Lucy, she'll go ahead with this journey. Can't you appear to someone else? My aunt, for instance? Lucy'd listen to her in a moment."

"Then you must tell your aunt," Emily declared promptly.

"I'd get no further with her than I have with Lucy."

"But—"

"No!" he snapped, and turned to stride angrily away.

Emily flew anxiously after him. "Oh, Lord St. Athan, you *have* to help me! What if I'm not allowed into heaven because I've failed?"

He halted. "There's absolutely nothing I can do. You've seen your dear cousin; if you were me, would *you* like the task of trying to persuade her about angelic warnings?"

"No, but—"

"There's nothing more to be said."

"You could always accompany them on the return journey," Emily suggested quickly.

"No!"

"Please, Lord St. Athan."

"When I leave here, it will be for Italy, not London."

Emily's eyes filled with tears again. "But you *must* help me; I need you," she whimpered.

"Don't start crying again, please!"

"It won't hurt you to return to England, and it might just save Lucy's life, as well as making sure I can go to heaven."

"This is blackmail; you know that, don't you?"

Tears welled from her eyes and her lips wobbled pathetically.

He gave a huge sigh. "Oh, very well."

An angelic smile lit her face.

Thirteen

Geoffrey was left in no doubt about Lucy's opinion of him at the dinner table that night, although to his relief, she considered the feelings of his aunt and the Weybridges, and declined to say anything in front of them. Even so, he knew she believed his new interest in her was based purely upon her changed expectations. She deemed him unutterably base for attempting to make her stay in Switzerland by saying what he had about her uncle and chaperones, and quite beyond the pale for bringing Emily into it the way he had.

He hardly dared contemplate the savagery of her thoughts when she learned he was planning to accompany them back to London. She was bound to conclude it was another ploy to stay close to the Trevallion fortune. Still, having given his word to Emily, who hovered watchfully in a corner throughout the meal, there was nothing for it but to make his bombshell announcement. He dropped it almost casually into the conversation.

"By the way, I, er, I've made up my mind to go back to England tomorrow with everyone else."

Astonishment and dismay riveted all eyes upon him. Lady Amelia, elegant in gentian silk and pearls, was on the point of taking her first mouthful of dessert, and put her knife and fork down with a clatter. "*You* mean to leave tomorrow as well?"

"Yes," he murmured, reaching for the sugar, and trying not to appear conscious of Emily as she glided to his side. He felt as if her glow bathed him in light, but dazzling as she was, he alone could see her.

His aunt dabbed her lips with a napkin and then stared at him. "And what, pray, has brought this on? I thought Italy was your destination."

"All this talk of Christmas in London has made me homesick."

"I find that hard to believe."

"It's true, nonetheless."

"But, there's too much to do at such short notice."

"It's all in hand. I've sent someone to hire a postilion in Vevey to take me as far as the French frontier, where I'll secure a new one to go to the coast. So our two carriages can easily depart together." He smiled blandly around the table.

James Weybridge looked sick, and suddenly lost interest in the meal. Dorothea toyed uneasily with the sleeve of her ruby marguerite gown, unconsciously returning Geoffrey's attention to the fact that some of her wardrobe was singularly inappropriate for someone in her claimed situation.

Lucy was appalled to realize she wasn't about to be free of him after all. She gazed furiously across the table, the leaf fustian of her gown bringing out the color of her eyes so much their greenness seemed almost luminous.

Emily studied them all curiously, and then glanced up at him. "The Weybridges are very cross, aren't they? And so is Lucy."

He almost made the error of replying, but at the last second clamped his lips closed. If he answered a question no one else could hear, he'd be deemed a suitable candidate for Bedlam! Embarrassed color suffused his cheeks, and without thinking he applied even more sugar to his plate. He'd have to make the angel promise never to speak to him when they were in company like this!

Lady Amelia watched him in puzzlement. "I had no idea you had such a sweet tooth, Geoffrey," she observed after a moment.

"Mm? Oh, I-I was miles away," he said, hastily setting the sugar aside.

She beckoned the footman to replenish her wine glass, and then looked at Geoffrey again. "I find your decision to leave somewhat quixotic. One moment you intend to remain until after Christmas, and now suddenly you're to return to England."

Somehow he managed to smile. "I've already explained, I have a fancy to be in London for Christmas, and what could be more sensible than for us all to make the journey together? We could even share, for what point is there in having three passengers in one carriage, and only one in the other? It seems to me an eminently sensible idea that two could travel comfortably in each."

Lucy's anger simmered. "And who would you suggest accompanied you, my lord?"

"I hadn't given it much thought, but if you wish to . . . ?"

"That would hardly be proper, sir," she replied in a voice that shook with outrage.

"Ah, well, if propriety is to be observed, then it's clear the two ladies should travel in one vehicle, the gentlemen in the other."

Geoffrey gave James a superficial smile. Get out of that, if you can, Weybridge, for it won't be so easy to pursue Lucy from a separate carriage!

James was equal to the moment. "Lord St. Athan, I see no reason to change our present travel arrangements. My sister and I are charged with Miss Trevallion's welfare; we will therefore all three use the same carriage, but naturally, we'll be delighted to sit at table with you, should we use the same inns along the way."

Geoffrey smiled again. Oh, he'd be using the same inns, every single one of them! He glanced at Lucy's stormy visage.

Emily followed the glance. "She'll be grateful to you in the end, my lord."

"I doubt that very much," he replied without thinking.

Hope lit up three pairs of eyes around the table—Lucy's, Dorothea's, and James's—but Lady Amelia was taken aback again. "What's that? You won't use the same inns? If that's the case, what on earth point is there in leaving with them?"

He could have bitten his tongue for falling into the very trap he'd been striving to avoid! On this occasion he was fortunate that what he'd said could be construed as a response to James, but it so easily might not. He gave Emily a furious glare, and the little angel hastily disappeared. As she did, he noticed one of the table candles suddenly go out.

Lady Amelia's fingers drummed on the table. "I'm awaiting your reply, sir."

"I, er, was thinking of something else, Aunt. Of course I'll be using the same inns."

His unwilling traveling companions' hope was extinguished like the candle, and Lady Amelia drew a long breath. "I really don't know what's the matter with you, Geoffrey; you seem, well, preoccupied."

He smiled. "I'm a difficult bear," he declared, deliberately reminding her of her pet term.

She smiled unwillingly. "You are indeed, and truth to tell, I shall miss you, in spite of your obnoxiousness."

"I'm touched."

"Yes, occasionally I believe you are," she replied promptly.

Lucy's expression spoke volumes. Touched? She thought him either completely mad, or more devious than Machiavelli! Probably both. As he met her gaze, Geoffrey knew he'd have to speak to her alone again. Her antagonistic reactions during this abominable meal warned him he'd probably be better able to watch over her by appearing to be exactly what he'd just claimed—

someone intent upon returning to London for Christmas. He'd have to avoid accusing the Weybridges and Robert Trevallion of anything, and certainly refrain from any mention of things supernatural. That meant satisfactorily explaining his astonishing story away in the meantime.

When the awkward meal ended, Lucy's fury was still at boiling point, so she deemed it best to withdraw in case she lost her temper completely. But as she murmured something about a headache and said good night to everyone, Geoffrey followed her into the candlelit passage.

"A word with you, if you please, Miss Trevallion," he said, carefully closing the door behind him so the others couldn't hear.

She turned with an irritated flick of fustian. "I've had enough of your words, Lord St. Athan."

"I realize I've offended, and wish to apologize. You see, I was a little in my cups by the harbor earlier."

"You seemed perfectly sober to me!"

"I hold my drink well."

One of the unlit candles on a nearby console table suddenly flickered into life, the flame small at first, but then gaining strength. It wouldn't really have been noticeable among all the candles that were lit, but he just happened to see it, and guessed Emily was somewhere nearby.

Lucy didn't observe anything. "Sir, you don't hold your drink that well, if you've started seeing things."

Oh, he was seeing things, all right! Emily's bright golden glow had now appeared by the staircase beyond her, and as he looked, the little angel smiled at him.

Seeing how oddly he gazed past her, Lucy turned to look as well, but, of course, saw nothing. She eyed him suspiciously. "Another angel, my lord?" she inquired acidly.

"Er, no, of course not. As I've just said, I was in my cups earlier."

"Am I to understand that you now claim there was no vision, and therefore no dire warning about my uncle or the Weybridges' vile intentions toward me during the journey?"

"Er, yes."

"Are you quite sure?"

"Yes." God forgive him such a whopper, but what choice did he have under circumstances like these? He held her eyes. "Miss Trevallion, I trust we can at least be amicable during the journey."

"Amicability is the very last thing I feel where you're concerned, sir, and I sincerely hope to see as little of you as possible."

If only she knew how much he reciprocated the sentiments! He was going on this journey under duress, and would much have preferred to see the back of Miss Lucy Trevallion. He glared past her at Emily, who returned the look reproachfully.

Then Lucy spoke again. "Why are you really doing this?" she demanded.

"Doing what?"

"Imposing yourself upon us all the way to England. You clearly don't like me, or the Weybridges, yet you insist on accompanying us. I wish to know why."

"Why won't anyone believe I'm simply intent upon being home for Christmas?"

She held his gaze. "Because it isn't true."

"But it is."

"You aren't even a very good liar, sir."

He read her thoughts, and was provoked into forgetting some of his earlier resolutions. "You flatter yourself if you imagine you or your fortune hold any attraction for me, and you deceive yourself if you think your appearance on the scene can have pleased Robert Trevallion. But for you, Emily's death would have been sure to have elevated him to the position of heir. Bear him in mind, Miss Trevallion, for in my aunt's view he's both scheming and grasping. Her words, not mine."

She knew that was how Lady Amelia had described Robert, for she'd eavesdropped upon the conversation! That was also how she'd learned of Geoffrey's financial problems. "Sir, being denied the inheritance doesn't automatically make my uncle my enemy, nor can it possibly have anything to do with the Weybridges, who, may I remind you, are here at my grandfather's instruction, not my uncle's."

The moment the words had passed his lips, he'd regretted them. He'd meant to damp all this down, not apply the damned bellows! He tried to be conciliatory. "Miss Trevallion, all I'm saying is that no one likes to be pipped at the post, and like it or not, that's what you've done to Robert Trevallion. Now, to return to the business of the journey, let me assure you I do indeed simply wish to be home in London for Christmas. That is all there is to it."

"I still don't believe you."

He was goaded again. "Then let me be as frank as you. I don't give a damn what you think, Miss Trevallion, for you are the most of a mule I ever knew, but like it or not, somehow I'll cope with being near you over the coming days."

"The words of a true gentleman," she replied acidly.

"I'm about to be even more gentlemanly. I warn you that if you mention any of this business to my aunt or the Weybridges, I'll deny every damned word. Which of us will look more foolish then, I wonder?" He inclined his head and returned to the grand saloon, where Lady Amelia had persuaded Dorothea to play pi-quet with her.

Lucy's lips pressed tightly together. She'd never have thought it possible to dislike someone as much as she disliked Lord St. Athan. His conduct toward her had been detestable, and according to Lady Amelia it was all because she reminded him of someone called Constance. Whoever Constance was, she was well rid of him!

With a toss of her head, she turned to hurry toward the stair-case, where, had she but known it, she passed right through Emily. If Geoffrey had been there, he'd have seen how the angel's beautiful light suffused her living cousin for a moment or so.

Emily accompanied Lucy to her room, and took up a position on the bed canopy, lying with her chin in her hands to watch her angrily trying to unhook her gown, never an easy task at the best of times. The angel was intrigued by her cousin's anger. Lucy was in a terrible pet, and no mistake. And it was all to do with Geoffrey. Grown-ups were really very puzzling at times, for Lucy was quite taken in by James, who was her enemy, but at daggers drawn with Geoffrey, who was her friend!

When Lucy at last succeeded in getting out of the gown, Emily left the canopy to stand by her as she sat at the dressing table in her nightgown, furiously brushing her hair. Emily smiled at their reflections in the glass, for they were so alike that there was no mistaking they were related. Oh, if only Lucy had been the one to see her at the harbor.

At that moment a man cleared his throat on the balcony out-side. Lucy turned, and Emily fluttered to see who it was. To the angel's dismay she found James standing outside, ostensibly to enjoy a cigar and the moonlit lake, but Emily knew he was hoping to lure Lucy outside.

His ploy was successful, for Lucy peeped out through the cur-tains, saw who it was, and quickly put on her cloak. Raising the hood over her unpinned hair, she opened the glazed doors and stepped out, pretending to be startled to see him.

"Oh, Mr. Weybridge, I didn't realize anyone was here."

He smiled, not fooled in the least by such arts. "Only two can play piquet, Miss Trevallion, and I didn't wish to inflict my cigar smoke upon Lady Amelia."

She moved to the rail, looking out over the lake. "I shall miss this view."

"I'm sure you'll find the lake at Trevallion Park equally to your liking."

"Have you been there?"

"No, I haven't had that honor; your grandfather engaged us in London."

"You and Miss Weybridge must come there to see me."

He smiled. "We'd be delighted." He glanced down at the silvery lock of hair peeping from beneath her hood. There was something innocently erotic about it, as if to touch it would be to touch her naked skin. From that, it was but a short step to imagine she wore nothing beneath her cloak. He felt a stirring of the loins that told him he'd need female company that night. One of Lady Amelia's maids was sure to oblige for a few coins.

Lucy looked at him. "I wish Lord St. Athan weren't accompanying us."

"You aren't alone in that," James replied, drawing deeply on the cigar to quieten his libidinous thoughts.

She gave a little laugh. "I'm almost tempted to stay here now, just to be rid of him."

"Your grandfather will be heartbroken if you do that."

"I didn't really mean it, it was just a pleasant thought. Anyway, with luck we'll lose him somewhere *en route*."

"We'll have to do our utmost," James replied, laughing.

"We can certainly pass the time plotting ways to avoid him."

"Dorothea and I will be your willing accomplices." He smiled.

She returned the smile, but then became conscious of the impropriety of being with him like this. They were utterly alone, and she was in her nightdress beneath her cloak! Hot color rushed into her cheeks, and she lowered her eyes quickly.

"I, er, I must go in, it's a little cold out here. Good night, Mr. Weybridge."

"Good night, Miss Trevallion." He took her hand and turned the palm uppermost. His lips lingered for a moment, and then he released her.

Her heart was thundering as she went back into her room and closed the door.

Emily had watched throughout, and thought Lucy very silly indeed. How could anyone be gulled by someone as horrid as James Weybridge! But then, Lucy didn't know the truth about him. Oh, if only she'd listen! All it needed was for her to be sensible enough to pay attention to what Geoffrey said; instead, she was deaf to everything!

The angel lingered on the balcony as James finished his cigar and then strolled away. She followed him down to the kitchens, where he soon engaged the services of a plump, giggling maid, who accompanied him to the stables.

Emily was about to follow them inside, when something warned her it was better she didn't.

Fourteen

The following day dawned cold and dry, and the air was so clear the Jura seemed to stand out in sharp focus. It was an excellent day for travel, and the carriages were bound to easily achieve their aim of reaching the Eagle Inn, in the shadow of the first high pass over the mountains. Dorothea and James had stayed there on their outward journey, and found it clean and comfortable. James had also found the landlady's daughter most accommodating.

Lucy's parting from Lady Amelia was tearful. Their relationship had always been fond, and it was therefore the most natural thing in the world for the old lady to hug her former employee. Then, when Dorothea and James had again assured Lady Amelia they'd take every care of their charge, the first heavily laden traveling carriage drove slowly out through the gates and took the road to Vevey and Lausanne.

Geoffrey's leavetaking of his aunt was equally fond, although Lady Amelia remained cross with him for his inexplicable conduct. With her handkerchief still clasped in her hand, she took him earnestly by the elbow. "Why are you going like this, Geoffrey? What is your real reason?"

He glanced at Emily, waiting impatiently in his carriage. "As I keep saying, Aunt, I merely have an itch to spend Christmas in London. That's all there is to it."

"I don't believe you, sir, but will you at least admit you dislike poor Lucy simply and solely because she reminds you of Constance?"

He hesitated, and then nodded reluctantly. "Very well, I admit it."

"Your behavior has been most reprehensible."

"I know."

"So unless you are able to temper your conduct with a little decorum, I trust you'll steer clear of Lucy during the journey."

He smiled a little ruefully. "I'll do my best."

Lady Amelia searched his eyes. "There's more to this than you're telling me, isn't there?"

"No."

"Geoffrey—"

"Good-bye, Aunt." He kissed her warmly on the cheek and then climbed quickly into his carriage.

She looked crossly after him, but waved as the Vevey postilion urged the team into action. As the vehicle drove out through the villa gates, she turned to go back into a house which seemed suddenly very empty indeed.

In the carriage, Geoffrey put his boots upon the seat opposite, made himself comfortable, and then eyed Emily sternly. "A word with you, miss."

"Sir?"

"I require a promise that on no account will you address me in company. I found that incident last night at the dinner table highly embarrassing, and I do *not* want a repetition. Is that clear?"

Emily pouted. "You didn't have to answer me," she grumbled.

"Have you any idea how difficult it is to behave as if you aren't there? *I* can see you; indeed, your brightness at times seems almost blinding, and yet no one else hears or sees anything! The last thing I need is to be made to look foolish because I respond to something you've chanced to say. Now, do you give me your word on this?"

Emily's lip jutted still more.

He drew a long breath. "Missy, there's very little that is angelic about you at this moment."

She lowered her eyes a little guiltily.

"Promise me, Emily."

"But—"

"Promise me! You'll never speak to me when others are present—unless, of course, it concerns something urgent."

"I-I'll try."

"You'll succeed!" Her resentful visage reminded him of Lucy. "What is it about you Trevallions? I swear you and your cousin share exactly the same mulish qualities; you certainly share the same disagreeable facial expressions!" He glanced out of the window, and when he turned to speak to the angel again, she'd gone.

In the first carriage, Lucy sensed nothing as Emily appeared on the seat next to her. The little angel scowled across at Dorothea and James, and wished anew she could make Lucy aware of the hazards ahead.

Lucy was struggling to master the sadness she felt at leaving

Lady Amelia. She kept her eyes averted, and was glad the brim of her gypsy hat concealed her face. She wore her lavender cloak over her warmest gown, a honeysuckle wool, and her hands were plunged deep into an ermine-trimmed muff, a parting gift from Lady Amelia.

Dorothea glanced at her. "Please don't be sad, Miss Trevallion, for I have no doubt you'll see Lady Amelia again soon." She smiled and held out a fresh handkerchief. She wore the strawberry merino pelisse and gown she'd had on when she'd arrived at the villa.

Lucy accepted the handkerchief and dabbed her eyes. "You must think me very foolish," she said apologetically.

"Not at all, in fact I think it charming that you and Lady Amelia think so highly of each other. One doesn't often find such warmth between mistress and servant. Oh, forgive me, I didn't mean to denigrate your position at all, I-I just . . ."

"It's quite all right, Miss Weybridge, for I understand what you meant."

Dorothea smiled, but the smile didn't extend to her beautiful brown eyes.

Lucy didn't notice. "I shouldn't be crying, not when I'm going to relatives I didn't know I had."

Emily glared at the brother and sister. How *could* they pretend to be so friendly! They were two of the nastiest people she'd ever known; the only nastier one was Uncle Robert!

Lucy fiddled with the handkerchief. "I-I can't believe Uncle Robert doesn't resent me little. After all, if it weren't for me, he'd be heir now, wouldn't he?"

"He doesn't resent you at all, Miss Trevallion," Dorothea replied smoothly. Oh, if only you knew, my dear!

Lucy smiled shyly. "Please call me Lucy, for we're to be thrust together like this for quite some time."

Dorothea nodded. "I'd like that."

James held Lucy's glance. "I will only permit such informality if it extends to me as well."

She blushed a little. "Yes, of course."

It was all he could do to resist the temptation of letting his glance wander hungrily over her. Rolling the maid in the hay last night hadn't eased the craving Lucy had aroused in him. There was something exquisitely virginal about the Trevallion heiress, something that bewitched and beckoned. He had to have her. And her fortune.

Emily watched his face. What was he thinking now? It was something about Lucy, but the angel couldn't guess what it was.

After passing through Vevey, the carriages followed the lake-side road for twelve miles to Lausanne. Emily divided her time between vehicles, and had just returned to Geoffrey's when it passed a wayside church. He couldn't help but notice how the angel's brilliance increased considerably for a moment before fading to her customary glow, and he felt he had to comment.

"That wasn't my imagination, was it? You did shine more when we were close to that church?"

Emily nodded. "It will happen every time I'm near something holy." She lowered her eyes and bit her lips. "I'm supposed to avoid it if I can, but how am I to know when a church or something is just ahead? It's not fair."

He smiled. "No, I suppose it isn't."

"They say He has strictly forbidden such things."

"He? Oh, you mean . . . ?" Geoffrey pointed up toward the sky. "Yes."

"Ah." Geoffrey observed her for a moment. "Actually, I've also noticed the effect you have on candles."

"Candles?" She looked puzzled.

"When you disappear, one goes out, and when you appear, one lights up. At least, that's how it seems."

She shrugged. "I don't know about that."

Lausanne swept into view more quickly than expected. Perched on hills above the lake, and surrounded by more vineyards, the steep medieval city faced south toward the snowclad peaks of Savoy, where on a day as clear as this the soaring summit of Mont Blanc itself was visible.

The first change of horses was to take place at the Blue Lion, where luncheon was to be taken before they pressed on to make the climb into the Jura before nightfall. The luncheon proved to be little more than Gruyère cheese, bread, and local red wine, which while tasty enough, was hardly the sort of fortifying fare required by travelers about to cross mountains. Geoffrey seemed impervious to the lack of welcome he received from the other three. He sat stolidly at the table, making no particular attempt to join in the conversation, and certainly evincing no concern when it went on around him.

Of course, he wasn't as isolated as the others might have thought, for Emily fidgeted around him all the time, sometimes standing at his elbow, sometimes behind him with her arm resting on his shoulder and her chin on her arm. She folded and unfolded her wings, reminding him of a preening bird, and several times he heard her inhale as if to speak, but then she remembered her promise and closed her lips again. Then, when the journey continued, she sat opposite him with a look of celestial self-satisfaction.

"There," she declared, "didn't I do well? I didn't say a single word to you."

"I congratulate you."

"Shall I go and see what's happening in the other carriage?"

"No, for whatever they plan won't happen today, you may be sure of that. They'll choose somewhere much more isolated, and I should imagine they'll try to head me off first."

Emily fidgeted a little more. "I don't like traveling, it's boring," she said after a moment.

"There's not much I can do about that."

"No. Can't we play I-Spy?"

He sighed. "We've only been on the road for a few hours; I trust you don't expect me to play games with you all the way?"

"You aren't much fun to be with," she replied sulkily.

"I'm not here for fun," he reminded her, "I'm here because *you* insist I must watch over your obstinate cousin. Believe me, I'd much rather be back at the villa, or, better still, already far away in Italy!"

Emily was stung. "It's all your fault in the first place. If you hadn't turned around to speak to Lucy when you did, I'd have been able to tell her everything I was supposed to. Instead, I have to talk to you, and I don't like it either."

"Were you as much of a saucebox when you were alive? Or is it something you've acquired along with wings?" he asked dryly.

"I'm not a saucebox."

"Oh, yes, you are."

She glared at him, and vanished.

He sat back with a sigh. This journey was already intolerable. Besides having a sulky angel, he had an equally sulky young woman who was guaranteed to misinterpret every single thing he said or did. Plague take Lucy Trevallion. And plague take all angels!

Fifteen

That afternoon the road began to climb, and the higher it went, the colder the temperature became. When the horses were changed for the last time before they reached the Eagle, heated bricks were purchased to keep the travelers' feet warm for the final few hours. Then, with rugs and sheepskins draped over their knees, they drove on through what was left of the short December day.

They were now in a region of pine forests, roaring torrents, and deeply cleft valleys, above which towered mountains which the previous night had received their first dusting of snow. The narrow road ran alongside a river that rushed noisily down a series of cataracts. Spray hung in the air, and the sound of water seemed to reverberate all around. In the summer months, it was a place of great beauty, with flowers in the lush meadows and crimson rhododendrons among the dark green pines, but with the river in spate like this, it was a little frightening, especially when the light began to fade and night approached.

Sleet began to fall, and they were relieved to see the Eagle's welcoming lights shining through the murk ahead. It was a rambling, uneven stone building in the lee of the mountain gorge that led toward France. The silhouette of the pass loomed behind it, not as grand as those in the alps, but still impressive.

Other travelers had already broken their journey for the night, and several diligences as well as two private carriages stood in the large yard adjacent to the main part of the inn. Leaving the postilions to attend to the horses and carriages, the four travelers hurried through the stinging sleet into the brightness and warmth of the tap room.

It was quite crowded inside, and the landlady's young son was entertaining the guests by playing the pipes. It was a cozy scene, made even more so by the appetizing smell of food. Local Jura sausages were hung to smoke in the huge open chimney, and hams were suspended from beams. Several kettles sang on the fire, and a shaggy mongrel sprawled by the dusty hearth.

The landlady and her daughter, both with the long plaits and white sleeves that were the custom in these parts, were anxious to make all travelers welcome. As far as James was concerned, the daughter's flirtatious smile of recognition promised all the pleasures he wished for the coming night, which was as well, for there was only one attic room left, and that was naturally allotted to Lucy and Dorothea. In theory, therefore, he and Geoffrey were expected to make themselves as comfortable as possible in the tap room, but in practice it would only be Geoffrey who was thus obliged.

The table d'hôte had already been served, so the newcomers were seated on wooden benches at a table close to a window, where they were served with a rather potent straw wine apéritif. Lucy, who didn't have much of a head for alcohol, soon felt the wine's rather dramatic effects, and so didn't drink much. She was glad when their meal was served, for food counteracted the rather unwelcome lightheadedness caused by strong wine on an empty stomach.

The Eagle more than made up for the poor fare they'd had earlier in the day at Lausanne. Courses of trout and bilberry tart were followed by as much cheese as they could eat. Afterward, feeling replete and comfortable, they joined the other guests to listen to the boy playing the pipes, while outside a rising wind drove the sleet against the windows.

Before the two women retired to their room, Dorothea drew James aside. Unknown to either of them, Emily listened to every word they said.

Dorothea was anxious. "James, if St. Athan clings as close as this, we'll find it virtually impossible to carry out our plan."

"I know."

"We must give him the slip somehow."

"I know that too, and I've already decided how to do it."

She looked swiftly at him. "What do you have in mind?"

"We're going to leave before St. Athan awakens in the morning, then take a much more circuitous route to Pontarlier."

"But what will that achieve? He knows we're going to stay at the Silver Apple in Pontarlier; in fact, we *have* to go there, so he's bound to catch up with us again, no matter how circuitous our wanderings in the meantime."

"Sis, we don't *have* to stay anywhere in particular," James replied quietly.

"But we do, you know we do. How else is Mansart to receive word?"

Emily listened urgently. Mansart? Who was Mansart? What were they talking about?

James smiled. "All we have to do is stay at another Pontarlier inn, and send word to the landlord of the Silver Apple, who'll inform Mansart as planned. It's really quite simple."

"Maybe . . ."

"It is, you know it is."

"Except we can't be sure of slipping away from this place without St. Athan's awakening. He hasn't drunk very much, and strikes me as a light sleeper, so he's bound to stir the moment the first maid begins her work, and since this is hardly suitable weather or country for traveling before it's light—"

He interrupted her. "He'll sleep heavily enough if he takes some of this." Surreptitiously, he showed her a little vial.

"What is it?"

"Laudanum."

"Laudanum's all very well, brother mine, but how exactly can you administer it?"

"I'll invite him to share a toddy of some sort before we put our heads down for the night."

She smiled. "Be sure not to drink his health," she said softly.

"I'll drink to his eternal damnation." He caught her arm. "All you have to do is warn Lucy we're going to slip away at dawn. I know she wants to be rid of him as much as we do, so she's bound to cooperate. But for God's sake, don't mention the laudanum, for I'm equally sure she won't go along with *that!* Little Miss Trevallion has principles, I fear."

"Do you take me for a complete fool?" A little irritated, Dorothea returned to the others, and a moment later she and Lucy took candles to go up to their room.

Emily hovered anxiously next to Geoffrey. She had to warn him about the laudanum and the plan to sneak away at dawn, but she'd promised not to say anything in front of anyone, and James was only too present. She retreated fretfully to the chimney corner, folded her wings, and tried to think what to do.

James gave Geoffrey a tentative smile. "I trust you'll share a glass of something warming before we attempt to sleep?"

"As you wish."

James called over to the landlady's daughter, a plump creature with flaxen hair and big blue eyes, who hurried away to prepare the toddies.

Emily was in a quandary. Geoffrey had said she could only speak to him if it was urgent. Well, this was definitely urgent!

The drinks were brought, and as the young woman withdrew again, James laughed and pointed at something across the tap room. "What do you think of those strange fellows over there? Are they bandits, or honest travelers?"

Geoffrey turned, and in a trice James tipped some of the vial into his drink. Emily glided determinedly in front of Geoffrey, so he had no option but to look directly at her.

"Don't drink the toddy, he's just put laudanum in it!" she whispered urgently.

Geoffrey's lips parted in surprise.

Emily spoke again. "He's putting the vial back in his pocket right now. Pretend to spill the drink! Do anything but drink it!"

Geoffrey was motionless for a moment, and then turned back to face James without a flicker of anything untoward. "Bandits or honest travelers? Why, I think the latter, who merely look like the former," he said lightly.

"You're probably right." James raised his glass. "Your health, my lord."

"And yours," Geoffrey replied, lifting his glass too, but only pretending to drink. Then he nodded past James to something the other side of the room. "Then what do you say to that couple over there? Are they married to each other, or merely playing their real spouses false?"

As James turned to look, Geoffrey deftly tipped his drink into the pot of geraniums on the table.

James shrugged. "A debatable point, my lord. Perhaps it could be said they appear too loving to be married."

"A cynical view, sir."

"Marriage is a cynical institution, only to be entered for practical purposes," James replied.

"From which I take it you approve of arranged matches?"

"Provided one has arranged it oneself," James murmured, glancing at Geoffrey's empty glass. "Shall I order another toddy for you, sir?"

"No, one is quite enough. Besides, I'm tired already, and I'm sure the landlady's daughter is impatient for your attentions."

James raised an eyebrow. "How observant you are, sir."

"Very little slips past me. Well, good night, Weybridge," Geof-

frey got up and stretched, before removing to a settle closer to the
fire.

"Good night, my lord." Humming to himself, James left the tap
room to find his ladylove for the night.

The moment he'd gone, Emily faced Geoffrey. "I did the right
thing, didn't I? I *had* to speak to you; I couldn't let you drink the
toddy, could I? And you did say that if it was something urgent—"

"I'm glad you warned me, Emily," he said, trying not to look as
if he was speaking at all, for as far as anyone else was concerned,
he was alone on the settle.

She beamed. "And I've got so much else to tell you too! I listened to everything the Weybridges said a short while ago." She
related the conversation word for word. "Who do you think
Mansart is?" she asked then.

"I've no idea. You are sure that's the name they used?"

"Yes, and the landlord at the Silver Apple in Pontarlier is going
to send word to him, whoever he is. Then something's going to
happen, but I don't know what." She looked anxiously at him
then. "Do-do you think it's what they plan for Lucy?"

"I fear it might be, but at least we can presume we have little to
fear between here and Pontarlier."

"What are you going to do now?"

"Regarding tomorrow morning's precipitous flight? Spike
their scheming guns by being wide awake and up before they
are," Geoffrey replied. "And for that I'll have to rely on you,
young lady."

"Me?"

"If I don't wake up in time, you'll have to make sure I do."

"All right."

"Then I bid you good night."

She watched as he made himself as comfortable as he could on
the hard wood. "Aren't you going to say your prayers, sir?" she
asked then.

"No," he replied, not opening his eyes.

"But—"

"If it bothers you that my soul may suffer a brush with hellfire,
you say my prayers for me," he interrupted.

"You shouldn't joke about things like that, Lord St. Athan," she
said reprovingly.

He didn't reply.

She waited a moment, and then knelt on the floor by the settle
with her hands together. "Now Lord St. Athan lays him down to

sleep, I pray Thee, Lord, his soul to keep, and if he dies before he wakes, I pray Thee, Lord, his soul to take."

Then there was silence, and Geoffrey opened his eyes. There was no one there, and a candle on the immense wooden mantelshelf had just gone out, for he could see smoke curling up from its blackened wick.

Sixteen

In the attic room, Dorothea quickly fell asleep, but Lucy lay awake, listening to the icy sleet being driven against the roof. There was no glowing fire, just a small black stove with an ugly flue, but at least it was warm.

The bed was packed with clean straw, the sheets freshly laundered, and the feather duvet cozy, but still she couldn't sleep. She kept wondering about the life waiting for her in England. She was going to people she didn't know, and suddenly she was a great heiress. Only a short time ago she'd been grateful for the post of companion; now she'd be paid flattering attention by hopeful gentlemen! She turned her head away then, for in the ignoble Earl of St. Athan she'd already had a disagreeable sample of that! If she hadn't suddenly been elevated to the status of Edwin Trevallion's heir, Geoffrey wouldn't have given a fig what happened to her. He was a dishonorable, self-seeking opportunist, and yet outwardly he seemed everything an English lord should be. It was such a pity that his particular book could certainly not be told from its cover!

She closed her eyes, her thoughts rambling back over the weeks she'd known him. What disagreeable weeks they'd been, with perhaps the visit to Chillon being the most disagreeable occasion of all. Yes, that was the day she'd really realized how great an aversion she felt toward him. . . .

Sleep began to overtake her, and the sound of the sleet became the rush of water beneath the prow of the boat conveying her to Chillon. Geoffrey stood to tighten a rope, and he smiled at her. It was a warm smile, quite unlike any he'd ever bestowed upon her before. It made her feel good. She found herself taking note of his clinging black leather gloves and the amazingly close fit of his breeches. Oh, such a close fit. When he stretched up to the rigging, she could see the enticing mound of his masculinity.

She was shocked that her gaze lingered where it shouldn't, but there was something about him today that turned her thoughts in a very improper direction. She was conscious of strange sensations deep inside, and for the first time understood whispered conversations she'd eavesdropped upon as a child. The maids at her parents' house had been very indiscreet, and very descriptive when they compared notes about their latest loves. Things had been said that a child couldn't understand, but when remembered now, their meaning was only too clear. And only too exciting. . . .

The maids were forgotten as the dream swept her irresistibly along. Soon the boat nudged the shore and Geoffrey stepped out to hold a gloved hand out to her. He caught her around the waist as she came toward him, and he held her hips to his for a moment before releasing her. In that heartstopping second she felt his dormant virility pushing toward her through their clothes. Electrifying emotions flared into being, and with a gasp she turned to hurry toward the castle bridge.

He followed, and in the courtyard he caught her hand, turning her roughly to face him. His blue eyes were dark and intense, promising no quarter. She didn't try to pull her hand away; she wanted him to do with her as he would. A faint smile played upon his lips, and without a word he led her toward the steep steps that descended to the subterranean dungeon.

She didn't resist, for her inner excitement was now a tumult of anticipation. There was nothing innocent in her thoughts or hopes as their shadows leapt against the walls of the fortress steps. She accompanied him knowing he was about to take her virginity.

The dark cell that had frightened her before, held no horrors now. His hand tightened over hers as they faced each other. She smiled and raised her lips to him. His kiss was brutal and arousing, and he caressed her breast through her gown, which was so flimsy it was as if she wore nothing at all.

He pushed her back against the cold stone wall, where ancient iron shackles still hung. "You're my captive now, Lucy," he breathed, winding the chains around her wrists.

"Do with me as you will," she whispered, hardly able to bear the pounding desire that coursed so imperatively through her veins.

With a cool smile he slipped her gown down to her waist, revealing her breasts, with their telltale pink tips standing out in excitement. He bent his head to take a nipple in his lips, sliding his tongue richly over it and then drawing it still further into his mouth.

Waves of forbidden emotion washed deliciously through her, and her breath caught as he moved to her other breast, kissing and caressing it in the same knowing way. His gloved hands moved over her, exploring her thighs and buttocks, and sliding luxuriously between her thighs as he kissed her mouth again.

His tongue flicked compellingly against hers, and a ferment of passion swept through her. Then he drew his head back to look into her eyes as he pressed his hips sensuously against her. His masculinity was now a pounding erection.

His eyes were compelling. "I've wanted you since the first day I saw you, Lucy," he whispered, moving against her so that she felt his entire length, like an iron bar within the confines of his breeches.

"Then take me," she breathed, closing her eyes as he kissed her again. Her heart was thundering and the blood racing through her veins. She felt him undo his breeches and take out that which she craved.

She wanted to run her trembling fingers down its length and feel its pulse. But she was helpless. At his mercy . . .

His lips were against her throat as he eased the throbbing shaft between her legs. She gasped as he raised her slightly, and then pushed forward until she felt his maleness pressing urgently to that place no man had ever touched before. She trembled, weak with expectation. He pushed again. Her body resisted, but, oh, the pleasure. . . . He pushed a little more, and suddenly he was inside her.

Shuddering gratification seized her, and she cried out as she felt him reach the hilt. "Oh, God, oh God . . . !"

His leather-clad hands clasped her buttocks, and he bent his lips to her nipple as he slowly withdrew and then sank into her again. Wild feelings scattered over her flushed skin, her heartbeats quickened to a frenzy. His mouth found hers and moved with lingering passion as he continued to slowly thrust and withdraw, thrust and withdraw. He took his time, savoring each leisurely stroke, and he knew exactly when she reached the peak of desire he sought.

He increased his thrusts, seeming to increase in size within her. It was as if all his strength and energy were marshaling in his virility, arming it for the final moment. His strokes were now as urgent as her need, and at last he gave a gasp as exhilarating satisfaction pulsed luxuriously between them.

She'd never known such delight. Tears were wet on her cheeks, her whole body seemed to quiver, and warm sensations carried her along, making her feel weightless. He clasped her hips, holding her onto him as his erection softened inside her. His mouth moved over her flushed breasts as he teased her pert nipples with little kisses, and then he kissed her lips again. It was a lingering kiss, with his tongue moving richly against hers, and when at last he pulled away, he withdrew from her body as well.

She felt the separation keenly. There was no shame in the way she felt now. She'd wanted to be taken, to be initiated into the joys of lovemaking, and this was the man she'd chosen to teach her. What sweet initiation, a lesson learned from a master of his art.

He eased his spent virility back into his breeches, and did them up, then he slowly unraveled the chains from her wrists, and took her in his arms. At last she could hold him, and press to him as he pressed to her. He kissed her, and it was a kiss that promised more sexual delights to come.

Suddenly the dream was halted as the wind rattled the attic window. Lucy's eyes flew open, and she stared up at the unfamiliar ceiling. The dream might have been shattered, but she could still recall every shocking detail. She was startled and dismayed. How could she have imagined such things? How *could* she! And with Geoffrey, of all men! She wished she'd never listened to those foolish maids!

She'd never be able to face him again. Never. Please let their sly early-morning departure succeed!

At dawn, the eastern sky bore only the faintest glimmer of light, because of lowering snow clouds. The wind and sleet had died away, but the temperature had plummeted, and high on the mountain there was deep snow.

Breakfast was brought to Lucy and Dorothea in their room. It was a tray of eggs, country ham, fresh bread, and hot milk, and the maid who brought it told them James had already ordered their carriage, and Lord St. Athan was still asleep in the tap room. The latter information relieved them greatly, especially Lucy, who was unable to shake off the effects of her dream.

Carrying their overnight valises, the two women crept down through the quiet inn to the firelit tap room.

Lucy peeped around the door, and then froze with dismay as her eyes met Geoffrey's. He was seated on the settle with a large cup of coffee. Next to him, but totally invisible, was Emily, her little face jubilant that the sneaky ruse had been foiled.

Geoffrey got up to don his outdoor things. "Good morning, Miss Trevallion, I trust you slept well," he said, according her a very civil nod of his head.

More hugely embarrassed than he could ever have guessed, Lucy advanced slowly into the room. Dorothea came in as well, and her face became a picture of disbelief. How could St. Athan possibly be as alert as this if James had administered the laudanum properly, she wondered angrily.

Geoffrey spoke again to Lucy. "Did you sleep well?" he repeated.

The mortification of the dream rendered her tongue-tied for a moment longer, but at last she managed to reply. "Yes, thank you," she said lamely.

"I'm glad to hear it, for I've just enjoyed the best night's rest I've had in ages," he declared, finishing his coffee.

She had to look away, for as far as she was concerned, *rest* was one thing he certainly hadn't had last night!

Meanwhile, Emily fluttered victoriously around him. "We showed them! We showed them!" she chanted.

Dorothea struggled to hide her fury. Damn James! He'd clearly bungled the whole thing! So much for his clever idea.

Just then James himself came in, rubbing his hands briskly because it was bitterly cold outside. He too halted in dismay on seeing Geoffrey, who bestowed upon him another blandly beaming smile.

"Ah, there you are, Weybridge. I trust you're ready to leave?"

"I, er . . . Yes, of course. I've just been seeing the carriage is prompt."

"Mine should already have been brought," Geoffrey replied, flexing his fingers in his gloves.

Lucy gazed wretchedly at the black leather as he gave them another beaming smile and then left the room.

Dorothea immediately hastened to her brother. "Bungler!" she breathed, keeping her voice down so only he could hear.

"I can't understand it. I put the laudanum in his drink, and he drank it. He must have the constitution of an ox."

"Or he didn't drink it."

"His glass was empty; he drank it all right."

Emily had glided up busily to listen to the exchange, and she put her tongue out impudently at them both. "No, he didn't drink it, because *I* told him what you were up to! So there!"

They didn't sense any supernatural presence as Dorothea spoke again. "We'll have to think of something else before we reach Pontarlier, won't we?" she said, giving a quick, bright smile as she perceived Lucy coming to join them. "Well, Lucy, I'm afraid we have to endure his lordship for at least another day, but I'm determined to slip away from him somehow."

"I pray so," Lucy replied, raising her hood to go out into the cold, where an occasional snowflake now drifted to the iron-hard ground.

Emily followed them, pulling horrible faces at the Weybridges with every step. Then, when they'd climbed into their carriage, she fluttered away to join Geoffrey, who'd observed her conduct throughout.

"What a decidedly unangelic cherub you are," he murmured dryly as the carriage jolted away from the inn.

Seventeen

Geoffrey's carriage led the way, and soon ice could be heard cracking beneath the wheels as they entered the gorge, where the mountaintops disappeared into a cloak of cloud. A river thundered between huge rocks, and spray filled the air. Pine forests covered the far side of the gorge, and just above the white water there were rhododendrons, their lowermost branches bowed down with icicles.

They were the only vehicles to be seen as the road climbed up the steep rock face above the pounding torrent, and snow began to fall more heavily, sometimes obscuring the far side of the gorge.

Dorothea was acutely conscious of the roaring water, and closed her eyes as the carriage wheels slid occasionally on the ice. She'd be glad when they'd crested the pass and were safely on their way down to Pontarlier on the other side.

Suddenly the road became a sheet of ice from the frozen spray of a small waterfall that was now a mass of icicles against the rock, and the first carriage slid so alarmingly close to the edge of the precipice that the postilion immediately reined in. Both vehicles came to an abrupt halt, and as Geoffrey alighted to consult with the postilion, Emily fluttered fearlessly above the rocky drop into the gorge. If she'd still been alive, she'd have been terrified, but she had wings now!

Snow flurried around Geoffrey as he and the postilion agreed it would be best for everyone to alight and walk across the ice, so the carriages could be led. It was when the two women had accomplished the crossing and stood waiting for the men to coax the frightened horses over the ice that Dorothea saw a sudden opportunity to rid the world of Lucy Trevallion. Everyone's attention was diverted to the carriages, and Lucy was standing tantalizingly close to the precipice. All it would take was one small push. . . .

But Dorothea reckoned without Emily, who saw her move stealthily toward Lucy, with an expression of malevolent determination in her brown eyes. The angel knew in an instant what she intended, and gave Geoffrey a warning scream.

"Geoffrey! She's going to push Lucy over the cliff!"

He whirled about, instinctively shouting. "Stand back from the edge, Miss Trevallion!"

Dorothea turned away as nonchalantly as she could, but James saw her, and knew exactly what she'd been on the point of doing. Lucy obeyed Geoffrey, but sensed nothing of the extreme danger she'd just been in.

Geoffrey saw the way James looked at his sister. It was a very telling moment. Weybridge didn't want Lucy dead. His sister did, but he certainly didn't! He was playing his own game, and there was no doubt the prize was Lucy and her fortune.

As soon as both carriages had crossed the ice, Geoffrey determinedly separated Lucy from her chaperones. He spoke in a tone that brooked no arguments. "For the time being I think it best if we divide evenly between vehicles. Miss Trevallion?" He opened the door of his carriage and held out his hand.

Without question, she again obeyed him, and neither Dorothea nor James made any protest. As the carriages continued, Emily sat with Geoffrey and Lucy, wondering how long it would be before her cousin received a sound telling off for standing so close to the edge of the cliff. The angel had only a minute or so to wait.

Geoffrey looked coolly at Lucy. "May I ask what on earth possessed you to place yourself within a foot or so of a sheer drop?"

"I just wasn't thinking."

"That's patently obvious," he observed sarcastically.

She went pink. "You've made your point, sir."

"Good, for I'm in no mood to labor it."

Her eyes flashed angrily as she looked out at the snow, which now fell more heavily than ever. She felt foolish for having been so unwary, but she wouldn't admit it to him. Nor would she again dream anything like she had last night!

Emily glanced from one angry face to the other, and then looked at Geoffrey. "Why can't you and Lucy be nice to each other?" she asked innocently.

His lips parted to give a short answer, but then he remembered in time and gave the little angel such a look that she hastily removed to the second carriage, where she found a very similar argument in progress.

James was furious with his sister. "What a damned fool thing to attempt!"

She was unrepentent. "There was a golden opportunity, and I took it!"

"Yes, in front of St. Athan! He very nearly caught you in the act!"

"But he didn't, so there's no harm done."

"There's a great deal of harm. Dorothea, I want your assurance that you won't do anything else on the spur of the moment." James looked out at the heavily falling snow. "Care is required at all times, and *we* don't need to take risks, because Mansart's going to do everything for us. Just remember that."

After a while he spoke again. "I know St. Athan is still with us, but I've decided not to stay at the Silver Apple anyway."

She was taken aback. "Why not?"

"I heard adverse reports at the Eagle. It seems the Silver Apple has an, er, unsavory reputation."

"In what way?"

"The way that just might jog St. Athan's memory as to where he saw you."

Color stained Dorothea's cheeks. "Thank you for reminding me."

"The less risk there is of him remembering, the better."

Emily listened to every word, and was deeply puzzled. What were they talking about? What might Geoffrey remember?

James drew a breath. "Anyway, I'm told an inn called the Boar is far wiser. It slipped my mind when we set off, but I'll tell St. Athan at the next halt. Damn him for persuading Lucy to travel with him. She's our responsibility, not his."

"True, but we seem increasingly stuck with him, and I suspect he'll stay at the Boar as well. Just remember to send the necessary word to the landlord of the Silver Apple, for Mansart *must* be warned we're on the way."

"I will." But he had no intention at all of sending word to the Silver Apple; indeed, the last thing he wanted was for Mansart to lie in wait. Lucy Trevallion was going to be his—lady, fortune, and all—so he had a little ambush of his own in mind for Lucy, a tender ambush of beguiling kisses and caresses, of gallant temptation and promises of happiness. In short, he was going to persuade her to elope with him. Once the ring was on her finger, and the marriage consummated, there was nothing anyone could do about it!

Dorothea pushed her hands deeper into her muff before glancing at her brother again. "St. Athan bothers me. I don't know what he's up to, but he clearly has every intention of cleaving to us every inch of the way."

"All the more reason to leave matters to Mansart. An ambush by bandits will leave us looking as much the victims as Lucy." The words fell easily from his lips. At all costs he wanted to prevent any more rash acts on his sister's part. And when he sprang his own plan, both she and St. Athan, if he presented any obstacle, would be dealt with. In the meantime, there mustn't be so much as a ripple to show the danger beneath his smooth surface. No one must suspect anything.

Emily's eyes had widened with horror. An ambush by bandits? So *that* was what they planned! Nothing more was said, and the angel flew swiftly out into the snowstorm to return to Geoffrey's carriage, where the occupants were seated in stony silence. The little angel sat next to Geoffrey, who gave her a dire look the moment she appeared. Don't you *dare* speak to me, the look said.

Emily's jaw jutted mutinously. She had so much to tell him! But as her lips parted, his blue eyes flashed so warningly she closed her mouth again. She'd have to wait until the change of horses.

But no easy opportunity presented itself. As soon as they reached the next stage, James hastened to the leading carriage to tell Geoffrey about the change of inn.

Geoffrey nodded his agreement, trying not to look at Emily, who was now fit to burst with impatience, and was gesticulating wildly for him to alight for a while. So as James hurried back to the other carriage, Geoffrey made his excuses to Lucy.

"If you'll excuse me for a moment, I think I'll stretch my legs," he said, turning up his coat collar and stepping down into the snow, which was now ankle-deep and falling ever more heavily.

Thrusting his hands into his pockets, he strolled along the road for a while. The gorge rose darkly behind, its sheer drop masked by the thickly flurrying snow. It was icily cold, and he was relieved that from now on they would be driving down from the Jura into France.

When he was far enough away from the carriages, he turned to face Emily. "Well? What is it?"

She told him everything she'd heard.

He listened with increasing anger and dismay. "Are you quite sure there's supposed to be an ambush?" he said when she'd finished.

"Yes, by the person called Mansart I told you about before. Geoffrey, you must stop it happening. You must stop James sending any message to the landlord of the Silver Apple!"

"I'd already realized that."

"What will you do?"

"Pay the Silver Apple's host a discreet call. Money talks, and I'm sure he'll prove informative if I cross his palm with sufficient silver." He eyed the little angel. "By the way, miss, I gave you no leave to address me by my first name," he said sternly.

"But you call me by mine," she replied with a pout.

"That's hardly the same thing. You're only a little girl."

"I'm not, I'm an angel," she said a little archly.

"Whatever you are."

"Oh, please don't be stuffy. We're in this together, and—"

"*I'm* in this because *you* made a mistake," he pointed out.

"You're quite horrid at times," she complained.

"I'm not horrid."

"Yes, you are!" she cried, her jaw beginning its familiar jut.

"Now listen, miss—" He broke off. God, he was becoming as childish as she was!

She came to stand in front of him, her little wings folded meekly, and her hands clasped before her. She looked very angelic indeed as she raised her large eyes pleadingly toward him. "*Please* may I call you Geoffrey?" she wheedled.

"Oh, all right, if it's that important to you."

She beamed. "Shall I go back to the Weybridges, and see if they say anything more?"

"Please do."

She unfolded her wings to fly off, but then remembered something. "Geoffrey, what did James mean about the Silver Apple having an unsavory reputation?"

"It's nothing that should concern you, Emily."

"Because it has something to do with fallen women?" she asked, remembering a phrase she'd heard once.

He hid a smile. "Something of the sort."

"Well, if it is, that means Dorothea must be a fallen woman. They're terribly afraid you'll remember where you've seen her before, and it must have been a place where you'll find fallen women."

She flew away through the snow, and Geoffrey gazed thoughtfully after her. Was she right? Had he seen Dorothea Weybridge in a house of ill repute? Well, that certainly narrowed things down, for he hadn't been to many such establishments. He'd never found it necessary to pay for feminine favors! He walked slowly back to the carriage, mulling over the various bordellos and so-called "convents" he'd been in over the years, and trying to recall the "nuns." Many a face and figure came definitely to mind, but not Dorothea Weybridge's. But he *had* seen her somewhere, and sooner or later it would come to him.

The journey continued. Soon they crossed the French frontier, and gradually descended into a softer countryside. The mountains became hills, and pine forests gave way to walnut and cherry orchards, vineyards, and sweeps of Spanish chestnuts. Snow still fell, but not as thickly as it had higher up, and the postilions were able to bring their teams up to quite a smart pace.

It was dusk when Pontarlier appeared ahead, and they were all weary as they drove past the Silver Apple. Dorothea and James exchanged knowing glances, his more knowing than hers. Geoffrey also looked out at the busy inn, which certainly didn't look like a house of ill repute. Clearly, James's claims about its reputation were a fabrication. The landlord's involvement with bandits *wasn't* a fabrication, however, and he would receive a visit later that night. After the necessary bribe, Geoffrey had no doubt the fellow would divulge everything about the ambush.

At last they saw the sign of the Boar, its new paintwork gleaming in the light from a street lamp. Snow flurried in the glow of the lamp, and lay in freshly cleared heaps around the busy yard as they alighted and made their way past the coaches, diligences, and other vehicles drawn up in the shelter.

Emily flew interestedly around the yard, and then glanced up toward the sky to see a church spire soaring up into the night. Without thinking, she sped up through the snowy darkness, forgetting that her glow would intensify. She could hear the church choir practicing a Christmas carol.

Il est né, le Divin Enfant . . . He is born, the Divine Child. Emily smiled. She knew the words because she'd once had a French nurse! Glowing brightly, and with gladness in her heart, she flew several times around the spire, singing with the choir.

But suddenly she saw how startled the roosting pigeons were. They could see her! With a gasp, she realized what she was doing, and swiftly she flew down into the inn yard again to rejoin Geoffrey.

He looked reprovingly at her. "You forgot, didn't you, miss?" he said when no one else could hear.

She nodded dolefully. "Do you think He'll be very cross with me?"

"I wouldn't presume to guess what He'll think, but I shouldn't imagine He'll banish you for a moment's forgetfulness."

A smile returned to her face.

Eighteen

The Boar was a large, five-story building with ample accommodation for the late guests, who arrived to find it was the landlord's birthday, and there was to be a celebratory dinner to which everyone at the inn was invited.

It was a diversion to which Lucy was looking forward, but she hadn't been in her room for long when she realized she'd mislaid one of her little pearl earrings. They weren't particularly valuable, but meant a great deal to her because they'd been the last thing her father had given her before he died. She'd definitely put both on that morning at the Eagle, but one had gone now. She could only hope it had fallen off in one of the carriages, because if she'd lost it on the pass, or at one of the stages, she'd never see it again.

She'd put her damp cloak in front of the fire to dry, but put it on again to go out to the stables. As she passed the entrance of the main tap room on the ground floor, James hailed her.

"Miss Trevallion?"

She turned to see him getting up from a settle by the fire, where he'd been enjoying a glass of local cognac. What she didn't see was Emily, who'd been whiling away time by invisibly pretending to do all manner of dire things to him, from hitting him on the head with a poker to tipping the settle over. It was great fun, but reprehensible, as the angel very well knew. But it was only make-believe, she told herself.

The little angel glided curiously toward Lucy, wondering where she was going in her cloak. James wondered the same thing, for he put his glass aside and came over. "You're going out, Lucy?" he asked.

"I've lost one of my earrings, and thought I'd search the carriages."

"You can't possibly go out alone," he said quickly.

"But the earring's important to me, James."

"Then we'll both look," he said promptly, offering her his arm.

Emily grimaced at his smooth gallantry. Ugh! How could Lucy not see through him? He was a *toad!*

Lucy gave him a shy smile. "I-I don't wish to inconvenience you."

"You could never inconvenience me," he replied warmly, taking her hand and drawing it firmly over his sleeve.

Emily pretended to be sick. Oh, how oily he was. His smiling attentiveness was just about the most disgusting display of dishonesty she'd ever seen. He positively oozed chivalrous concern.

Lucy blushed a little. "You're very kind."

"Not at all, it's the least I can do," James said, ushering her toward the door.

Emily accompanied them as they stepped out into the snowy yard. A diligence from Ornans was just arriving, the passengers looking half frozen in the light of a lamp by the yard entrance. It was very noisy as the cumbersome vehicle halted, and porters hastened about their business. Ostlers came from the stableyard to take the weary horses, as Lucy and James hurried through the archway that led to the coachhouses.

They soon found their carriages, standing among various others in the barnlike shadows, where the only light came from a lamp hanging from a beam. There was melting snow on most of the vehicles, and the sound of dripping seemed oddly loud as James led Lucy toward the first carriage, which happened to be Geoffrey's. He opened the door, and assisted her inside before climbing in himself. Emily flew through them both, but they felt nothing.

"I'm afraid it's only a very small earring," Lucy said, beginning to look around.

"I know, but very charming, as I recall," he said softly.

She glanced swiftly at him. "I'm surprised you noticed."

"I notice everything where you're concerned."

Color flamed into her cheeks.

He smiled a little, for her flustered reaction was a good sign, but he didn't say anything more as he helped her to make a thorough search.

It was while Lucy was looking under one of the seats that she found the secret compartment. Puzzled, she opened the little hinged flap in the floor, and to her surprise found a pistol hidden there. It was a beautiful weapon, and kept well oiled and polished.

Realizing she'd found something, Emily leaned over her shoulder. The angel's eyes widened. Geoffrey kept a pistol in his carriage?

Lucy closed the compartment without saying anything. It was

no business of hers, nor of James's. She continued to search, but after several minutes it was clear the earring wasn't in the carriage.

Lucy couldn't hide her dismay. "I hardly dare look in the other carriage, because if it isn't there either . . ."

James put a practiced hand over hers. "We'll find it, I'm sure. Don't be disheartened yet."

He allowed his hand to linger, and she didn't immediately pull hers away. It was a hesitation that couldn't help but encourage him. He knew when a woman was attracted to him, and when she wasn't. Lucy Trevallion was.

The way their hands met bothered Emily, who frowned at her cousin. Don't be so easily taken in! He's not a knight in shining armor, he's-he's a fallen man! It was the most dire thing she could think of calling him.

The angel's displeasure passed completely unnoticed as James alighted from the carriage and helped Lucy down to lead her to the other vehicle. Again he held her hand longer than was necessary, and again she didn't pull immediately away, so this time he made so bold as to take her hand properly.

When Lucy didn't snatch her fingers away, Emily was appalled. Oh, Lucy, you're being such a gull. He's utterly odious. For heaven's sake, open your eyes!

They commenced the second search, and luck favored James, who found the earring and held it up triumphantly.

Lucy gave a glad gasp. "Oh, you don't know how pleased I am to have it back again!"

"And you don't know how pleased *I* am to be able to restore it to you," he said softly, pressing the pearl into her palm.

"I'm truly grateful," she said, trying to put it on, but her hands trembled, and she couldn't.

"Allow me," he said, taking the earring again. "Lean forward a little."

She obeyed, and he gently put the earring in place. "There, all is well again," he murmured, brushing a stray curl of hair back from her cheek.

Emily fluttered desperately around them. What could she do to distract them? Surely there was *something?* But there wasn't, she was completely helpless, and could only watch James's relentless progress.

His hand rested against Lucy's cheek for a moment before with mock self-consciousness he lowered it again. "Forgive me, I didn't mean to take undue liberties, it's just that I'm so very happy to have made you smile again. These past days in your company have been among the brightest of my life."

His flattery made Lucy feel warm, for it was in marked contrast to the treatment she received from Geoffrey. Besides, she was by no means indifferent, but still she knew she mustn't encourage too much. "You're very gallant, James, but I doubt I've brightened your existence quite that much."

"But you have."

Emily hopped furiously up and down on the seat. *Lucy Trevallion, you're the greatest goose there ever was, and I'm ashamed of being your cousin!*

Lucy made to alight from the carriage, but James detained her.

"Lucy, there's something I must say to you."

"What is it?"

"That I think you quite delightful; indeed, I find you everything I've ever admired in a young lady. You're gentle, refreshingly natural, and very beautiful." He put his hand to her cheek again, caressing her skin with his thumb. "If there's anything I can ever do for you, you only have to ask," he breathed softly.

His touch sent a frisson of excitement through her, and as he leaned forward to put his lips to hers, she made no move to prevent him. It was a skilled kiss, conveying tenderness, love, and desire, but it was also the chaste kiss of a gentleman who held her in high respect. There was nothing to alarm her, but a great deal to entice her into response.

Emily was motionless with consternation. Oh, Lucy! Lucy! You-you nincompoop!

Lucy's lips trembled beneath his, and she closed her eyes, but then the enormity of her misconduct caused them to fly open again. "No!" she breathed, pulling away.

Emily was relieved. Just keep saying no from now on, she instructed silently, glaring at her foolish cousin.

James pretended guilty dismay, but read Lucy like a book. She'd enjoyed the kiss, and would be ripe for more if he chose the right moment. "Forgive me, I . . ." He allowed his voice to trail wretchedly away.

"There's nothing to forgive, James, it-it's just I know I shouldn't have allowed this to happen."

"I'm the one at fault, Lucy, and will not permit you to accept any blame. I've transgressed, and crave your pardon."

She met his eyes. "If-if that is your wish, then I-I forgive you," she whispered.

"You're the most of an angel I ever knew, Lucy," he said gently.

Emily momentarily forgot her dismay to become indignant. *She's* not an angel, *I* am!

James climbed out of the carriage and held his hand out to Lucy again. This time he was careful to release her hand as swiftly as possible, as if anxious to return matters to their former status. He knew exactly how to proceed from here. All he had to do was appear reluctantly enslaved by his emotions. She was like a beautiful fish, to be reeled carefully into his waiting net.

Lucy kept her eyes lowered as they returned to the inn, and couldn't bring herself to look back at him by the tap room entrance until she reached the staircase. But then she did look back. He was waiting for her to do just that, and gave her a smile laden with honorable longing and devotion.

Her heart beat swiftly as she gathered her cloak to hurry on up. Emily glided crossly at her side, but didn't accompany her to her room; instead, the angel went in search of Geoffrey. She found him enjoying a hot bath in front of the fire in his room. There was a Spanish cigar between his lips and his eyes were closed as he luxuriated in the steaming water, but his eyes flew open as Emily addressed him.

"Oh, Geoffrey, Lucy's allowing James to do all sorts of things he shouldn't."

He almost choked on the cigar, and sat up in the bath. "Eh? What things?" he demanded.

"Kisses and things."

"Kisses and things?" he repeated.

"Yes. In the coachhouse."

He blinked, and began to get out of the bath, but then remembered he didn't have a stitch of clothes on, and so sat back in some embarrassment. "You'd better tell me exactly what's been going on," he said then.

Emily explained. "And Lucy really liked that horrid kiss," she finished incredulously. "Oh, he's so slimy and disgusting, but she thinks he's wonderful, I can tell she does!"

Geoffrey exhaled slowly. Weybridge was making relentless progress, and foolish Lucy seemed to be ripe for plucking.

Emily was impatient. "What are you going to do about it?"

"There isn't a great deal I can do for the moment," he replied tetchily. "All I can promise is to keep a close eye on things this evening."

"And tonight? What about tonight?"

"I can hardly stay with her all night! But you can, and if anything, er, undesirable, should occur, you can come for me."

"Oh, yes. So I can." She felt a little better then, and sat down on a chair as if to stay a while.

Geoffrey eyed her. "I'd appreciate it if you toddled off for the moment, Emily," he said.

"Why?"

"Because I wish to get out of this damned bath."

"I'm not stopping you. And don't swear."

"All right, I won't swear, but go anyway. *Please*," he replied with exaggerated patience.

In a blink she'd disappeared, and with her went the light of the only candle in the room. With a curse that would have shocked her, he climbed out of the bath and relit the candle at the low fire.

But as he reached for a towel, Emily reappeared.

"Geoffrey, you *do* promise to watch Lucy carefully tonight, don't you?" she asked, her interested gaze moving over every inch of him.

He snatched the towel to his loins. "Yes, I do!"

She vanished again, and he gave a furious sigh as the candle was extinguished once more. "God give me patience," he muttered, holding it to the fire a second time.

Then he began to dry himself, wondering as he did if all Trevallion females were as vexatious as the two he was unfortunate enough to be involved with. Both Emily and Lucy had far too much to say for themselves, and Lucy's conduct now was questionable to say the least. He was of half a mind to let her go her own foolish way, for her persistent ingratitude was becoming hard to endure. But then he drew himself up. Lucy might be many things, but she didn't deserve to be ruined by the likes of James Weybridge. And there was still Dorothea to consider, for although James no longer intended Lucy's death, his sister certainly did.

With another sigh, he slipped into his dressing gown and then went to the window to hold the curtain aside and look out. Through the snow he could see the nearby church spire reaching up into the night. It was a very seasonal scene, reminding him that this accursed journey was supposed to end at Christmas. He'd be damned glad when it did, for then he could wash his hands of Lucy Trevallion, and, hopefully, at the same time see the last of Emily!

Earlier, when James parted from Lucy and resumed his seat in the tap room, he called for more cognac, and then sat in quiet thought. He'd made much progress with the lady, so why not hasten things along a little? He recalled the previous evening at the Eagle, when she'd confessed to not having much of a head for wine, and a cunning smile began to curve his lips. There would be wine in plenty at the landlord's birthday celebrations tonight, and if a little of the exceeding potent local *eau-de-vie* were to be added to Lucy's drinks . . .

Nineteen

Guests had already begun to assemble for dinner an hour later when Lucy emerged from her room to go downstairs. She wore the pearl earrings and her sage dimity, the primrose brocade evening gown being packed away in her luggage on the carriage. She'd put her hair up into a knot, with several ringlets falling to the nape of her neck, and there was a simple brown velvet reticule looped over her wrist.

She was still blushing because of what had happened in the coachhouse, and didn't know what she was going to say to James when she saw him. She knew she'd permitted far more than she should, but also knew those few minutes had been more than a little agreeable.

She entered the dining room, where highly polished brass lamps cast a fine light over the long white-clothed table, gleaming cutlery, and dazzling glassware. The landlord's birthday repast was to be a memorable occasion, with nothing but the very best for everyone in the inn that night. The room was filling rapidly, and the musicians had begun to play, although the dancing wasn't to be until after the meal.

She glanced around, hoping to see James, but he and Dorothea hadn't come down yet. Instead, she saw Geoffrey alone on a bench in the corner next to the fireplace. In such French surroundings, his Englishness was only too apparent, for he wore an indigo corded silk coat and white trousers. He looked very London, and, she conceded, very elegant indeed. She decided to avoid him, and so crossed the room in the opposite direction to examine the table.

Emily was enjoying herself flitting from group to group, trying to understand what was being said, but her French wasn't all that good, and they spoke too quickly for her. So she amused herself making up ridiculous conversations, and then squealing with laughter at her own wittiness. But even while she played, she remembered what was frowned upon in heaven, and so studiously avoided a little crucifix fixed to the wall above the fireplace. It wouldn't do at all if she were suddenly to shine brightly in the middle of such a gathering!

Meanwhile Geoffrey observed Lucy, and got up to approach her. "Good evening, Miss Trevallion."

Her heart sank. "My lord."

"Will you join me?" He indicated the bench.

Reluctantly she consented, and he procured her a glass of the strawberry liqueur which was being liberally provided.

"Is it very strong?" she asked. "I become very dizzy."

"I really can't say what it's like, Miss Trevallion, but maybe you'd prefer something else?"

She glanced at the liqueur, and then at the various other ladies who were sampling it with obvious relish. If they could drink it, surely she could too? "I-I'm sure it will do, sir."

He sat down, observing the blush that had been on her cheeks since he'd noticed her a moment or so ago. Memories of the coachhouse, no doubt! He decided to amuse himself at her unwitting expense. "Would it be in order for me to say I think you look delightful tonight?" he said suddenly.

The compliment caught her unawares. "I, er . . . Thank you, sir."

"Don't look so startled, madam, for I have been known to give praise where it is due, and besides, I can't help noticing how dazzling you are. Evidently something highly agreeable has occurred."

More color stained her cheeks. "Well, if a bath can be termed an agreeable occurrence . . ." She left the sentence unfinished in a way that was meant to close the subject.

"I'm sure it can, but . . ." He deliberately didn't finish either.

"But what, sir?" She was beginning to bridle.

"But a bath can hardly be the cause of such, er, radiance."

Her green eyes darkened. "Lord St. Athan, permit me to inquire if your compliments, few and far between as they may be, are always accompanied by an interrogation?"

"An interrogation? Miss Trevallion, why on earth would I do that? Indeed, what possible reason could there be for me to question you about anything?"

"Precisely." But she knew her cheeks were aflame with guilt. Oh, plague take him for having the unerring ability to rattle her.

He decided he'd tweaked her enough, and so changed the subject. "Miss Trevallion, I trust that from now on you'll refrain from being as adventurous as you were today."

Her thoughts were still of the coachhouse. "And what do you mean by that?" she demanded coolly.

"Precipices are dangerous things, and your, er, daring, was bad for my heart."

She relaxed a little. "I'm sure there's nothing wrong with your heart, sir."

"I didn't think there was either, but you caused it to leap into my mouth, and I'd thank you not to repeat the exercise."

She smiled a little then. "You have my word, sir."

"Just be careful."

Her smile extinguished as she realized he was reminding her he didn't trust James and Dorothea. "Please don't spoil this evening, my lord. It is a birthday celebration, and I'd thank you not to bring unpleasantness into the situation."

"Unpleasantness? Miss Trevallion, I—"

She interrupted heatedly. "Please, Lord St. Athan! If you're about to harp on about the Weybridges, I'd much prefer it if you didn't say anything at all."

"Well, since you're clearly far too sensible and levelheaded to get into scrapes, I'm sure there's no need for me to say anything more, is there?"

She had to look away. Sensible and levelheaded? She hadn't been either in the coachhouse! She drank the strawberry liqueur.

He read her face like a page. Yes, miss, he thought, well you might look away, for your conduct hasn't been what it should be. And with Weybridge!

She glanced at him again, saw the expression in his eyes, and furiously beckoned to a waiter to bring another glass of liqueur.

Geoffrey was concerned. "Take care, Miss Trevallion, for I have no idea how strong—"

"Don't lecture me, sir!"

"As you wish." He drew a long breath. There were times when he'd like to shake her, and this was one. He was only here because he'd been coerced, and yet she'd behaved as if he were the devil incarnate! More than that, she was guilty of misconduct with Weybridge, and thus showed an abysmal lack of wisdom, standards, and even basic taste. She was, without doubt, the most aggravating creature imaginable! What she needed was a good—!

He pulled his thoughts up sharply, for to have completed them wouldn't have been at all gentlemanly. But it *was* what she needed! A lusty session between the sheets would give her something worthwhile to think about. And James Weybridge wasn't the man to do it!

*   *   *

At that moment, Dorothea was coming down the staircase from her room on the fourth floor. Her chestnut hair was worn in an elegant pleat, with little curls teased around her face, and she wore blue velvet.

Reaching the second floor, where James's room was, she paused before going on down. She saw his door was slightly ajar, allowing the candlelight within to shine into the shadowy passage. But as she approached, she heard playful female giggles, and a frown darkened her face.

She pushed the door open a little more, and saw James had lured one of the inn maids onto the maroon-curtained bed. The girl's skirts were up around her waist, and James's expert fingers were stroking her white thighs as he leaned over her.

Dorothea interrupted sarcastically, using French for the maid's benefit. "Don't you ever tire of such vulgar creatures, brother mine?"

The maid gave a mortified gasp, and scrambled up to run from the room, leaving James to roll irritatedly onto his back to look at his sister. "Was that really necessary, Dorothea dear?"

"If you must satisfy your lust with servants, at least do it behind closed doors."

He got up to put on his coat. He was otherwise dressed, and needed only to tidy his neckcloth.

She watched him. "Have you sent word to the Silver Apple?"

He paused. "No, not yet."

"Then don't you think you should?"

"There's ample time."

"Do it now," she insisted, nodding toward a table where writing implements were set out.

"Very well. I'll join you downstairs when I've done it," he said, sitting down and selecting a sheet of paper.

"I'll wait," she replied, going to hold her hands out to the stove that warmed the room.

He glared at her, and snatched up a quill. As he dipped it in the well, he realized there wasn't any ink, but he wanted to convince Dorothea the task had been done, so he scratched the quill over the paper as if writing.

Dorothea glanced toward the dressing table mirror, in which she had a perfect view of him. It took only a moment for her sharp eyes to perceive the inkless page. She remained silent as he made a great pretense of dusting and sealing the folded sheet.

"There, I'll see someone takes it straight away," he said.

"And Mansart will be lying in wait for us tomorrow as planned?" She smiled coolly.

"Yes."

The smile hadn't reached her eyes. "I'll be glad when it's over, and we can shed crocodile tears for poor little Lucy," she murmured.

"Yes," he said again, pushing the note into his pocket and then extinguishing the candles before offering her his arm.

She accepted, but as they reached the staircase, she suddenly gasped. "Oh, I didn't bring a handkerchief. I-I'll just go to my room again. I'll see you downstairs."

"As you wish."

Dorothea hurried to the fourth floor again, where, in French, she wrote a letter of her own to the landlord of the Silver Apple. *We are in Pontarlier. Tell Mansart as agreed. —James Weybridge.*

Once downstairs, she gave the note to a waiter, together with some coins if he'd deliver it immediately. This he did.

When James had gone down a few minutes earlier, the first thing he'd done had been to seek out one of the other waiters, a shifty-eyed fellow he'd spoken to just after returning from the coachhouse with Lucy.

"Have you done as I asked?" he demanded.

The man nodded and glanced at Lucy. "Yes, *monsieur*, I have put the *eau-de-vie* in her liqueur. She has had two glasses now."

"Good." James slipped another coin into the man's palm. "A little in her wine during dinner as well, mm?"

"As you wish, *monsieur*, but it is very strong indeed," the waiter warned.

"So much the better."

James then made his way through the crowd to join Geoffrey and Lucy. Geoffrey stood, and gave a very brief nod. "Weybridge."

"My lord." James hardly glanced at him, but bowed over Lucy's hand. "Good evening, Miss Trevallion," he said softly.

"Good evening, Mr. Weybridge," she replied. His touch made her pulse quicken, and there was a warmth in his brown eyes that was quite unsettling.

A few moments later the gong summoned everyone to the table, and Dorothea entered just as the guests began to sit down. James had been too quick for Geoffrey, who'd intended to deny him the chance of escorting Lucy to her seat, and he put his hand over hers as they crossed the room.

"You look very beautiful tonight, Lucy."

"You're still very gallant, James."

"You must know by now that I think everything about you is beautiful," he said smoothly, "and the more I think about what happened earlier, the less sorry I am to have given in to my feelings."

She lowered her eyes blushingly as she sat in the chair he drew out for her.

Geoffrey escorted Dorothea to the table, obliging her to sit on her brother's other side, so he himself could take the remaining chair next to Lucy. What good it would do, he didn't know, but at least he could hear what she said to Weybridge.

Dorothea was elated. Mansart's ambush would take place after all, and she was the only one here who knew it! She didn't know what her brother was up to, but could guess by the marked attention he was paying Lucy. James had always been greedy, and he clearly wasn't satisfied with the generous sum Robert was paying him. No, James wanted all the Trevallion fortune, and so was going about his own sly business. Well, two could play at that game, as her dear brother would very soon discover. By this time tomorrow it would all be over, and so would James's hopes of getting his scheming hands on the fortune that was Robert's by right!

Dorothea had seldom enjoyed a meal more than she did that one. She felt so triumphant it was as if the vile deed had already been done. She could almost feel Robert's wedding ring on her finger, and see herself as mistress of Trevallion Park. Respectability, wealth, and comfort were as good as hers, and all because she'd been vigilant where her own brother was concerned!

Meanwhile, Emily had become bored with silly imaginary conversations and was hovering by the corner of the ceiling wondering what to do next to pass the time, when she noticed the sly smile on Dorothea's face. Then she noticed the equally satisfied glint in James's eyes, for, like his sister, he thought he'd stolen a march. The little angel's heart sank. Something new had taken place, and she'd been so taken up with her stupid games she didn't know what it was.

She fluttered anxiously to Geoffrey, who was just pouring a glass of wine for Lucy, but he refused to look at the angel, even though she appeared on the table right next to his plate.

Emily was incensed. "Don't ignore me, Geoffrey! They're up

to something, I know they are! Just look at them!" she cried, gesticulating wildly toward Dorothea and James.

He gave her a ferocious look, but reluctantly leaned forward to glance past Lucy at the other two. They were both getting on with their meal, and appeared quite natural to him.

Emily looked at them again too. "They *are* up to something, I can tell! It must be something to do with the ambush, so you have to go the Silver Apple right now!" she said urgently.

He kept his lips determinedly closed. He wasn't going to say anything aloud, not with Lucy sitting right next to him, and he certainly wasn't about to visit the Silver Apple until much later on. Such things were always best accomplished in the dead of night, not when inns were still doing brisk trade

Emily was almost in tears. "You *must* listen to me, Geoffrey!"

It was too much. "I'll speak to you later!" he said firmly.

Lucy, who was vaguely aware of far too much of a warm glow from the liqueur before the meal, and the wine during it, glanced at him in surprise. "I-I beg your pardon, my lord?" she asked, feeling obliged to speak much more carefully than usual because her lips wouldn't do quite what she wanted them to.

She was tipsy! Far from shocking her, the realization made her want to giggle, but she was still sufficiently mistress of herself to resist the temptation. Indeed, anyone observing her now would have found it hard to believe she was under the influence at all.

Geoffrey certainly didn't realize anything was wrong. "I, er, asked if you'd dance with me later." He managed a smile and nodded toward the rich dishes with which the table was laden. "So much cream will require a good deal of energetic hoofing, don't you agree?" he went on, trying to divert her.

"Yes, I do. I'd like to dance with you, my lord." She smiled, astonished at the enthusiasm with which she'd accepted his unexpected invitation. She'd *like* to dance with him? She didn't even like *him*, let alone anticipate with any pleasure the thought of dancing with him!

James overheard, and looked sharply at her. He knew her doctored drinks were taking effect, but the last thing he wanted was for St. Athan to reap the benefit! He smiled at her. "Would you care for some of this cheese, Miss Trevallion?" he asked, indicating the selection on the board to draw her attention away from Geoffrey.

Emily, meanwhile, was very angry with Geoffrey. She scowled at him, her lower jaw jutting in a childishly defiant way. Then, in a considerable huff, she vanished, snuffing several candles on the table. Geoffrey heaved a sigh of relief, but her warnings hadn't fallen on stony ground, and from that moment on he kept a close eye on Dorothea and James. It wasn't long before he concluded the angel was right; they both looked far too pleased with themselves.

The meal came to an end, and the musicians struck up again. The table was moved aside, the floor cleared, and the dancing began. James moved quickly to ask Lucy to partner him, but this time Geoffrey was alert enough to step in first.

"You promised me this honor, I believe, Miss Trevallion," he said with a smile.

She glanced regretfully at James, but accepted Geoffrey's hand. It was warm in the room, the atmosphere was heady, and the dance unexpectedly affecting. Geoffrey's arm was around her waist, his fingers enclosing hers as they whirled to the intoxicating folk music. She smiled at him, remembering her dream and how abandoned she'd been. Forbidden excitement began to pound through her again. What would it be like to kiss him? To have his arms properly around her? To submit to him . . .

She felt relaxed and slightly dizzy. Oh, she'd definitely had too much strawberry liqueur before the meal, but it was a nice feeling—a wicked sort of feeling, as if she were now permitted to do things she wouldn't normally. Like indulge her curiosity about kissing him. She moved closer, disengaging her hand from his in order to link her arms around his neck.

He was startled to say the least. He could see the flush on her cheeks, and the shine in her green eyes, and there was something unbelievably erotic about the way her hips swayed to the music. This was Lucy Trevallion as he'd never seen her before! He put his hands to her waist, savoring the litheness of her body, so warm and pliant beneath the sage dimity.

Lucy was uninhibited now. She decided definitely to kiss him! After all, that was the only way to find out how it would feel. She stretched up toward him, her lips parting invitingly, and before he knew it she was giving him the sort of kiss no proper young lady should give. Her body molded to his, her breasts pressing wantonly, and he felt her tongue teasing against his in a way no mortal man could resist.

His arms tightened around her and he returned the kiss. Dear God, she was temptation personified, and certainly not the sweet little innocent she appeared on the surface! There was an unmistakable ache in his loins, and a visible arousal he'd have preferred not to experience in public, but what red-blooded male could withstand a sensual assault like this?

The thought of bedding her seemed more and more enticing, as she moved her hips against him, savoring the hardness she'd excited into existence. She knew that hardness, for she'd surrendered to it in her dreams! Oh, to surrender like that again now, to have him inside her, thrusting as he had then.

But her lips suddenly softened beneath his. Then her entire body softened, and she went limp. He managed to catch her before she lost consciousness, and there was quite a stir as he lifted her into his arms, for everyone had observed what had gone on in the moments before she fainted.

Geoffrey was hugely dismayed, both at himself for succumbing, and at the fact that it had all been so public. The incident had brought the dancing to a startled halt, and he knew practically everyone in the room deemed him guilty of lamentably lecherous conduct toward a young lady who was unfortunately the worse for wear.

But some experienced other emotions too. He felt Dorothea's quizzically angry gaze. The woman clearly suspected him of having ulterior motives, not seducing Lucy Trevallion for her charms, but for her fortune! As for James Weybridge . . . Geoffrey glanced at him and saw an expression that was much more difficult to fathom. Was it resentment, perhaps?

As soon as Dorothea and some of the other ladies took Lucy in hand, he guiltily made himself scarce. The time had come to visit the Silver Apple! A minute or so later, he went out relievedly into the snowy night.

Twenty

Emily accompanied Geoffrey to the Silver Apple. She'd reappeared during the dance and so had seen what happened, but when she tried to ask him about it, he declined to reply because he was embarrassed, and more than a little ashamed of himself. The angel was miffed to be denied an explanation, but soon gave up questioning him.

She hovered at his side as he confronted the landlord of the other inn. Bribery soon had the desired effect, and although the message had long since been sent on to the bandits, by the time Geoffrey left to return to the Boar, he knew the time, place, and outline of Mansart's planned ambush. He also knew that the landlord had apparently been informed of the victim's arrival in Pontarlier by a note from James Weybridge, but Geoffrey had little doubt it was Dorothea's handiwork, not her brother's. James clearly no longer desired Lucy's demise, but his sister certainly did—her promised marriage to Robert Trevallion depended upon it!

It was still snowing lightly, and his top hat was pulled low and his collar turned up as he walked back to the Boar, with Emily, golden and shining, flying next to him. His thoughts turned briefly from the ambush to the puzzle of Dorothea's past. If only he could recall where he'd seen her, but try as he would, it remained shrouded in mystery. He shrugged the riddle aside to consider the more immediate matter of the ambush, which was set to take place the very next morning, halfway between Pontarlier and Ornans. Lucy had to be protected, and the obvious course was to change the route, but he knew the others wouldn't agree—Dorothea because she wanted the ambush to take place, James because he believed he'd prevented the ambush by not sending word to the Silver Apple, and Lucy because she'd regard it as a matter of principle to oppose any suggestion from loathed Lord St. Athan!

This latter thought brought a sour expression to Geoffrey's

face, for the more he thought of Lucy, the more obstinate she seemed. Obstinate, but unexpectedly warm and passionate! The sour expression lifted guiltily, for it had ill become him to respond to her as he had. With hindsight it was clear she'd had several drinks too many, but he'd done nothing to deter her, and what's more he'd thoroughly enjoyed the astonishing erotic kiss that had ended only when she lost consciousness in his arms.

As he reached the Boar, he paused to glance toward a livery stable further along the street. He began to smile as without warning he saw a way of foiling the ambush. He hadn't come to the continent unarmed, and apart from the small pistol he always kept hidden in his carriage, he possessed a rare pair of repeating magazine pistols by Cox of London! It was highly unlikely the bandits had guns that came even remotely close to a capability of firing nine times in quick succession, and if Mansart himself were picked off with the first shot . . .

Emily looked inquisitively at him. "What are you thinking?"

"That all is far from lost."

"What do you mean?"

"Emily, tomorrow morning you and I are going to leave before the others even wake up." Humming to himself, he went into the inn.

Lucy awoke the next morning to find Dorothea and one of the inn maids by the bed. The maid had brought some vervain tea, locally reckoned a sovereign remedy for the aftereffects of too much alcohol. Lucy felt dreadful, but didn't know why, because she remembered very little of the previous evening.

Dorothea was solicitous. "How are you?" she asked.

"Awful," Lucy replied with masterly understatement, for she'd seldom felt worse in her life.

The maid poured a dish of the tea, and held it out to her. *"Vous avez la gueule de bois, oui?"* she said.

Lucy translated the inquiry. "I've got a wooden mouth? What do you mean?" she asked, but then the truth dawned. A wooden mouth was the French expression for how one felt the morning after the night before!

Dorothea urged the tea upon her. "You'd better take it, I'm told it's the very thing for someone with your, er, indisposition."

Slowly Lucy sat up, and winced as her head pounded. She closed her eyes for a moment and then looked in puzzlement at Dorothea. "How can I possibly be as bad as this? All I had was a little liqueur before dinner, and about two glasses of wine during the meal."

"I fear that what you drank wasn't quite what it seemed."

"What do you mean?"

"That a particularly potent *eau-de-vie* was mixed in your drinks."

"But . . . why?"

Dorothea avoided her eyes. "I, er, believe a certain person had your seduction in mind," she said slowly.

Lucy stared. "My what? But who . . . ?"

"Well, for the culprit, you need look no further than the person who procured your drinks."

Lucy's lips parted. "Lord St. Athan?"

"Who else?" Dorothea believed what she said, for Geoffrey had been with Lucy throughout, and his reaction to the kiss had been most illuminating, so when James said someone had paid a waiter to spice up Lucy's drinks, it didn't seem necessary to look further than his lordship. The waiter had prudently disappeared, and James's obvious outrage seemed to eliminate him from suspicion. Therefore, it had to be Geoffrey. It wasn't until that revealing moment during last night's dance that his motives had suddenly become clear. Now she didn't doubt that his purpose was exactly the same as her own dear brother's—the securing of Lucy's inheritance. The opportunity of acquiring a very large and convenient fortune was apparently as irresistible to a peer of the realm as it was to a lowly adventurer. Dorothea gave a secret smile, for it wouldn't benefit either man to pursue dear Lucy, who a few hours from now would be no more.

Lucy was still reeling from learning what Geoffrey had done to her drinks. "I—I can't believe he'd stoop so very low," she said at last.

"I believe he's after your fortune," Dorothea replied coolly.

Lucy lowered her gaze to the cup of vervain tea. "It's no more than I already suspected," she said after a moment. "I, er, overheard Lady Amelia and him talking one morning. It seems he's in debt, and Lady Amelia suggested he be nice to me because of who I am. Evidently he took the advice to heart." Her anger flared then. "How unutterably vile he is! No doubt he had some reason for thinking it would impress me, but he even went so far as to pretend he'd seen a vision of my cousin Emily."

Dorothea blinked. "A-a vision of Emily?"

"Yes. Afterward, when he saw how disgusted I was, he was at

pains to explain it away as a nonsense brought on by being in his cups. I can't imagine why he said it all in the first place."

Dorothea was mystified, but then remembered how James had believed Lucy to be devout. "Maybe he thought you were pious."

"I go to church on Sunday, but that's all," Lucy replied.

"You *did* make that bookmark with angels and so on," Dorothea reminded her, having seen the embroidery in question.

"Yes, but it wasn't for me, it was for Lady Amelia's cook to give to the pastor."

"Maybe Lord St. Athan didn't realize that," Dorothea said, for James certainly hadn't.

"Maybe."

"What did he say about the vision?" Dorothea asked curiously.

Lucy hesitated, for she could hardly tell Dorothea everything Geoffrey had said. "Oh, nothing very much," she replied dismissively, and to her relief the point wasn't pressed.

The maid leaned forward to pour more vervain tea, and made a smiling remark only Dorothea heard.

Lucy looked sharply at the latter. "What did she say?"

"That you must have drunk vervain last night as well. You see, vervain isn't just a remedy for aftereffects, it's put in love philters as well. She thinks there was some in your drinks yesterday, as well as the *eau-de-vie*."

Lucy's heart began to sink. "Why would she think that?" she asked quietly.

Dorothea shifted uncomfortably. "Because you were so amorous toward Lord St. Athan," she said reluctantly.

"Amorous? What did I do?" Lucy asked faintly.

"Well, you were clearly a little, er, intoxicated, but you insisted on dancing the first dance with him. Your conduct then was, well, very affectionate."

Lucy's dismay knew no bounds. "Affectionate? With Lord St. Athan?"

"Yes." Dorothea went to look out at the cold but sunny morning. Pontarlier lay beneath a blanket of snow, and the air was so clear the Jura mountains seemed close enough to touch. It made her think of Christmas. Oh, what a memorable yuletide it would be this year. With Lucy gone, Robert was bound to achieve his dream of becoming Edwin Trevallion's heir, and that would mean that she, Dorothea Weybridge, one-time *belle de nuit* at the Devil's Den in St. James's, would become a respectable and wealthy married woman!

If she had but realized it, there was someone on the other side

of the glass, looking in at her. Emily had lingered at the inn after
Geoffrey's departure, and had been about to follow him when she
noticed Dorothea's duplicitous face at Lucy's window. Looking
past Dorothea, the angel saw Lucy's mortified expression, and so
she flew invisibly into the room to see what was going on.

Lucy's cheeks were aflame, and she pushed her dish of tea
back into the maid's hands. "Please leave us," she ordered.

The maid quickly obeyed, and as the door closed behind her,
Lucy pressed trembling hands to her fiery face.

Emily was consternated. What had happened? Why was Lucy
so upset? The angel made herself comfortable at the foot of the
feather bed, and prepared to watch and listen. Lowering her hands
at last, Lucy looked hesitantly at Dorothea. "What *exactly* did I do
last night?"

"I don't think you really want to know."

"But I do."

"Very well, you kissed Lord St. Athan in front of everyone, and
I don't mean a chaste peck on the cheek, but a full-blooded, pas-
sionate kiss that brought the entire proceedings to a standstill.
Then you fainted clean away."

Lucy was shaken. "I-I did what?"

"Do you really want me to say it again?"

Lucy shook her head. She was shocked, and so appalled she
didn't know what to say or do. But then her mortification flared
into a blaze of indignation. Why should *she* feel embarrassed and
wretched? *He* was the one who had set out with purely opportunist motives, and *he* was the one who had had her drinks tam-
pered with. "How *dare* he behave so villainously! How *dare* he
put something in my drinks so I'd allow him to take liberties!"
she breathed.

At the foot of the bed, Emily blinked at her cousin's quivering
fury. What was Lucy talking about? Geoffrey would never behave villainously, or do something to anyone's drinks!

Dorothea was quick to set the record straight. "I only said he
seemed the obvious culprit," she corrected.

"It's perfectly clear he was the one behind it," Lucy replied
flatly.

Dorothea nodded then. "Yes, and if you hadn't fainted, I don't
doubt that what he began in public would have been completed in
private. You'd have surrendered everything last night, Lucy, then
your reputation would have been ruined. On the grounds of propriety alone, your grandfather would probably then insist you
marry your seducer, and that would suit Lord St. Athan down to

the ground!" *And* it would suit my brother, who also aspires to be your seducer and husband!

Emily was confounded. Complete what in private?

Lucy couldn't say anything, for the picture Dorothea drew was only too graphic and humiliating.

Dorothea glanced at her. "From whichever direction you view Lord St. Athan, he is the lowest of the low."

"I know, but I've made a complete fool of myself now, haven't I?" Lucy's brief fury dwindled into wretchedness as she thought of James. What did *he* think of her now? In the coachhouse she'd permitted more than she should, and then, in front of everyone, it seems she'd virtually thrown herself at Geoffrey! She summoned what composure she could. "What does James think of me?" she asked in a small voice.

Dorothea gave a bright smile. "James blames Lord St. Athan for everything." She was tempted to turn Lucy against her brother, but knew that might seem odd.

"Are you sure?"

"Absolutely."

Dorothea took a deep breath. "Take comfort in the fact that his lordship failed last night, and from now on you aren't likely to fall into any more of his traps, so let's think about today's traveling."

"Dorothea, I can't travel feeling like this." Lucy leaned her aching head back and closed her eyes again.

"I'm told the vervain will soon take effect, and it's best we press on," Dorothea insisted. It was more than best, it was positively *vital*, for Mansart would have received her message by now, and would be setting up the trap.

Emily scowled at her. Oh, you viper! You want Lucy to fall into the ambush! I hate you!

Lucy shook her head. "I simply can't."

Emily was jubilant. That's the way, Lucy! You stay safely here in Pontarlier!

But Dorothea was determined. "We have to continue if we're to have any chance of reaching London in time for Christmas. Besides, you're going to have to face Lord St. Athan sooner or later, so you might as well get it over with."

"That's easy enough for you to say; you weren't the one who behaved so shockingly last night."

"Lucy, you weren't to know what had been done to your drinks," Dorothea said reassuringly. "And James and I have decided that on no account will we leave you alone with Lord St. Athan. You'll always be with us from now on."

"You—you promise?"

"Yes."

Dorothea smiled as Lucy reluctantly pushed the bedclothes aside and got out of bed.

Emily floated unhappily toward the window. Lucy had allowed herself to be persuaded after all, which meant she'd be in the carriage when it drove into Mansart's trap. It was time to go after Geoffrey and tell him what she'd heard.

Twenty-one

Geoffrey had set off over an hour earlier, after discreetly purchasing a good saddle horse from the livery stable he'd noted the night before. With the horse tethered to the rear of his carriage, and a new French postilion to replace the Swiss, he drove swiftly north out of Pontarlier just as the sun rose over the Jura.

Behind him, the snow-covered mountains were blushed to crimson by the brilliant morning light, and all around the beautiful Franche-Comté countryside lay beneath a crisp carpet of snow.

The frontier town had disappeared behind when Emily appeared on the seat at his side. He listened as the angel told him what she'd heard, and then he sighed resignedly. So something had been done to Lucy's drinks, and the finger of suspicion was directed at him. He didn't doubt that James was the real offender. Lucy's seduction would be the perfect answer for a fortune hunter like Weybridge, but he supposed it was inevitable that this particular damsel-in-distress would blame long-suffering St. George, not the dragon! Still, it was agreeable to ponder how the dragon felt when it was St. George who reaped the sensual benefit! Geoffrey couldn't help a slightly wry smile at the thought of James's fury.

Emily saw the smile. "Is something funny, Geoffrey?"

"Eh, no, of course no." He quickly resumed a sterner expression.

"Why did you let Lucy kiss you like that if you don't like her?" the angel asked suddenly.

What an impossible question to answer! How could he explain to a child about such things as sexual desire? In short, he couldn't. He glanced at her. "I'm afraid you wouldn't understand."

"That's what grown-ups *always* say!"

"Perhaps because it's true."

"Or perhaps it's because you're too embarrassed to tell me," she replied with damning accuracy.

"Perhaps, but whatever the reason, I don't intend to discuss it with you."

"It's not fair!" the angel declared mutinously.

He didn't reply, and after a while she lapsed into a sulky silence. He was being horrid! She wanted to know, but he wouldn't tell her. Oh, how she loathed being treated like a child.

The carriage continued swiftly along the almost deserted road. The air was freezing, and hard-packed snow crunched beneath the wheels. Geoffrey flexed his fingers in his gloves, and turned his collar up a little more.

At last the road forked, one branch continuing north, the other plunging northwest into the rocky valley of the River Loue, where the ambush was to take place. As previously instructed, the new postilion halted the carriage, and Geoffrey alighted. Untethering the horse, he watched as the carriage then drove on toward Ornans, where it would wait at an isolated spot on the outskirts of the town. As the carriage disappeared from sight, Geoffrey mounted the horse and then rode quietly along the deserted road.

Snow-covered pine trees hung over the way, and the roar of water echoed between the rocks. The valley was very beautiful, but dangerous too, with far too many opportunities for the likes of Mansart. Geoffrey felt inside his coat to make sure his pistols were secure and easy to reach, for it wouldn't do to be waylaid himself!

There was no sign of his carriage as he reached the place described by the landlord of the Silver Apple. Mansart would approach from the Ornans direction, but Geoffrey knew the carriage would be safely out of sight before the bandit and his men left the Black Unicorn. The ambush was to be launched from a jumble of large rocks at the very narrowest point of the road, and Emily flew ahead to scout the scene.

She returned to tell him that the place was as yet deserted, and that she'd found a spot where he could hide without detection. On the slope above the road there was a small fir copse which offered the perfect vantage point.

He left the road and his horse picked its way along the incline above the river. Progress was slow, but at last he was in position in the copse. Now came the wait. He made himself as comfortable as he could, and gazed down at the Loue as it rushed endlessly over the rapids.

It was nearly an hour before he heard hoofbeats approaching from the Ornans direction. A moment later, Mansart and his men rode into view. They dismounted, hid their horses among the pine trees, and then dispersed among the rocks. Geoffrey had no trouble picking out Mansart himself, for the bandit leader was clearly visible issuing instructions.

It seemed an age after that that Emily suddenly gasped and looked back along the road. "I can hear a carriage!"

"I'm damned if I can hear anything above the noise of the river," Geoffrey replied.

There was a sudden bright flash from the top of a tree along the road toward Pontarlier, and he realized a look-out was stationed there, with a mirror to send a warning. Glancing down at the bandits, he saw they were suddenly much more alert, crouching down in their places, their various weapons at the ready. Some carried pistols, some swords, and others daggers, and they presented a very bloodthirsty and dangerous sight as they waited for their prey to drive into view.

Geoffrey mounted his horse and maneuvered to a part of the slope he'd already chosen earlier, because it offered a relatively easy descent to the road. Then he waited again.

In the swaying carriage, Lucy was still feeling dreadful. The vervain had helped to a point, but she still had a headache, and now felt sick as well. Her hair was pinned up very loosely beneath the raised hood of her lavender cloak, and she'd dispensed with either hat or bonnet, but the headache wouldn't go away. Beneath the cloak she wore her honeysuckle gown, and her hands were once again pushed deep into Lady Amelia's ermine-trimmed muff, for although they'd now traveled down from the Jura, it was still bitterly cold.

She sat opposite Dorothea and James, and tried her best to avoid the latter's gaze, because although she'd been spared a confrontation with Geoffrey, she was still hugely embarrassed at what James might think of her. Last night she'd been anything but shy, proper, or innocent—in short, she'd behaved like a common strumpet—and now she wished she could hide away from everyone. But it was impossible to hide in a carriage, so all she could do to save her blushes was look steadfastly out of the window.

She took what comfort she could from Geoffrey's unexpected departure, telling herself it proved his guilty conscience, for if he were innocent, surely he wouldn't have scuttled off at first light like that.

James gazed out of the carriage window as well, but he wasn't thinking of Geoffrey. They'd almost reached the place where

Mansart's ambush would have taken place, he thought, and then looked at his sister, whose tense face revealed that at any moment she expected the attack to commence. But dear Dorothea was about to be disappointed, for Lucy was safe—from bandits, if not from the man seated opposite her now!

His glance moved to Lucy. It was a pity things had gone as they had last night, but at least he was in the clear. St. Athan was held to be the villain of the piece, and the way he'd returned Lucy's kiss was ample proof of his fortune-hunting intentions. His lordship was made of the same base metal as James Weybridge! But Lucy despised St. Athan now, and James, who knew about such things, was confident it wouldn't be long before she fell into his palm like a ripe plum. And then, oh, and then . . . His hot gaze lingered on the curve of her breasts, outlined by the soft folds of her cloak.

Perfectly turned out in the strawberry merino, Dorothea looked expectantly out of the carriage window. They were almost there now, and excitement rose through her as she glanced swiftly at Lucy. You're about to breathe your last, my dear, she thought. She felt nothing, no pity or even vague regret. When it came to the realization of Robert Trevallion's dreams, and thus her own dreams as well, Lucy was completely dispensable.

Suddenly there was a shout, and the carriage came to a sharp halt. A shot reverberated around the valley like a thunderclap, and the horses reared and plunged as the postilion fell wounded. Mansart and his men had commenced the attack.

Geoffrey and Emily observed the ambush from the safety of the slope above, but the moment the shot was fired the little angel panicked. "You must do something now, Geoffrey!" she cried.

"All in good time," he murmured.

"But what if they shoot Lucy?"

"They won't, not just yet."

"But—"

"I've made it my business to find out how Mansart operates, and if the Weybridges think they'll escape scot-free, they're very much mistaken. Mansart will rob them first, and then attend to Lucy." Geoffrey reached inside his heavy coat with both hands, and drew out his dueling pistols, which were loaded and ready. Then, unobserved by anyone below, he gently urged his horse down the slope. He needed no reins, for he was horseman enough to control his mount with knees and heels alone.

In the carriage, James had gone pale at the sound of the shot. The ambush? But it couldn't be; he hadn't sent the message!

Swiftly he lowered the window glass and looked out. His heart missed a beat as he saw the groaning postilion lying on the frozen snow, and Mansart and his men emerging from the rocks.

"Dear God," he breathed, drawing hastily back inside as the bandit leader leveled a pistol at the carriage door.

Lucy's eyes were wide and frightened. "What is it? What's happening?"

"Bandits," he replied numbly. How had Mansart found out? The answer came in a flash. Dorothea! His bitter gaze swung to his sister's triumphant face.

Mansart intended them to know he meant business, and so fired into the bodywork of the carriage. The shot thudded into the wood, and Lucy screamed, pressing her hands to her mouth. James swallowed, his gaze still upon Dorothea. Suddenly he hated her. She'd ruined his plans, and if it was the last thing he ever did, he'd ruin hers!

There were more shouts, and then the carriage door was flung open. The roar of the river swept in as with beckoning gestures, two bandits ordered the occupants out. Dorothea was stiff with fear, not as yet of the bandits, but of the shining Loue as it spilled noisily over the rapids only a few feet away. But then, as one of the men seized her arm and almost hauled her from her seat, she at last began to feel more frightened of the bandits than the river. What if Mansart decided to kill them all, not just Lucy? As she was flung aside, she pressed against the carriage, as far away from the water as she could.

James's mouth was dry as he clambered down, but as he turned to assist Lucy, Mansart knocked him scornfully aside with a rifle butt. James fell to the ground, pretending to be far more badly hurt than he really was. He was a past master at such feigning, for he'd long since learned that it spared him the risk of showing any courage. Dazedness precluded action.

Dorothea knew him only too well, but Lucy screamed his name in dismay, fearing he'd been killed by the blow. In that moment, Dorothea realized exactly how much progress her brother had made toward winning the Trevallion fortune. She wondered how adoring Lucy would remain if she knew James wasn't badly hurt at all, but merely faking it to save his own skin. Dorothea closed her eyes then, for what did any of it matter should Mansart choose to kill them all?

Lucy's scream for James was stifled as she was dragged from the carriage even more roughly than Dorothea. Her hood fell back, and her hair tumbled down from the few pins that held it.

She dropped her muff, and it rolled softly away over the hard-packed snow, coming to rest by the feet of one of the bandits, who gave a grin and kicked it into the river.

The current snatched it almost gleefully, and in a few seconds sent it spinning wildly over the rapids. Soon it would sink to the bottom. A dread echo sounded silently through Dorothea. *Sink to the bottom . . . the bottom . . . the bottom . . .*

Mansart went up to Lucy, taking her chin roughly between his dirty fingers. She stared at him, too terrified to move, but then to her relief he lost interest in her, flinging her aside so roughly that she went sprawling into the snow.

Emily was outraged. She swooped furiously over to the bandit, trying to claw his face and snatch his hair. But her little hands passed straight through him, and he felt nothing.

Fury blazed through Geoffrey as well, and he knew he dared not delay any longer. He shouted out in perfect French, "Tell your men to throw their weapons away, Mansart, or I'll shoot you right between your brutish eyes."

Twenty-two

Mansart whirled about to see the tall newcomer leveling two exquisite dueling pistols at his head. Dorothea and James stared. Lucy sat up in amazement. Geoffrey? But how could he possibly be here? Then she closed her eyes with relief. It didn't matter *how* he was here, just that he was.

Geoffrey spoke to Mansart again, his tone almost amiable. "Don't take any unwise chances, for pretty as these weapons are, they aren't toys, nor are they average dueling pistols. Both are capable of firing nine consecutive shots, and by my reckoning there are only ten of you. By the way, I'm also an excellent shot, and can assure you I've never been known to miss."

Emily's eyes widened and she stared at him. "How often have you done this sort of thing?" she asked.

"A man doesn't purchase costly dueling pistols merely for decorative purposes," he murmured, still keeping a watchful eye on the scene in the road.

Mansart clearly didn't believe the newcomer was the shot he claimed, and nodded at one of his men, who immediately raised a pistol. Geoffrey's response was instant. He fired directly between Mansart's legs, just high enough to make the bandit fear he'd never enjoy a woman again. Mansart cursed and froze, and the other bandit quickly lowered his weapon again.

Geoffrey then slowly and deliberately recocked the pistol to show it was still loaded. Even above the noise of the river the bandits all heard the unmistakable click. There was a stir, and they glanced uncertainly at each other. They were brave when they had the upper hand, but cowards when at a disadvantage.

Emily clapped her hands delightedly. Oh, how masterful Geoffrey was! His stock went up and up in her eyes.

Still watching them all very closely, and holding a pistol in either hand, Geoffrey moved his horse onto the road. Then he gestured toward the river with one of the pistols. "Throw your weapons in, gentlemen."

They made no move to obey.

"Your weapons, gentlemen!" he snapped, loosing another shot, this time at the road by Mansart's feet.

They hastened to comply, and the River Loue received an assortment of knives, swords, and handguns. Mansart's rifle was the last to be consigned to the water.

Geoffrey looked at Lucy. "Come here," he ordered her.

His supposed crimes the night before were of no consequence now as she scrambled up to run to him, her hair bouncing loose about her shoulders.

James clambered to his feet, giving his sister a hateful look. "This was your doing!" he breathed, his voice too low to carry to anyone but her. "Well, you've failed, thanks to St. Athan!"

"And you'll fail too, brother mine," she hissed back. "The fortune is Robert's, not Lucy's, and I'll see he gets it!"

"If you believe Robert Trevallion really means to marry you, you're a bigger fool than I thought! He won't take a whore to wife, of that you can be sure!"

"He's a man of his word!" she breathed.

"Yes, the lying word!"

Geoffrey was still intent on Mansart. "Step well back, and tell your men to do the same," he said, gesturing along the road toward Pontarlier, but as he spoke, Emily became suddenly alarmed.

"I can hear something, Geoffrey!" she cried, looking anxiously in the Pontarlier direction.

"Well, go and look!" he ordered urgently.

As Emily flew invisibly away, Mansart looked uncertainly at Geoffrey, and then at the other bandits. The Englishman was clearly unhinged, for he spoke to someone who wasn't there!

Lucy was uneasy as well. Geoffrey didn't seem to be talking to her, but maybe he was. She looked up at him. "I—I don't understand . . . "

"Don't concern yourself, Miss Trevallion, for I'm only conversing with the angels," he said dryly.

Her green eyes flashed resentfully. They were in utter danger, and *he* chose to mention angels again!

Emily rushed back. "I can't see anything, Geoffrey, but I *know* someone's there!"

As she spoke, a pistol shot exploded from the tree where earlier they'd seen the mirror flashing. The ball whistled past Geoffrey's head to enter one of Dorothea's trunks on the back of the carriage. Lucy shrank fearfully against Geoffrey's leg, and Dorothea and

James glanced anxiously around to see who'd fired. But Mansart knew, the smile on his face was sufficient evidence of that.

Too late, Emily knew as well. "It's the look-out, Geoffrey! We forgot all about the look-out!"

The shot had caught Geoffrey completely unawares for a vital second or so, and one of the bandits leapt forward to snatch his bridle and jerk the horse's head roughly to one side. The animal reared, and Geoffrey almost lost balance.

Lucy screamed, trying to cling to his stirrup leather as the other bandits surged forward, and Mansart himself snatched a pistol from Geoffrey's hand.

Emily was distraught. It had all gone wrong in the blinking of an eye! Why, oh why hadn't they remembered the look-out! Hovering agitatedly above Geoffrey as he struggled to break free, she willed him to greater effort. Try harder, Geoffrey! Much harder!

Suddenly he managed to regain control of his horse. Dropping the second pistol, he leaned down to grab Lucy. There was no time for finesse; he seized her however he could, and his hand slid briefly over her breasts as he swept her from her feet onto the saddle in front of him. Then he kicked his heels and urged his frightened mount away toward Ornans.

Dorothea screamed after them, "What about us? What about us?"

But he didn't glance back. As far as he was concerned, she and her brother could fend for themselves. The ambush was their doing, and they could face the consequences. His arm tightened around Lucy as she clung to him. "It's all right, they won't catch us now!" he said reassuringly.

"We can't just leave the others!" she cried, trying to look back.

"Even if I wished to save them, I couldn't. Mansart has the only pistols, and they're mine, damn it!" he replied, kicking his horse faster. The danger was far from over, for a horse with two up couldn't long outpace horses carrying only one.

They were still just in range, and Mansart snatched up one of the pistols to fire a wild shot after them, but his aim was poor when the target was moving so swiftly away from him. The ball whined harmlessly past as Geoffrey spurred the horse still more. Another shot whistled through the air, and struck a tree trunk, scattering splinters of wood in all directions, but a moment later they'd reached the next bend and were out of view.

In the air above them, Emily fled as well. Her light was very dim and sorry, and there were tears on her cheeks. It had nearly gone wrong, and she didn't dare think of what might have happened if Geoffrey hadn't gotten free and taken Lucy with him. What if Lucy had died? What fate awaited guardian angels who failed in their duty? Would the gates of heaven be closed to her? Would she be refused permission to go to her parents? Tears stung the little angel's eyes.

After riding away for several minutes, Geoffrey reined in to glance back. The river was quieter now, winding along level ground, and he listened for any sound of pursuit, and then breathed out with relief. "They've decided to let us go," he said, his arm still tightly around her.

Lucy stared fearfully back along the road. "Are—are you sure?" The hectic gallop had left her hair in a hopeless tangle, with several tresses clinging damply to her cheeks, and he could feel her heart pounding.

"As sure as I can be."

"We *can't* leave Dorothea and James, we just can't! We must go back."

"Don't be idiotic! What can we two possibly do against so many? Will them into submission? Just be thankful we've escaped with our lives!"

"But something dreadful may happen to them!"

"And something dreadful *will* happen to us if we're stupid enough to ride back into the lion's mouth."

"Please, for I couldn't bear it if we did nothing."

He felt a pang of conscience. James and Dorothea Weybridge didn't deserve any consideration or pity, but he knew it would be dishonorable to abandon them to their fate. Reluctantly he nodded. "Very well, we'll go back, but very cautiously, do you understand?"

"Yes."

He turned the horse.

Emily was dismayed. "You can't do this, Geoffrey! You can't take Lucy back to the ambush, especially not for the sake of those two horrid Weybridges!"

He didn't reply. He *knew* he shouldn't be doing it, least of all for the Weybridges, but in spite of their utter worthlessness, he still couldn't ride away and leave them.

Twenty-three

Geoffrey wasn't about to fall into Mansart's clutches again, so well before the scene of the ambush, he turned the horse from the road and up the slope to his earlier vantage point. Emily stayed with them, still from time to time telling Geoffrey he was being very foolish. He didn't need telling.

To Lucy's relief, nothing terrible had yet happened to either James or Dorothea. One of Mansart's men was holding them and the wounded postilion at gunpoint by some rocks, while the rest of the bandits ransacked the carriage. They'd already found Dorothea's money and most of her jewels, and had almost immediately located James's purse hidden behind the carriage upholstery. Lucy's small trunk had been emptied, and nothing of interest found. Her volume of *La Nouvelle Héloïse* lay open on the riverbank, its pages fluttering slightly in the draft from the rushing water.

Furious at having lost face because of Geoffrey and Lucy's escape, Mansart was determined to steal anything of value. What he intended to do with his prisoners remained to be seen.

Lucy looked anxiously at Geoffrey. "What's going to happen?"

"I'm not really sure," he replied, his sharp eyes moving over the scene. Mansart was clearly in a rage, and who could say what such a man was capable of?

Down by the carriage, James and Dorothea were equally uneasy as they watched their luggage and belongings being strewn over the snowy road. Dorothea had to look away as two of the bandits pranced around with her undergarments.

Mansart was determined to do all he could to restore his standing with his men. As soon as the contents of the carriage had been gone through and everything of value set aside, he turned his attention to the vehicle itself. He ordered some of his men to unharness the team and lead them away, and the rest of the men to overturn the vehicle into the river.

James was dismayed. "No, you can't!" he cried, but any further protest died on his lips as the bandit leader's bright glance swung coldly toward him.

Dorothea looked contemptuously at her brother. "You fool, do you want to antagonize him?" she breathed.

Mansart's men rocked the carriage to and fro, then heaved it into the Loue. There was a splintering sound as the current dragged it into the rapids, where it caught fast on the rocks. Then, while his men were gathering the things they intended to steal, the bandit leader turned to look at Dorothea. She wasn't as much to his taste as the little blonde had been, but she'd do.

Her response was swift. She had to save herself as best she could. So she raised her chin defiantly, but made sure her pose was slightly provocative by thrusting her breasts forward and moving her hips slightly. It was a ploy that had seldom failed at the Devil's Den, where gentlemen invariably found her spirited attitude both challenging and arousing.

Mansart was no gentleman, but he read the signals just as accurately. Slowly his smile returned, and he came over to her, taking her chin between his rough fingers and forcing her to look up at him. "What is this? The lady is perhaps not a lady after all?"

"The lady knows a man of consequence when she sees him, sir," she replied.

James watched her. This was the real Dorothea Weybridge, a whore to her fingertips, he thought disparagingly, at the same time admiring her courage. But would she succeed, that was the point? She was accustomed to drunken English lords and wealthy young striplings eager to lose their virginity; the bandit was a world away from both.

Mansart grinned at Dorothea. "And this man knows a *fille de joie* when he sees one," he murmured, jerking her head forward and pressing his parted lips over hers.

Quelling the shudder of distaste that swept through her, she put her arms around him and returned the kiss.

On the hillside above, Lucy, Emily, and Geoffrey watched in astonishment. Emily was perplexed. Here was yet another example of how strange grown-ups could be! Dorothea couldn't possibly *like* a horrid brute like Mansart, yet she kissed him as if she did!

Lucy watched in startled silence, but Geoffrey gave a low laugh as he suddenly recalled exactly where he'd seen Dorothea before. "Of course, the Devil's Den," he murmured.

Lucy looked up at him. "What do you mean? What's the Devil's Den?"

"The St. James's gaming house and brothel where I saw Dorothea Weybridge."

She stared at him. "I—I don't believe you."

"That's up to you, but it's still where I saw her. Your dear Dorothea is nothing more or less than a whore. No, perhaps that's not entirely fair, for the clientele at the Devil's Den were wealthy and, on the whole, well born, so perhaps she should be more accurately described as a courtesan."

Her glance fled back to Dorothea, who was now pressed against one of the rocks, with Mansart's hand roaming intimately over her as he continued to kiss her. "I—I still don't believe you," she whispered.

"Look at her, is *that* the conduct of a lady?" Geoffrey observed caustically.

"No, but then, thanks to your despicable actions, nor were mine last night, or so I'm given to understand," Lucy replied, hot color flaming her cheeks.

"Ah, yes, the *eau-de-vie*. Well, let me assure you I was not the guilty party. What possible reason could I have for wishing to seduce you?" He was angered by her complete conviction that he was the villain, and so paid her back by implying there was nothing about her, either personally or financially, of sufficient attraction to arouse his interest.

"Even Lady Amelia believed you to be concerned with my fortune, sirrah, so don't adopt that lofty tone with me. The moral high ground certainly doesn't belong to you!"

"Nor to you, madam, because whether it was alcohol-induced or not, your behavior last night was immodest, importunate, and downright—" He broke off, for Mansart was preparing to make love to Dorothea standing up against the rock. With James and the rest of the band looking on, he pulled her skirts up to her waist and undid his breeches. Geoffrey swiftly put his hand to Lucy's head, forcing her face to his shoulder, and at the same time he fixed Emily with a stern look.

"Don't watch, for it's not at all suitable," he said, choosing words that could be addressed as much to Lucy as the little angel.

Emily needed no second bidding, for she was a little frightened by what was taking place down on the road. She turned away, her hands to her eyes, and Lucy made no protest as she too kept her head averted. She didn't want any of this to be really happening. There wasn't an ambush, and Dorothea wasn't doing what she was right now . . .

She could feel Geoffrey's heartbeats, and suddenly needed reassurance. It didn't matter that a moment ago they'd been ex-changing bitter words, he was her comfort now, and she needed him. "Hold me tight, please," she whispered.

Without a word he put his arms around her, his fingers twining in her hair as he continued to watch the scene below.

Suddenly there was a shout and Mansart turned sharply as the look-out of earlier now gave warning of something approaching from the direction of Pontarlier. Whatever it was was clearly not to be taken lightly, for the bandit leader abandoned Dorothea and nodded swiftly to his men. The bandits melted away toward the trees where they'd left their horses. A moment later they rode off toward Ornans.

Geoffrey glanced up at Emily, who immediately rose into the air to look toward Pontarlier. She returned excitedly. "It's an armed mail coach with an escort of soldiers!" she cried.

Relief surged through Geoffrey. "It's all right now, Miss Trevallion, help is at hand," he said, taking his arms from around her, but still steadying her by the waist. "Oh, and by the way, I don't think it would be prudent to mention the Devil's Den to Miss Weybridge, do you?" he murmured as he urged the horse from the copse and down the slope just as the open-topped mail coach and its escort swept into view around the corner.

At that moment Dorothea herself was almost as sick with relief as she had been with apprehension a short while before. Help had arrived at the very point of capitulation to Mansart's loathsome advances, but with it had come Lucy and Geoffrey, who must have seen everything she'd done. Somehow she had to explain it all away, and convincingly!

Geoffrey's horse reached the road as the mail coach and its escort came to a halt, and he lowered Lucy gently to the ground before turning to speak to the French officer in charge, a handsome young lieutenant of very Gallic appearance, who, most unexpect-edly after the long years of war, was well disposed toward the British. His name was Armand Coty, and he came from Brittany, where his family had long had close connections with Cornwall.

Dorothea ran to Lucy and with a huge sob flung herself dis-tractedly into her arms. "Oh, it was dreadful, quite dreadful! That awful man would have-have . . . "

Her whole body shook with simulated shock, and James looked on with grudging admiration. His sister could have been another Mrs. Siddons!

Lucy was taken in, and held Dorothea comfortingly. "It's all right now; it's over."

Dorothea drew back, searching for a handkerchief. "I-I didn't know wh-what to do. I-I wanted to resist, b-but then I thought he might not h-hurt me if I . . . " Again she pretended to be too upset to finish.

Geoffrey came up to them just as Dorothea dissolved into fresh tears. His glance was withering. "It's regretful but true that one cannot always sup with long spoons when one is with the devil, Miss Weybridge," he murmured.

Her brown eyes flew briefly toward him at the word *devil*. Had he remembered? But his face was expressionless, and her swift alarm subsided.

Lucy didn't hear what he said, for she'd already turned to James. "Are you all right? I was so afraid when that brute struck you with his rifle . . . "

He smiled, looking deep into her eyes. "I'm quite all right, Miss Trevallion," he said softly, stroking her with his glance.

She felt the caress, and smiled too.

Dorothea was swift to turn attention from herself to Geoffrey. "How did you come to be here, sir? You left the Boar before everyone else was up, and then you appear providently at this very spot!"

"What are you insinuating, Miss Weybridge? That I somehow knew of the ambush in advance?" he challenged quietly.

"Hardly, but—"

"But?"

"Well, you have to admit it's rather odd. Don't you agree, Miss Trevallion?"

Lucy shifted uncomfortably, and looked at Geoffrey. "How *did* you come to be here, my lord?"

"Pure chance. I learned there was supposed to be excellent shooting hereabouts, and decided to see for myself. I hired a horse, and just happened to be in the vicinity when the attack commenced."

James laughed derisively. "Shooting? With *dueling* pistols? Oh, come, sir."

"They're excellent weapons, Weybridge. At least, they were," Geoffrey added regretfully, for the pistols were among the bandits' ill-gotten gains.

"Excellent or not, I've yet to come across the use of such guns in shooting. And besides, what game is there here? Sparrows?" James glanced scornfully around.

"White buzzards," Geoffrey replied levelly.

"*White* buzzards?" James repeated.

"Yes." Geoffrey held his gaze.

The glint in the other's eyes alarmed James. "Well, I trust you had good sport," he murmured, backing down.

"No, as it happens. They're damned difficult to spot in the snow."

James flushed. "To be sure," he muttered.

Emily thought it exquisitely funny, and dissolved into squeals of childish laughter that only Geoffrey heard.

Dorothea couldn't have cared less about white buzzards. "What does it matter right now? We're stranded here, without any money, our belongings stolen or ruined, and our carriage wrecked!" She glanced wretchedly at what was left of her beautiful wardrobe. Lieutenant Coty's men were gathering what they could, but she saw gowns that had been spoiled by the look-out's shot, and others that had been trampled beyond redemption. Lucy's things, on the other hand, were undamaged.

But Geoffrey had already made arrangements. "The mail coach is at your disposal, Miss Weybridge. It isn't very comfortable and, being open, is rather exposed to the elements, but I'm sure you'd prefer it to the indignity of walking." He gave another of his bland smiles. "As it happens, luck is further on our side, for after seeing the mail coach safely to Ornans, the lieutenant and his escort are riding on to their barracks in Besançon, where he assures me he can secure us excellent accommodation for tonight at the best inn in the town. I'll willingly convey you in my carriage."

"That won't be necessary, my lord," James began stiffly, for accepting Geoffrey's charity was the last thing he wished to do, but then he remembered that Mansart had stolen his and Dorothea's money.

Geoffrey's smile didn't falter as he read the nuances on the other's face. "But it *will* be necessary, won't it, Weybridge? How else are you, Miss Weybridge, and Miss Trevallion to reach England? Of course, if you still prefer to decline, that's entirely up to you."

Dorothea spoke quickly. "We gladly accept your offer, Lord St. Athan."

"Yes, I rather thought you might," he replied coolly.

Lieutenant Coty came over. "*Milord*, we must continue."

Geoffrey nodded, and looked at Lucy. "Your mail coach awaits, Miss Trevallion," he murmured, taking her hand and leading her toward the odd vehicle.

As he was about to help her into it, she turned to look at him. "I don't believe a word about white buzzards, sir; in fact, I think you know a great deal more about this whole thing than you've seen fit to admit, and when we reach Besançon, I expect you to tell me the truth."

He didn't reply, but he knew she meant what she said.

Minutes later, as Geoffrey stepped back for the mail coach and its escort to continue toward Ornans, Emily hovered curiously beside him.

"What will you do? Will you tell her everything?" she asked.

"I don't know," he said, crossing to the riverbank to retrieve Lucy's book. He smoothed the pages and closed it gently.

"Will you tell her about me?" Emily asked, watching his hands upon the beautifully worked cover.

"I don't know that either."

"She won't believe you if you do," the angel warned.

"That I *do* know," he said with a sigh, as he returned to his waiting horse.

Twenty-four

Geoffrey rode after the little cavalcade, handed Lucy the book, and then joined the lieutenant.

In the open mail coach, which, unlike its elegant counterparts in England, was little more than a cart with a wickerwork body, the three travelers made themselves as comfortable as they could among the mailbags. It was an ignominious mode of travel, but they knew they couldn't complain, for without it they'd be walking. Nothing was said, but all three were deep in thought about the Earl of St. Athan's mysterious appearance at the scene of the crime.

Lucy was determined to get to the truth. He'd warned her the Weybridges weren't all they claimed to be, but in fact it seemed to be Geoffrey himself who wasn't all he claimed to be! Something very odd was going on, and she was determined to get to the bottom of it.

She watched him with Lieutenant Coty at the head of the little procession, and then she glanced down at the book he'd rescued and given back to her. Any lingering embarrassment over the night before had now vanished completely, leaving only anger, but she had to concede that if it weren't for him, she, James, and Dorothea might not have emerged unscathed from Mansart's clutches.

Opposite, James was also disturbed by Geoffrey's activities, and by his whole demeanor. The fellow behaved for all the world as if he were *au fait* with the entire plot on Lucy's life, but that was impossible. There wasn't any way he could know anything, and yet . . . James shifted his position to try to keep as much out of the draft of cold air as possible. He prayed the alarming scrape they'd just escaped would make Dorothea think twice before doing anything more to further Robert Trevallion's cause.

But Dorothea's resolve had hardened. It was belatedly hitting her that the plan by which she'd set such store had failed. Now, not only had Lucy survived, but she and her fortune would still pursued by both James and Geoffrey! If either man should succeed, the fortune would once again slip through Robert's fingers, and thus through her own as well. That was something she'd fight against to the last, so she'd have to try again.

There'd be no more errors. Next time, Lucy Trevallion's demise would be certain.

The road to Besançon climbed out of the Loue valley, and the December sun was sinking toward the horizon as the little convoy breasted a very high hill above the plain of Franche-Comté. Ahead was a three-mile descent toward their destination for the night. Shadows lengthened as they reached the foot of the hill and followed the road along another river valley that was thickly wooded on either side.

Besançon was built on a tight loop in the river, and was virtually an island with a rocky outcrop in the middle, from where a military citadel presided over the town. They entered the gates only just before curfew, and Lieutenant Coty honored his promise to secure them accommodation at the best hostelry in the town. He took them to the Hôtel de la Poste, in a square by a church, and was greeted fondly by the buxom landlady, who had a soft spot for his winning Breton charm. The travelers were given rooms, and promised an excellent table d'hôte, all at Geoffrey's expense, of course.

When everyone had adjourned to their rooms to prepare for dinner, Dorothea decided to see James to attempt to allay all his suspicions, and maybe even regain his trust, not because she was a reformed character after all, but because it would be easier to make plans without her brother's close eye on her all the time.

Wearing a cornflower fustian gown that had escaped the bandits' attentions, she went to James's room.

He was wary of her. "You and I don't have anything to say to each other now, Dorothea."

"But we do, for no matter what, we're brother and sister," she said with a tentative smile. She knew how to smile, whether it was flirtatiously, winningly, amiably, or anything else. This smile was one of shyly making amends, and was gauged to perfection. She saw his uncertainty, and went closer. "I'm sorry for what happened today, James, truly I am."

"I find that hard to believe."

"It's true, because I think you're right about Robert. He doesn't intend to marry me." She lowered her eyes, which shimmered with sudden tears.

But James wasn't about to be so easily taken in. "You cry too easily, Sis," he said softly.

She went a little nearer. "I'm ashamed of the reason we came here, and I think you are too." She paused. "This may have started out as one thing, but it's now something very different, isn't it? I came here to do Robert's bidding, and so did you, but then you decided to win the Trevallion fortune for yourself, and so you began to lay siege to Lucy. Only it wasn't that simple, was it? You've fallen head over heels in love with her, and I can't blame you. She's so sweet and gentle, so adorably kind and considerate, that you'd have to be made of stone not to succumb."

He searched her face. "I find this *volte face* a little hard to take in, Sis. This morning you were venomous toward me, and bloodily intent upon Lucy's demise; now, quite suddenly, you've turned full circle."

"I admit it, but we had a brush with death today, and it opened my eyes to what's really important. That's why I want to make up with you again. You're my brother, and I love you, James. Neither of us is perfect, but we should be friends, not enemies."

Her brown eyes were huge with pleading, and James believed every word. He held out his hand, and she ran to hug him, but he was as two-faced as she, for what he said wasn't what he meant.

"I'm sorry too, Sis, and just think, if I marry Lucy, you'll be her respectable sister-in-law. I see happiness ahead." He smiled slyly as he rested his cheek against her hair. Happiness ahead? He'd see her in Hades first!

Emily was bored, and after wandering aimlessly around the inn, she drifted out into the dark square, where she immediately heard carol-singing coming from the church. It was so beautiful she couldn't resist, and, forgetting she wasn't supposed to go near anything holy, she flew through the doorway.

The music seemed to beckon her. She felt great joy, just as she had when she'd first dreamed of going to her parents in heaven, and she floated above the high altar, her hands together in prayer. It was only when the singing faltered into gasps that she realized everyone was staring at her. Confusion broke out, and the priest fell to his knees in joy, extending his arms toward the vision.

"It is a sign from God!" he cried.

Emily's eyes widened. God? Oh, no, He'd be very angry indeed when He realized how badly she failed again! Her lips began to quiver, and she fled the church. Her appearance had caused such a stir that she hid on the inn roof for some time, watching the priest and congregation in the square below. They hurried about, spreading word of what had happened, and soon it seemed the whole town had heard. Feeling dreadful, Emily could only think of finding Geoffrey. The little angel felt more and more wretched as she searched the inn for him. Oh, where was he? At last she found him sitting alone in the writing room, composing a letter to Lady Amelia.

As the candle before him brightened suddenly, and Emily appeared, he put his quill down to look sternly at her, for word of the angelic manifestation had spread through the hostelry. "And what have you been up to, miss?" he asked.

"I didn't mean to do it, truly I didn't. I just forgot."

"Not for the first time," he said, recalling her excursion around the spire in Pontarlier.

"I know." Emily bit her lip and sniffed again.

"If it's strictly forbidden, you'll just have to try harder," he said, but kindly.

"I know."

"I'm sure He knows you're still learning," Geoffrey went on gently.

"Do you really think so?"

"Of course, for He knows everything."

She was reassured. "I feel better now," she said, perching on the edge of the desk and peering at what he'd written.

He turned the page over. "One misdemeanor a day is sufficient, miss, so don't add nosiness to your list."

She looked a little crossly at him, but then gave a knowing smile. "You haven't written anything interesting; you've only come in here to avoid Lucy, haven't you?" she observed, with more accuracy than he cared for, but before he could reply, the door opened and Lucy herself entered.

She closed the door and came to stand before the writing desk. She wore her sage dimity gown and her hair was freshly pinned in a knot. Her green eyes were coolly determined.

"Now, sir, it's time for you to explain exactly what you're up to," she said quietly.

Twenty-five

Geoffrey looked at Lucy. "I don't understand, Miss Trevallion," he murmured unconvincingly.

"I'm not a fool, sir. I want an explanation for, among other things, the amazing coincidence of your arrival at the ambush, and don't bother with that tall story about shooting white buzzards with your dueling pistols, for it was clearly a nonsense. You *knew* about the ambush, and I want to know how, and why."

"Am I to believe, from your tone, that you suspect me of organizing the entire episode?" he asked coolly.

"Did you?"

"No, madam, I did not." His manner was stiff, but he knew she was justified in her suspicions. Were he in her position, he'd think the same.

"Then how did you come to be there?"

"I've already explained."

"And I've already told you I don't believe it. I want the truth, sir."

He drew a heavy breath. "There's little point in telling you what really happened, Miss Trevallion."

"Why?" she demanded.

"Because you won't believe me."

Her eyes darkened. "You surely aren't about to mention angels again? Not even you would stoop to such ignominy!"

He looked away.

All that Dorothea had told her at Pontarlier now came flooding back, but she managed to hold her temper in check. Just. "Sirrah, let me assure you I'm not the devout soul you apparently suspect me to be."

He was taken aback. "I have no opinion one way or the other concerning your religious beliefs, Miss Trevallion, except to say that from my experience last night at the Boar, you're an exceeding long way from taking the veil!"

Fresh embarrassment shot through her, but she remained outwardly icy. "Well, such a low observation is all I expect from you, Lord St. Athan, for you are the most iniquitous, pernicious—"

At that he interrupted. "No, madam, *I* am not the pernicious element in all this, the Weybridges hold that title!" He said caustically.

"They are above reproach."

"Above reproach. Ye gods, woman, what will it take to remove your blinkers?" he exclaimed.

"Adopt that sarcastic and condescending manner if you wish, my lord, but the fact remains you are full of accusations without proof."

That was true enough, he acknowledged privately, turning away for a moment to look at Emily, who was still perched on the writing desk. The little angel pulled a sympathetic face, knowing as well as he that convincing Lucy of the truth was tantamount to impossible.

Now it was Lucy's turn to be scornful. "How silent you are, sir. Could it possibly be because you have nothing to say, because this whole thing is a despicable ploy to—"

Stung, he rounded on her. "A ploy to hunt your damned fortune? No, Miss Trevallion, it most certainly isn't, for I find you disagreeable, and your fortune of no interest, but since you challenge me to explain myself in full, I will oblige! Just do me the service of holding your tongue until I've finished. Sit down, if you please," he indicated a chair.

She flinched at the iron-bright light in his eyes, and obeyed silently.

Steeling himself for the inevitable outcome, he told her everything, except that Emily was in the room with them at that very moment, and he finished— "Your cousin Emily is now your guardian angel, and she's watching over you because of the Weybridges. They've come at Robert Trevallion's behest, to do away with you so he can become your grandfather's heir. Dorothea is Robert's mistress, and has been promised marriage for her part in this. James does it simply for the money Robert promised him—at least, he did; now I believe he's pursuing you for his own gain. As far as the ambush is concerned, they were both in league with Mansart in the beginning, but I fear James reneged on the deal, because he's every bit the fortune hunter you say I am!"

Lucy interrupted witheringly. "This is the most preposterous invention I have ever heard!"

"The truth is often unbelievable, Miss Trevallion," he replied resignedly.

"And lies usually masquerade as truth, sir."

"I agree, but in this instance I'm not lying. Now, I requested you not to interrupt, and I'd be obliged if you'd remain silent until I've finished."

A nerve flickered at her temple, but she said no more.

"As I was saying, James Weybridge decided to exclude Dorothea and go after you for himself, and he's making a complete gull of you with his smiles and charm. The fellow's a blackguard of the highest order, and is almost certainly behind the doctoring of your drinks last night."

At that she leapt to her feet. "How dare you say such vile things! You have no honor, sirrah!"

"It's Weybridge who lacks honor, madam," he replied levelly.

"James has been all that's chivalrous toward me," she declared, but specks of color marked her cheeks because she remembered the coachhouse at the Eagle.

"So it's James now, is it? How cozy and reprehensibly familiar. Well, let me point out that a true gentleman doesn't make so bold as to put his arm around a young lady when they've barely met, and I saw Weybridge do precisely that at the villa," Geoffrey replied bluntly.

"Hardly gross misconduct, sir, which is more than can be said of your behavior since the moment you saw me. You've been unforgivably rude because I remind you of someone called Constance!"

"You trespass upon that which doesn't concern you, madam," he warned coldly.

"Oh, it concerns me very much, because I've suffered on account of it!"

"Constance has no bearing on this, Miss Trevallion."

"Your aunt doesn't think so."

"My aunt knows nothing."

"I suspect she knows you only too well, sir. She accused you of treating me shabbily because I reminded you of Constance, and from your reaction now, I'd say she was right."

"Is it your habit to eavesdrop upon private conversations, Miss Trevallion?"

"It isn't always possible to avoid so doing, sir."

"Indeed? I would have thought it perfectly avoidable."

She managed to hold his gaze, but wished her cheeks hadn't

gone so hot. "Avoidable or not, I have to point out that I have no need to invent angels in order to put my case."

"This particular angel is no invention, Miss Trevallion," he replied, glancing at Emily. "Nor was it heavenly intervention that reminded me where I'd seen Dorothea Weybridge."

"Ah, yes, the so-called Devil's Den. Well, I don't believe a word of *that* either!"

"I'm hardly surprised, for you run true to form. Not even the evidence of your own eyes will convince you, will it? You saw how she behaved with Mansart, but you choose to be blind to the facts," he replied dryly.

"She was afraid for her life, and thought to lessen the danger."

"Which doesn't explain how expertly she knew how to set about seducing him. She's a whore to her fingertips."

"Perhaps you think the same of me, sir?" she challenged.

He smiled a little. "You were under the influence of alcohol. Miss Weybridge, believe me, was very sober indeed."

"Believe you? I'd as soon believe the Devil, with whose den you seem to be shamefully well acquainted. Is that where you discovered the effect *eau-de-vie* could have upon unsuspecting victims?"

"I've already told you I wasn't responsible for that."

"James wasn't at my side throughout, nor was he the one with whom I was so foolish to dance at the end. I'm told you made the most of the situation!"

She touched a guilty nerve. "You flatter yourself, madam!" he replied shortly.

"No, sir, I merely draw the comparison between your conduct and James's. What you did was an infinitely greater liberty than his. He merely put an arm around me; you—"

She'd cornered him, and it wasn't a feeling he relished. His instinctive reaction was to turn the tables on her, and he did so by interrupting. "Madam, it's debatable as to whether I took a liberty with you, or the other way around. I assure you that I wasn't the one who made the first move, but I concede the whole thing culminated in a full-blooded kiss that we *both* thoroughly enjoyed."

She drew back. "I loathe you," she breathed.

"Be my guest, Miss Trevallion, for right now the feeling is mutual, but I swear I haven't told a single lie. Emily is very real, and so is the danger you are in."

"Please stop this."

"I would if I could, believe me, but I've been dragged into this against my will, and now it's a millstone around my neck. No, correction, *you* are a millstone around my neck. But much as I dislike you, I refuse to stand by and watch you suffer the fate intended by your enemies."

She looked bitterly at him. "Don't put yourself out on my account, sir," she said coldly.

Something potentially convincing suddenly occurred to him. "Miss Trevallion, can you deny that it was Dorothea Weybridge who told you I'd meddled with your drinks?" he asked, remembering what Emily had told him.

Lucy shifted a little uncomfortably. "No, I can't, but—"

"How do you think I would know it was her?"

"Perhaps you were low enough to listen at the door, sir," she replied crushingly, alluding to his sarcasm about her eavesdropping.

"But I'd already left the inn."

She paused. "So you claim, sir, but who's to say *where* you were? Maybe there were white buzzards outside my door!"

"No, but there was a small angel at your bedside, who listened to a great deal you and Miss Weybridge said." Geoffrey glanced at Emily.

Lucy lost her patience. "Oh, *please* stop this!"

He stepped swiftly over to her and caught her wrist to drag her to the window and point down into the square, where excited townspeople still gathered by the church. "Did you hear all the clamor a little earlier, Miss Trevallion?" he demanded, forcing her to stand there.

"I, er . . . No, not really. I was dressing after taking a bath in a room at the back of the inn." She tried to pull free, but still he held her.

"How very clean, to be sure," he breathed. "Very well, I'll tell you what happened, and you can confirm it with whomever you choose, for it's the truth. An angel appeared above the church altar tonight, a little girl who was seen by the priest and choir. They believe it to be a miracle for Christmas, a sign from on high, but the fact is that the manifestation was the result of the angel's inexperience. You see, Emily Trevallion hasn't been an angel for long, and isn't used to it yet. She liked the carol-singing and forgot that the high altar was such a sacred place that when near it she'd actually become visible to everyone!"

He paused then. Of course! Why hadn't he thought of it before? If Emily could appear to the people of Besançon, she could appear to Lucy too! He turned sharply toward the angel, but Emily understood what he was thinking, and shook her head fearfully.

"No, Geoffrey, please don't ask me to do that!"

"But you must, Emily, it's the perfect way to convince Lucy you really do exist!"

Still trying to pull free, Lucy looked up at him in consternation. He was talking to himself again! He *was* mad!

Emily's voice became a wail. "But He might not allow me into Heaven to be with Mama and Papa!"

"Emily—"

"No!" Tears filled the angel's eyes, and in a trice she'd vanished.

The candle on the desk went out, and suddenly the room was engulfed in shadow, the darkness softened only by firelight. Geoffrey was dismayed. This whole sorry business might have been resolved if he'd been able to persuade the angel to accompany Lucy and him to the church. An actual manifestation would convince even Lucy, resulting in the Weybridges and Robert Trevallion's being brought to book for their villainy. But Emily would never agree, he knew that now.

With a huge effort, Lucy at last pulled free. "I think you're demented!" she breathed.

He was resigned, but there was one thing he needed to know. "It's your prerogative to think me mad, but it's my prerogative to know if you mean to tell the Weybridges any of this."

"Tell them the terrible things you've said? How can I possibly do that? I wouldn't dream of it, for I like and respect them too much to want to cause such distress."

"How good it must feel to be so sure of one's friends, Miss Trevallion."

"Yes, sirrah, I'm sure they are my friends, and I'm equally sure I shouldn't trust you! Oh, I know you came to my rescue today, but I still despise your lies, and believe your real motives to be far more mean and mercenary than a desire to protect me!"

Something perverse overtook him then, and he seized her wrist again, twisting her much closer this time, so her body arched against his. "So I'm mean and mercenary, am I? Well, if that were the case, I could make sure of you right now. All I have to do is have my evil way with you, and then broadcast the fact!" He knew he was behaving badly again, but felt provoked beyond endurance.

Fear lightened her eyes. "You wouldn't!"

"Why not? You've accused me of base intentions, and if you give a dog a bad name . . . "

"You disgust me!" she hissed.

"Oh? That's not how it seemed last night," he said softly.

"I wasn't responsible for my actions!"

"No one forced you to behave like that, madam; you did it of your own volition. Was it a case of *in vino veritas*? Yes, I think it must have been." His conduct worsened by the second, but he was bitterly angry with her. "Is *this* what you really wanted last night, Miss Trevallion?" he breathed, pushing her to the wall and kissing her passionately on the lips.

She struggled. He was conscious of her sensuous curves, her perfume, and her warmth. He felt arousal begin to rob him of control. Desire began to pump into him, and his hands moved down to her hips, holding her against his needful masculinity.

She should have been frightened, but instead she felt forbidden sensations flitting wildly over her body. Memories of her dream swept back, and her breasts tightened with wanton sexual hunger. A voluptuous heat flamed along her veins, turning all thought to the exciting pressure of his virility as he continued to hold her to him. Her lips softened, and for a heartstopping moment she yielded.

Control slipped further and further from him. He wanted to take her there and then, to relieve the fury of desire she'd aroused, but suddenly a wave of icy common sense washed soberingly through him. Dear God, what was he doing?

Abruptly, he released her, turning away to run his trembling fingers through his hair. The urgency of desire began to subside, but it didn't go away, no, it didn't go away. . . .

The physical separation allowed her own guilt to flood in. Shame and mortification snatched at her. She'd given in! She'd wanted him as much as he wanted her! *Please* don't let him have realized, let his own arousal have been such that he hadn't detected her brief response. But she knew it was a futile hope, for in those few shocking seconds he'd been conscious of everything about her.

Her shame intensified and, just as he had earlier, she took refuge in attack. "How *dare* you, sirrah!" she cried, dealing him a stinging slap, and then fleeing from the room.

He exhaled very slowly. What was the matter with him? He was scornful and disapproving of Weybridge's actions, when his own were infinitely worse! How *could* he have done what he'd just done? It went against every principle he'd ever possessed! And yet . . . He closed his eyes. And yet it had felt so right to hold her like that, to respond to her like that, to *want* her like that.

He opened his eyes again, remembering how she'd yielded for

that telltale moment. The ghost of a smile played upon his lips then, for one thing was certain, he and Lucy Trevallion might despise the very sight of each other, but by *God* they'd be good together in bed!

Twenty-six

When Lucy fled from Geoffrey, she cannoned straight into James in the passage outside. She cried out in alarm, and he steadied her swiftly before looking concernedly into her flushed face and wide eyes.

"Lucy? What's wrong?"

She glanced back at the closed door, and then gave him a rather self-conscious smile. "Er, nothing, nothing at all. You startled me, that's all."

"With all due respect, I feel there's a little more to it." He gazed intently into her eyes.

"I-I've merely had words with Lord St. Athan."

His eyes hardened. "Has he upset you? Because if so, I swear I'll . . . " He chose words expected of a gentleman, but the last thing he wanted was to face up to Geoffrey!

"It was merely a verbal crossing of swords, so please think nothing more of it," she said hastily.

"Are you quite sure? I mean, if he's said or done anything to cause you distress, I will not hesitate to—"

"It was nothing, just a foolish disagreement," she said again.

He hesitated, and then put his hand gently to her cheek. "I can't bear to think of your distress, Lucy," he said softly.

His fingers were warm and tender, but although she felt a frisson of pleasure, his touch didn't affect her like Geoffrey's. There was no forbidden excitement, no powerful craving, no sense of fire passing through her veins. With James, she remained completely in control, and now, completely indifferent too. She might *like* him infinitely more than Geoffrey, but she didn't desire him. Geoffrey's scornful, contemptuous glance had always wrought havoc with her presence of mind, but she'd mistaken her reaction for loathing! She should have realized the truth when she dreamed about the dungeon at Chillon.

Her long silence disturbed James. He could feel her withdrawal. There was a barrier between them that hadn't been there before, and he was only too conscious that the Trevallion fortune was a little further away than it had been. Perhaps the time had come for more boldness. "Lucy, I know I shouldn't say this, but I have to let you know how I feel. I've tried not to let it happen, but I've fallen hopelessly in love with you, and can't bear to think of the moment we reach England and I lose you forever."

She was embarrassed. "You-you shouldn't say such things, James . . . "

He pressed her. "I can't help it, Lucy. Please say you feel something for me. Throw me a crumb of hope to ease my pain."

After her momentous experience with Geoffrey, this was too much for her. "Please don't say any more!" she cried, and then gathered her skirts to hurry away.

He stared after her in dismay. He knew he wasn't losing his touch, but he was certainly losing this particular lady. From being vulnerable to his advances, she was suddenly immune. Why? His glance moved toward the door. St. Athan? Was *he* the cause of the change in her?

James's brown eyes hardened. He wasn't about to let the Trevallion heiress slip through his fingers. If stronger action was called for, he wouldn't hesitate to use it. Marriage was the surest way to secure his aim, and although he'd have preferred the bride to be willing, it wasn't essential. Abduction and an unscrupulous priest were all that was needed for Lucy Trevallion to become Lucy Weybridge!

That night, Geoffrey had a sensuous dream. It was twilight a day or so before Christmas, and he was by the entrance to the maze at Hurstfield House, his country seat at Dover. He glanced toward St. Athan village on the hill behind the estate, and could tell by the lights in the church's stained glass windows that advent evensong was in progress. There were stars in the deep turquoise sky, and it was bitterly cold, with frost already beginning to shine on the tall close-clipped hedges.

An unknown woman laughed mockingly at him from somewhere in the maze, and he followed the sound, hurrying further and further from the entrance. He caught a glimpse of her fur-lined crimson cloak disappearing around a corner ahead, and was spurred to greater effort. He had to catch her!

She was still laughing at him, a light, flirtatious sound that taunted. She was like a will-o'-the-wisp, always just beyond his reach, and he grew angry. Why couldn't he get closer?

Suddenly there was silence. He ran the final yards into the

clearing in the center of the maze, where there was a summer-house. As he emerged from the tall hedges, he saw her standing on the steps of the white-painted pavilion. Her hood had fallen back, and at last he saw her face. It was Lucy. Her ash-blond hair was a tangled confusion of curls because she'd been running, and her cheeks were flushed, but it was her eyes that commanded his attention, for there was challenge in their green beauty.

She didn't move away as he approached, and the closer he came, the more aware he was of how much he desired her. It was more than just the thrill of the chase, it was a culmination of emo-tion, a realization that he'd wanted her from the outset. And now he was about to have her. He knew it as surely as night would fol-low day. She'd led him here in order to surrender, and his body was already anticipating that sweet moment.

His fingers closed warmly over hers as she stretched out a hand, and she came willingly into his embrace, raising her parted lips to meet his.

In spite of the cold, she wore nothing beneath the cloak, and a sigh escaped her as his knowing hands moved over her body. He felt how she trembled at his touch, and it seemed the desire pounding through him wouldn't wait for the moment of entry. But it did wait, and for several minutes he caressed her, kissing her throat and breasts, and exulting in her soft sounds of pleasure.

At last he was free of his doomed affair with Constance. The fierce sexuality he'd suppressed for these long months had been liberated, and pounded needfully through the hard shaft at his loins. His breath caught as she moved her fingers to undo his breeches buttons. His erection seemed to spring into her hand, and he groaned as she caressed him, sliding her palm over the tip until he felt his desire would explode.

How he contained himself he didn't know, for suddenly she knelt before him to take him deep into her mouth. Her arms were around his thighs and he closed his eyes in ecstasy. He ran his trembling fingers through her hair. Oh, Lucy, Lucy . . . The final moment was close now, he couldn't hold back much longer, and he wanted to share the climax with her.

And so he pulled away. His eyes were dark with passion as he looked down at her. She knew his thoughts, and smiled as she lay down on the summerhouse floor. Her cloak spread around her like a fur bed as she stretched her arms up toward him, and at last he lay with her, covering her body with kisses until she begged him to take her.

His breath caught with elation as he pushed deep into the delicious warmth that seemed to have been created just for him. His body shuddered as he drove slowly in to the hilt. A tumult of erotic sensations flooded over them both as he withdrew before pushing in again. He couldn't restrain himself now, and soon his thrusts were imperative.

She moved voluptuously beneath him, her need as great as his, and when the final moments came, they were in complete harmony. He'd never known such magnificent gratification. His whole body melted as he took possession of her—or was it that she took possession of him? He surrendered the essence of his male soul, and her femininity seemed to gather it close, as if to cherish it forever.

As the waves of pleasure died gradually away, he pulled her into his arms, holding her to him out of sheer joy. "I love you, Lucy. I love you with all my heart. Stay with me forever . . . "

But suddenly a strange voice intruded. "Milord, it is morning and time to awaken!"

His eyes flew open and he stared up at the bed canopy. Where was he? Realization flooded through him then, and he sat up, running his hands through his hair. In his dreams, he'd run his fingers through Lucy's hair. Lucy . . . He closed his eyes.

The inn maid spoke at the door again. "Milord?"

"Yes, I'm awake."

"We are serving breakfast soon, milord."

"I'll be down directly."

Her light steps hurried away, and he drew a long breath. The sensual tendrils of sleep began to thread away into the early morning light that shone palely through the curtains. The temperature had risen, and rain fell against the windowpane.

He flung the bedclothes aside and got up, shivering a little as the chill air touched his naked skin, but then he heard a childish gasp, and whirled about to see Emily staring at him from the top of the bed canopy.

With an embarrassed oath he snatched up his dressing gown and held it in front of him. "What in God's name are you doing up there?" he demanded.

She recoiled a little, her cheeks bright pink. "You shouldn't swear, Geoffrey, especially not to angels."

"Well, I'm pretty certain angels shouldn't lurk in gentlemen's bedchambers!" he snapped, turning away to don the dressing gown and then pad to the fireplace.

"I-I didn't want to sleep on my own. I've been here all night," Emily explained.

He couldn't bring himself to look at her. All night? He felt as if she'd been spying on him in that damned summerhouse!

"Why are you in such a disagreeable mood?" she asked, peeping down at him again.

"I'm not in a disagreeable mood."

"You are."

He glared at her. "All right, so I'm not in a sweet humor, but can you blame me? You could have solved all this at a stroke last night; instead, you decided to cut and run."

"That's not fair," she protested.

"Isn't it? What's so damned fair about the predicament you've forced on me?"

"It was an accident, I didn't mean to appear to you instead of Lucy!"

Her little face threatened to pucker, and he hastened to prevent that. "Please don't cry, I didn't mean to bite your head off." He flung himself in the side chair by the fire.

"What's wrong?" she asked, floating concernedly down to kneel beside him.

He glanced at her. "Nothing you can do anything about," he murmured, glancing toward the rain on the window.

"Are you really cross with me for disappearing last night?"

He had to smile. "No, I'm cross with you for *not appearing*," he corrected. Forgetfully he reached out to fondly ruffle her hair, but his hand passed right through her.

"I'm afraid to do it again. You do understand, don't you?"

"Yes. If I were you, I'd probably be afraid as well."

"Do you mean that?"

"Of course." He smiled again.

She smiled too. "I do like you, Geoffrey," she said candidly.

"I'm honored."

She was silent for a moment. "What shall we do now?"

"Do?"

"About saving Lucy."

"I haven't the slightest idea, except to stay out of her way for a while. When I think of the story I was obliged to tell her last night, I could curl up with embarrassment."

"You only told her the truth."

"Precisely."

Emily lowered her eyes. "I suppose it *is* a little hard to believe, isn't it?"

"That's putting it mildly. I can only hope that I've at least managed to instil her with a little wisdom where her precious Weybridges are concerned, although I doubt it. Wisdom is a commodity that's sadly lacking in Miss Lucy Trevallion." With a sigh, he got up. "And now, if you don't mind, I'd like to get dressed."

"All right." In a twinkling she'd gone, and with her went the lingering glow in the fire.

Sighing again, he went to the wardrobe to get his clothes. Now to face Lucy at breakfast, then in the carriage. It wasn't going to be easy, not after the appalling liberty he'd taken when last they'd met. Whether or not she'd tell the Weybridges about *that,* he didn't know, but he was confident she wouldn't divulge the outlandish story he'd told her. Telling it would be to invite complete disbelief. He should know; he'd tried it!

Steeling himself for the meeting, he went down to the dining room, where his three traveling companions were already at the table. Lucy barely looked up at him, but he couldn't help noticing the way a little escaped curl rested lightly against her downy cheek, and how her lashes cast a soft shadow when she lowered her glance. This morning he was conscious of everything about her, especially of her lissom figure, silhouetted so daintily by her honeysuckle gown. In his dreams he'd possessed that delightful body. Ah, such sweet possession . . .

James spoke. "It would seem the weather has changed dramatically, my lord," he said.

Geoffrey didn't hear.

"My lord?"

"Yes?" Geoffrey roused himself from his musings.

"The weather has changed dramatically."

"Yes." Geoffrey deliberately looked right through him.

James shifted uncomfortably, and abandoned all attempt at conversation.

Lucy was too embarrassed to look at Geoffrey. All she could think of was the way he'd kissed her last night, and the way she'd so forgotten herself as to respond. Hot color rushed into her cheeks and she lowered her coffee cup quickly. Just being across the table from him upset what was left of her equilibrium! Last night, for the first time in her life—well, the first time she could remember, because being under the influence of *eau-de-vie* didn't count—she'd experienced a man's sexual potency. It hadn't been a dream, she'd really felt Geoffrey's erection against her, hard, imperative, and unbelievably exciting. It was a memory that gave her much to think about, and much to come to terms with about herself, so she said very little.

After breakfast, they went to the barracks to take their leave of

Lieutenant Coty, to whom Geoffrey made a gift of the fine horse he'd purchased in Pontarlier. After that, they set off once more. The rain had already turned the snow to slush, and the sound of water seemed to be everywhere as they drove west out of Besançon toward their next overnight halt at the town of Dale.

Franche-Comté would be behind them when Dorothea found an ideal opportunity to relieve Robert Trevallion of his unwanted stepniece.

Twenty-seven

Dorothea's chance came well over a week later, deep in the heart of Burgundy, where constant heavy rain had wrought havoc with the chalky vineyard-studded countryside.

They were about ninety miles southeast of Paris, on their way to Auxerre on the banks of the River Yonne. It was early afternoon on December the eighteenth, and the state of the roads made their progress so slow it seemed they'd never be able to reach London for Christmas. Now they'd taken a wrong turning somewhere, and weren't even on the right route.

The wide, usually placid Yonne was swollen and dangerous, and the carriage rounded a bend to find the way ahead completely submerged for a hundred yards or so beneath muddy, fast-flowing water. A line of spindly willows marked the bank, and beyond them the main river channel flowed even more swiftly. Miniature whirlpools dimpled the shining brown surface of the flood as broken branches and other flotsam were swirled helplessly downstream.

The rain had ceased for a while, and as the carriage came to a standstill, suddenly the air seemed to be filled with the gurgle, rush, and roar of water. The passengers alighted in dismay, for the short winter afternoon would soon begin to draw in.

Emily had been sleeping next to Geoffrey, snuggling up beside him as any living child would, but now she fluttered interestedly around, wondering how the journey could possibly continue. Surely they'd have to return to the last town?

James echoed the angel's thoughts, for he glanced at Geoffrey. "We'll have to go back, won't we?"

"There hasn't been a suitable inn for miles," Geoffrey replied, tilting his top hat back on his head and gazing thoughtfully at the road as it disappeared beneath the floods.

"All right, but there *was* an inn. I think we should turn around and—"

"I have no intention of turning around," Geoffrey interrupted.

"Oh, come now, you surely don't think we can continue?" James exclaimed.

"I see no real reason why not. Judging by the willows and that fence over there, I'd say we can not only be sure where the road is, but also that the water is only a few feet deep. You and I can assist the postilion by riding two of the horses, and the ladies can remain in the carriage, with the doors open to allow the flow to pass harmlessly through."

Dorothea, who had as yet to realize the potential of the situation, stared at the water in complete terror. "We can't possibly! You must have taken leave of your senses to even suggest it!" she cried. She'd borrowed Lucy's cloak, and the lavender color was oddly bright in the dull winter light.

Geoffrey turned to her. "Miss Weybridge, it's common practice to traverse floods in the way I suggest; how else do you imagine the mail is delivered at times like this? Every stagecoach in England takes these measures as a matter of course in order to complete its journey. Believe me, the current has to be very strong indeed to overturn a carriage if the doors are open to lessen resistance, and I can see by the direction and force of this flood that it's perfectly feasible for us to cross. I therefore intend to do just that. Now, if you and your brother wish to remain on this side, you are at liberty so to do, but it's my carriage, and I intend to see Miss Trevallion safely across." He glanced at Lucy then. "Or are you too timid to proceed as well?" he asked.

"Timidity isn't one of my faults, sir," she replied, drawing her other cloak, older and made of plum velvet, more tightly about her shoulders, for if the air wasn't exactly icy, it was still very cold and damp.

A glimmer of cool humor touched his eyes. "No, I'll grant you that," he murmured, his voice almost lost in the noise of the water.

She raised her chin. "If you're confident it's safe to cross, then I won't raise any objection." Secretly she was frightened, but wasn't going to let him realize it!

"Then we cross," he said.

Emily watched Lucy, and then looked knowingly at Geoffrey. "She's not as brave as she's pretending," the angel declared.

It was on the tip of his tongue to reply, but at the last moment he remembered no one else could see the angel. Damn it all, why couldn't he get used to being the only one? Giving her a dark look, he turned to Dorothea again. "What is your decision, Miss Weybridge?"

She glanced at the water and then the carriage. Her terror was suddenly checked as she perceived her golden opportunity. Open doors, a flood, attention diverted while she and Lucy were alone in the vehicle . . . One push, and Robert's upstart stepniece could be consigned to the Yonne! Summoning all her courage, she nodded at Geoffrey. "Yes, I've decided. If Lucy feels able to cross, so do I."

James happened to look at his sister in the second before she spoke, and he knew something was afoot. He turned quickly to Geoffrey. "I don't think it's wise for the ladies to be left alone in the carriage. Someone should be with them, and I willingly volunteer."

Dorothea hid her fury.

Geoffrey nodded. "Very well, you remain in the carriage; the postilion and I will manage the horses." Then he moved away slightly, summoning Emily with a slight nod of his head.

She flew obediently to him. "Yes, Geoffrey?"

"You stay in the carriage too. I want you to keep an eye on things."

"All right."

Five minutes later, with the horses as calm as could be managed in the face of so much water, Geoffrey and the postilion coaxed the animals forward. The team were unwilling, dancing around a little as the current swirled against their fetlocks, but the two riders were firm with them, making them go on.

Lucy, Dorothea, and James looked out of the open-doored carriage until the water reached the axle, then the two women drew back inside with their feet on the seats as the flood rose closer and closer to the floor. Emily sat with them, although no one knew.

Dorothea's mouth was dry and her heart pounded as she watched the water creep inexorably toward the sill. Then, with a gurgling sound, the Yonne swept through the carriage. Dorothea felt sick with dread, but kept a tight grip on her nerve. She glanced at Lucy, providentially occupying the seat by the door closest to the fast-flowing main channel, which swept rapaciously past the willows as if it would uproot them. It wouldn't be long now. Soon the right moment would arrive . . .

James's attention was upon the team. He continued to lean out of the carriage on the side away from the river, observing Geoffrey and the postilion ease the frightened horses slowly through the water, which was now up to their bellies. His back was toward Dorothea, and he didn't see her move surreptitiously closer to Lucy.

Lucy didn't sense the danger either, but Emily did, and with an alarmed squeak flew swiftly to Geoffrey. "Geoffrey! Geoffrey! Something's going to happen!" she cried, fluttering agitatedly around his head.

He glanced up sharply. "How do you know?" he asked, much to the postilion's consternation.

The Frenchman turned. "Milord?"

"Not you!" Geoffrey looked at Emily again. "Well? How do you know?" he repeated.

"I just do! Dorothea's moving closer to Lucy, and I can tell by her face she's about to do something dreadful!"

He turned back to James. "Is all well?" he shouted.

James nodded.

"No! Inside, man!" Geoffrey cried impatiently. God damn the dimwit!

As he shouted, Dorothea was ready to give Lucy the violent push that would send her reeling into the waiting water, but at the final moment, Lucy turned to speak to her. For a breathless moment the women's eyes met, and awful realization swept sickeningly through Lucy. Geoffrey had been telling the truth! Her lips parted to scream, but no sound came out. She raised her arm defensively, as with bitter fury Dorothea tried to overwhelm her.

At last James turned. "No, Dorothea! No!" he cried, clinging to a handgrip as he somehow managed to wrench her away from Lucy. He caught her by surprise, and she fell sideways, but as she struggled to her feet, she forgot the flood rushing through the carriage. The water swept around her cloak and skirts, and she screamed as she lost her balance completely. For a moment she teetered in the doorway, trying desperately to claw at something to save herself, but then she fell into the water, striking her head on a submerged post as she did. The current snatched her away, sweeping her unconscious body into the main river channel like a bundle of lavender cloth. She was face down, and could not possibly survive.

Emily gasped, forgetting for a moment that Dorothea had borrowed Lucy's cloak. For a split second it seemed to the little angel that it was Lucy who'd perished. She pressed her hands to her mouth, and stared in dismay, but then remembered. It was Dorothea!

Stunned, James was absolutely motionless in the carriage. Still clinging to the handgrip he stared after his sister until the speck of lavender could be seen no more. He knew she was dead. He'd killed her. . . .

Lucy trembled like a leaf as she tried to get up. Dazed by the swiftness of what had happened, she too forgot the water flowing through the carriage, and stood up. She was too confused to save herself, and in a split second was swept into the river.

The icy Yonne engulfed her, and she struck her head on the same submerged post, but then her cloak caught on the willows, which by some miracle kept her head above the water.

Emily whimpered as she watched, for it was clear the trees might at any moment relinquish her cousin to the river. Geoffrey had felt nothing as Dorothea fell to her death, but his heart froze within him when it seemed the same fate had happened to Lucy. "No!" he cried, his glance flying to James, who remained motionless in the carriage. "Do something man, you're closest!" he shouted.

James didn't respond, and Geoffrey flung off his greatcoat to leap into the water. There was no time to kick off his boots, for the willows were beginning to give audibly, and the current seemed to tug willfully at Lucy's unconscious body. Her hair waved like golden weed in the muddy water, and he could see the plum velvet of her cloak billowing in the flow.

Emily hovered distractedly above her. Oh, don't let her drown! Don't let her drown!

Geoffrey swam against the current, but he was strong, and soon fought his way through the tangle of branches, reaching Lucy just as the willows gave up the struggle. He seized her hand, but the river still tried to take her. He clung to the sturdiest branch, clasping Lucy's cold, limp fingers as tightly as he could, and at last he managed to pull her toward him.

Releasing her hand for a moment, he flung his arm around her waist, holding her close as the icy water almost forced the breath from his body.

Twenty-eight

Emily gave a cry of joy, but Geoffrey knew the angel's relief was premature. He looked desperately across at James. "For God's sake, man, I need some help!" he cried.

At last James found his tongue. "I-I can't . . . "

"You must, damn it!"

"I can't swim." James's gaze moved fearfully away from him toward the rushing torrent.

Geoffrey knew then there was no hope of any help from the shore. James was clearly in a state of shock, and the postilion had all his work cut out to keep control of the horses, which had been unnerved by the screams and shouts of the past minutes. He glanced desperately around. He was a strong swimmer, but not strong enough to swim against the fierce current and reach the shore with Lucy's dead weight.

Then he saw a small landing stage about fifty feet downstream. If he let go of the branch, surely the current would carry them directly to it?

Emily followed his glance, and knew what he was thinking. "Do you think you can do it, Geoffrey?" she asked, her voice shaking a little.

"I have to try." He glanced at Lucy. Her lashes were motionless against her ashen cheeks, but he knew she wasn't dead because he could feel her heartbeats even through their wet clothes. He spoke to her. "Lucy? Can you hear me?"

She stirred a little.

"Lucy?"

Her eyelids fluttered and she looked up at him in puzzlement, but then she realized where they were and began to panic.

His arm tightened reassuringly around her. "It's all right, you're with me. I won't let anything happen to you."

She stopped struggling, and clung to him, hiding her face against his shoulder.

"Do you trust me, Lucy?" he asked gently.

"Yes."

"Enough to put your life in my hands?"

"Yes."

"I ought to be flattered, but I fancy your faith is born of fear."

She raised her eyes to his. "I do trust you, Geoffrey," she said with quiet sincerity.

"Then hold on tightly, and I'll try to get us to safety."

Emily watched in trepidation. "Oh, do be careful, Geoffrey!"

"I'll be as careful as I can," he replied, knowing the assurance would be appropriate for both Lucy and the little angel. He let go of the branch, holding Lucy tightly around the waist as the river swept them toward the landing stage. Please God, let him be able to seize hold of one of the piers before they were swept past!

Suddenly they were almost upon it. He reached out desperately, and managed to grab hold of one of the reassuringly solid piers, but almost immediately the force of the current wrenched him away again. They were sucked beneath the landing stage, and he knew he only had one more chance. With a superhuman effort he reached out to the piers on the other side, and this time managed to wrap his arm around one.

He glanced toward the carriage, which was again moving slowly through the flood. James had recovered a little now, and had waded through the water to help the postilion.

Geoffrey turned to Lucy again. "Can you hold on to this pier? I mean *really* hold on, while I try to haul myself out, and then pull you up too?"

"Don't leave me!"

"I must, Lucy, for both our sakes."

Frightened tears filled her eyes, but she nodded bravely.

He smiled. "Just cling to the pier. Whatever you do, don't let go, and above all, don't close your eyes. Stay awake, do you hear?"

She nodded again, and he kept his arm around her as she did as he instructed. Terror swept through her again as he released her, and she felt the full force of the current, but she resolutely clasped the pier. To keep herself alert, she tried to think of something to recite, and for some reason, all she could think of was the Christmas carol "The Holly and the Ivy."

Her teeth chattered as she spoke. "Oh, the holly and the ivy, When they are both full grown, Of all the trees that are in the wood, The holly bears the crown . . . "

Geoffrey heard her as he began to drag himself out of the water. It took a huge effort, for the river was loath to surrender him, but at last he flung himself onto the safety of the wooden boards above. Within seconds, he stretched a hand down to Lucy.

Her eyes were wide. "I-I'm afraid to let go . . . "

"No, you're not; just reach up to me," he replied firmly.

Her lips pressed determinedly together, and slowly she reached up. Their fingers touched and he clasped her fiercely, dragging her bodily from the river.

She came up easily into his arms, and he held her tightly. "It's all right, you're safe now," he whispered, hardly realizing he was twining his thankful fingers in the wet hair at the nape of her neck and kissing the top of her head.

She put her shaking arms around him as huge sobs rose in her throat, while above them Emily was whirling about with joy. Lucy was safe! Lucy was safe!

Lucy clung to him. "It-it was dreadful. Dorothea tried to push me into the river, but then James pulled her away. She lost her balance, and then so did I . . . "

"Don't talk about it now," he said softly.

"I should have believed you, I should have listened . . . "

As James helped coax the frightened horses finally out of the flood, he turned toward the landing stage in time to see what appeared to be a very tender moment indeed! In a split second, his numbness over Dorothea's fate was replaced by cold fury.

"Oh, no, my fine lord," he breathed, "I'm not about to relinquish the Trevallion fortune that easily!"

Then, as Geoffrey picked Lucy up and began to carry her to the carriage, James's gaze went beyond them to the wide, swirling river. Briefly his thoughts returned to his sister. Dorothea had always dreaded death by drowning, and that was what had happened to her. By now, her body would have been swept miles downstream, and might never be found. His face bore no expression, for Dorothea had tried to thwart him, and that he could never forgive.

Geoffrey walked past him to lay Lucy gently on the carriage seat and cover her with traveling rugs. Then he took her hand for a moment. "I'll just check with the postilion that all's well to proceed. The afternoon's wearing on, and I mean to reach Auxerre before nightfall."

She nodded, unaware that Emily was kneeling protectively beside her. The little angel scowled as James climbed into the carriage. "Don't trust him, Lucy! He's as wicked as his sister!"

But Lucy no longer needed warning. Geoffrey had been proven right about Dorothea, and so was probably right about James as well. He'd attacked his sister to save the Trevallion fortune, not because he loved the Trevallion heiress!

He was aware of the change in her, but affected not to notice. "Oh, Lucy, forgive me for failing you. I-I was so shocked by what Dorothea did, that I . . . "

"I understand," she replied, looking quickly away from him.

"If you'd suffered the same fate as Dorothea, I-I don't think I could have borne it," he whispered, taking her hand. "I love you, Lucy."

"Please don't say that," she said, pulling her fingers away.

"But I must say what's in my heart, Lucy. I knew we were meant to be together that evening when we searched for your earring. Nothing can change that, and if I failed you today, I also saved you. If I hadn't pulled Dorothea from you . . . " He managed to make his voice catch, and turned away as if overcome.

"I'm grateful for what you've done, sir, but that is all I feel. I wish to forget everything that passed between us before, and I think it best if we are a little more formal from now on."

He'd been given his congé! Fury bubbled through him, but he hid it. Well, at least he now knew beyond all doubt that persuasion and soft words would no longer work. He sat back, and looked out at the river. Now it *had* to be a matter of abduction and an unscrupulous priest.

Geoffrey returned, and as the carriage drew away, he noticed Emily's pleased smile. He raised an inquiring eyebrow, and the little angel almost hugged herself with delight as she told him how cool Lucy had been with James. "She doesn't like him in the least now, Geoffrey; in fact, I'm sure she believes everything you've told her. Well, almost everything. I don't know if she believes about me yet."

Geoffrey smiled, but remained thoughtful about James. He owed Weybridge nothing at all, and didn't intend to carry him any longer. Lucy's remaining so-called chaperone was going to be left behind at Auxerre, which would only leave Robert Waverly Trevallion himself to deal with!

The light had almost gone when Auxerre appeared in the gloom ahead. The capital of Lower Burgundy was built on two low hills on a bend in the river, and had a skyline crowned by three great churches, one a cathedral. It was a beautiful walled town, with gabled stone houses, steep cobbled streets, and boulevards leading to the quay, where the Horseshoe inn stood.

For once, Emily was wary of possibly passing a church, and prudently removed herself into the night air, soaring high above the town to watch the vehicle's progress from a safe distance. Her precaution proved wise, for there was a church on a corner which would have made her glow quite brightly if she'd remained in the carriage.

James gazed sourly out at the lamplit streets, and saw the church. Its door was open to reveal a bright candlelit nave. An old woman rose from prayer, placed some coins in a dish, and then walked away. A priest immediately moved from the shadows to pocket the coins. As the carriage drove on, a sly smile crept to James's lips. He'd found his unscrupulous priest!

Before going to the inn, Geoffrey ordered the postilion to halt at the town hall, for Dorothea's death had to be reported. It took some time, for there was much paperwork, but at last they were able to drive on to the Horseshoe. Rain began to fall heavily again as they entered the inn yard, but in such a downpour no one noticed James slip away to go to the church, where he was soon deep in conversation with the priest. A pact was made, and when James left, Lucy's fate was sealed.

During the coming night, legally if not willingly, she would become Mrs. James Weybridge.

Twenty-nine

Emily saw James return to the inn. Startled to realize he'd been out, the little angel glided curiously around him. Where had he been, and why? She noted the anticipatory smile on his lips, and a horrid feeling of foreboding began to seep through her. He was so pleased with himself about something that he was oblivious to the rain!

She hurried to find Geoffrey, and found him with the doctor who'd been sent for to examine Lucy, to be certain she wasn't injured more than had been realized. The doctor had been very thorough, with special attention to the knock she'd received on the head. He declared that no lasting harm had been done, and that since she hadn't swallowed any river water, or taken any into her lungs, all she needed was warmth and rest to recover from her ordeal. He prescribed laudanum to ensure a good night's sleep, but said she should not take it until she'd first had a good bath and then eaten properly.

Emily waited impatiently until the doctor had gone, and then spoke in Geoffrey's ear. "James has been out!"

He gave a start, for he hadn't realized she was behind him. "Don't do that!" he replied, glancing around to be certain there was no one to observe him apparently talking to himself.

"I'm sorry, but I thought you should know. He looks nastily pleased with himself, as if he's just done something very clever. I think you should ask him where he's been."

Geoffrey thought for a moment. Why would Weybridge go out in a town he didn't know, and on a night such as this? It was odd, to say the least. Emily was right, the fellow should be questioned—and then told that his company was no longer required. The time had come to see the last of anyone with the name Weybridge!

He confronted James in the tap room, where he was shaking the rain from his greatcoat. "Where have you been, Weybridge? It's hardly the weather for an evening stroll," he said, only too con-

scious of Emily peeping over his shoulder as she tried to keep
well away from a crucifix on a far wall.

James faced him smoothly. "I went to light a candle for
Dorothea," he replied glibly, placing his coat on a settle. "I know
that what she did today was terrible, but she was still my sister,
and—"

"And you couldn't care less that she's gone," Geoffrey interrupted. "Don't take me for a fool, Weybridge, just tell me where
you've really been."

James's face hardened. "With all due respect, St. Athan, it's
none of your business."

Emily rose indignantly. "Don't you take that from him, Geoffrey!" she cried, and then ducked hastily down again as she remembered the crucifix.

Geoffrey needed no urging. "Weybridge, given your sister's
vicious attack upon Miss Trevallion, I think your activities are
very much my business."

"You surely aren't implying I was party to what Dorothea
did?" James inquired hotly.

"Possibly not latterly, but I certainly believe you and she origi-
nally set out with a shared purpose." The kid gloves were off.

James became very still. "What are you suggesting, St. Athan?"
he said then.

"That as Robert Trevallion's agents, you and your sister left
England to dispose of Lucy so that Robert could become heir in
her place. I'd go so far as to hazard a guess that Robert also disposed of Emily Trevallion."

Emily nodded vigorously. "He did! Oh, he did!"

James stared at Geoffrey. How in God's name had St. Athan
deduced so much?

Seeing his amazement, Emily hugged herself with glee. "Go
on, Geoffrey, go on!"

"Have you nothing to say, Weybridge?" Geoffrey challenged,
doing his best not to glance at the little angel.

"Only that I haven't any idea what you're talking about. I was
engaged to assist Dorothea in chaperoning Miss Trevallion safely
home to England, and that's *all* I was engaged to do. Given my
sister's appalling act today, I have to concede that her intentions
were clearly not so innocent, but I swear I knew nothing."

"I know you for a liar, Weybridge."

"Are you questioning my honor?" James replied stiffly.

"What honor? Don't come the outraged innocent with me, for I
know far too much."

"You can't possibly *know* anything!"

"But I do, and now I'm no longer prepared to put up with you. You're not going to travel with us any more, is that clear? I'll meet the bill for tonight, but as from tomorrow morning, you make your own way. Do you understand?"

James stared at him. "But, how am I supposed to—?"

"I neither know nor care."

James snatched up his coat and left the tap room. He was shaken by the extent of Geoffrey's knowledge, but there was still a gleam in his brown eyes. To hell with his lordship, for come tomorrow morning, it would be too late anyway!

Geoffrey gazed after him, and so did Emily. The little angel's brows drew together disappointedly. "Why didn't he protest more?"

"I don't know," Geoffrey replied slowly. Something about James's reactions bothered him, and the fellow still hadn't divulged where he'd been or why.

Emily drew a long breath. "Well, at least we know that Lucy doesn't like or trust him at all now, and so won't be taken in by anything he says. She made it very clear to him in the carriage after you'd rescued her."

Geoffrey's eyes sharpened. "You're right, which means that if he is to stand any chance, he must do something quickly. And tonight is now his only opportunity!"

Emily's lips parted with dismay. "Then you must stay with her all the time!" she declared.

He couldn't help a wry laugh. "I fear that would hardly be proper."

"But she can't be left alone."

"No, so you are hereby nominated as sentry."

Emily sighed. "Oh, all right." Then she looked curiously at him. "Why wouldn't it be proper? You'll only be guarding her."

"A gentleman cannot remain all night with a lady unless he's married to her."

"But—"

"The matter is closed, Emily. You must watch over Lucy; after all, you *are* her guardian angel."

Emily nodded again, but still grumbled a little. "I think it's silly. If you were with her, Horrid James wouldn't dare do anything."

There was no denying her logic, but etiquette was etiquette, and he and Lucy certainly could not spend the night alone together in an inn room. He sighed, and looked at the angel. "Silly or not, it's what must be. Now then, I've ordered a bath which should be ready, and I intend to enjoy every steaming hot moment, so if you don't mind . . . ?"

Emily sighed and vanished, and a candle on the tap room mantelpiece went out.

As Geoffrey went upstairs, his thoughts returned to the moment he realized Lucy might drown. He'd thought he'd lost her, and it was a fear that cut through him like a knife. Like it or not, Lucy Trevallion meant a great deal to him. Perhaps everything.

It took quite an effort for Lucy to prepare for dinner. She was tired, and her hands shook with delayed reaction to the dreadful events in the Yonne. She sat at the dressing table and somehow managed to dress her hair up into a knot, but knew she looked far from her best. She wore her sage dimity gown, the honeysuckle wool having been torn beyond redemption by the willows that had saved her life. It crossed her mind that before leaving Auxerre in the morning, she'd have to acquire a new cloak. She'd only possessed two, and both had perished that afternoon. What color should she choose? Certainly not lavender, or plum. . . .

She wasn't thinking clearly, and knew it, for what did the color of a new cloak matter? She put her comb down, and drew a steadying breath. She'd had the bath the doctor prescribed, and would obey his instructions about eating a good meal, but all she really wanted to do was go to sleep in the large, comfortable-looking bed she could see in the mirror behind her.

She got up and went to the window, holding the curtain aside to look at the endless rain. The room had two doors, one from within the building, the other opening onto the gallery surrounding the busy yard. Lanterns shone in the darkness, their glow picking out the falling rain. A diligence was just leaving, its passengers huddled as best they could against such a torrent.

How far away the Villa Belmont seemed, she thought, remembering how often she'd stood on the balcony gazing at the lake shimmering in the sunlight. Unbidden, a more disagreeable memory of the villa returned. Suddenly she recalled some of the unpleasant things she'd overheard Geoffrey saying about her. Truly unpleasant things. Hurtful things. Tears sprang to her eyes, and she swallowed. Was he really any better than James? After all, wasn't he also only interested in her inheritance? What had he really rescued from the Yonne today? The woman? Or the fortune?

She wished she wasn't so susceptible to him. His smiles twisted her heart, his touch brought her flesh to life, and his kisses threatened to set fire to her soul. She wanted him to love her. *Her*, not her expectations! Closing her eyes, she mustered her fortitude. She'd be a fool to trust him too much, and certainly shouldn't succumb to the yearning that wrenched longingly through her now.

"Keep him at arm's length, Lucy Trevallion," she whispered.

There was a tap at the door. It was Geoffrey. "Are you ready to go down, Lucy?"

She turned. How subtle the change had been. Only this morning they addressed each other formally, now they were on first name terms. "Yes, I'm ready. You can come in."

He entered. His hair was tousled and still a little damp after his bath, and his blue eyes swept over her. He wanted to take her in his arms and kiss her, but instead confined himself to a compliment.

"Green suits you; it brings out the color of your eyes," he said, smiling.

Her answering smile was uneasy. "Thank you, sir."

He sensed her reserve. "Has something happened?" he asked, thinking of James.

"No. I-I'm just tired, that's all."

He relaxed again. "Well, soon you can sleep, but first you must eat."

"Yes, I suppose so," She avoided his eyes.

He came closer, putting a hand to her chin and making her look at him. "What's wrong, Lucy? Perhaps we should send for the doctor again . . . ?"

She pulled away defensively. "Forgive me, I-I can't relax after all that's happened."

"That's understandable."

She looked at him. "How kind and understanding you are."

"You make that sound a criticism."

"Not a criticism, merely an observation."

"Then it was a critical observation," he said, leaning back against a table and folding his arms. "What's all this about, Lucy?"

"I can't help remembering that until very recently you didn't like me in the least; in fact, you found me virtually abhorrent. Now you're all friendship and first names."

"Maybe I realize I was wrong about you."

"Or maybe . . . " She didn't finish.

He straightened, and his voice became cold. "Or maybe I'm still after your fortune, and therefore not to be trusted any more than Weybridge? After all, I *did* behave monstrously at Besançon! And maybe I'm completely mad, too, for I claim to see angels!" he said angrily.

"I-I don't want to talk about that," she answered awkwardly, for she now knew all about the heavenly vision at the church in Besançon, including that the angel had been a little blond girl with green eyes. She didn't know what she thought, she was too confused and tired to be sensible about anything any more.

He bowed coldly. "If you can bring yourself to endure my company for dinner, I suggest we go down now."

Color stained her cheeks. "You have to understand . . . "

"Oh, I understand perfectly, Miss Trevallion. You were glad enough of my assistance earlier, but now it suits you to resume our antagonistic formality. Well, I'm obliged to you, for I was in danger of thinking you far more worthwhile than you actually are. In your instance, my first impression was completely accurate. You're vainly opinionated, disagreeably perverse, and downright exasperating, but I'm stuck with you. Like it or not, you still need me, my money, and my carriage if you're to reach your grandfather safely in time for Christmas, and in spite of your grave doubts concerning my honor and mental faculties, I'm still gentleman enough to feel responsible for you. However, I feel no such responsibility toward Weybridge, who will no longer be accompanying us, so if you have any qualms about traveling alone with me, you'd better say so now."

Oh, God, this wasn't how he wished it to be. . . .

"Look, Miss Trevallion, this achieves nothing. I don't want to quarrel, nor do I wish to compromise you, so I intend to hire a maid in the morning, to satisfy all the rules. I trust that will be in order?"

"Yes, of course," she replied in a tight voice.

"Good. Now, please, let us go down to eat, the quicker to bring this odious evening to a close, for I assure you I have as little desire to be in your company as you have to be in mine."

He offered her his arm, and reluctantly she took it.

If he'd looked at her eyes in that moment, he'd have seen how close to tears she was, but he didn't look because he was too angry and disappointed. He'd hoped their relationship had changed for the better, but it hadn't, and the fact mattered to him far more than he found comfortable. Just to glance down at her little hand on his sleeve made him want to rest his own over it, but he had to be as cold and unforgiving with her as she was with him.

Thirty

As Lucy and Geoffrey dined in stony silence, James set about arranging the abduction. Palms had to be crossed with silver, so he crept along the rain-swept gallery to let himself into Geoffrey's room with a key he'd persuaded a maid to hand over. Apart from the rain, the only sounds came from the kitchens below, where light and voices drifted from an open window. After glancing around to see if anyone was about, he went into the room.

It was firelit, and shadows moved over the walls as he began to search for money. He found it in the boots Geoffrey had worn that day. They stood drying before the fire, with several fat purses stuffed into the toes. It was more than sufficient for James's purposes, and he grinned as he pocketed them and let himself out again.

He went stealthily along the gallery to the steps leading down into the yard, but halfway down he had to stop, for the landlord and a cook were talking in the kitchen doorway. In spite of the rain, he heard everything they were saying.

They were discussing *le réveillon,* the traditional dinner served in France on the night of Christmas Eve. The cook wished the main course to be turkey stuffed with chestnuts and truffles, but the landlord favored goose. To the two Burgundians, it was clearly a matter of immense importance, but James wished them in Hades.

"Damn it, have goose and be done with it!" he said under his breath, turning up his collar against the onslaught of the rain.

To his relief, at last they finished and went inside, closing the door. He hastened down the rest of the steps and made his way to the stables, where he sought the French postilion who'd replaced the Swiss one at Pontarlier.

Lucy and Geoffrey were glad to bring their unhappy meal to a close. Emily had hovered nearby as they ate, and she was puzzled as to why they were so dreadfully cold with each other. After the rescue that afternoon, they'd seemed so well disposed; now it was all horrid again. The little angel was upset, for she'd been so happy when they clung so lovingly to each other on the landing stage.

There was still nothing said as Geoffrey took a candle to escort Lucy to her room, where she accorded him a brief nod before going in and closing the door.

Emily looked accusingly at him. "Why aren't you speaking to each other?"

"Because I'm tired of being falsely accused."

"Accused of what?"

"The same base purpose as Weybridge. Look, it's a long story, and I have neither the time nor the inclination to go into it all now"; he turned toward his own door. "Don't forget to watch over her tonight," he said over his shoulder.

"I won't. Good night, Geoffrey."

"Good night."

His door closed, and Emily gazed unhappily at it.

Lucy stood miserably in her room. How she wished she were far away from here, far away from Geoffrey, Earl of St. Athan. If only he'd never come to the villa, and the truth about her family background had never come to light. She'd been happy just to be Lady Amelia's companion.

She undressed in front of the fire. The warmth of the flames was pleasant on her skin, and when she caught a glimpse of herself in the dressing table mirror she saw how sensuously the dancing light moved over the contours of her breasts, picking out the small shadows cast by her nipples. She ran her fingertips over herself, and then closed her eyes as the tears had their way. She wished Geoffrey were with her now, that his were the hands that stroked her. Instead, she was alone, with far more than just inn walls standing between her and him.

If only she hadn't given in again to her ill-founded suspicions, for they *were* ill-founded, she was now as suddenly certain of it as earlier she'd been convinced of the contrary. Now she'd probably alienated him forever. He'd see her safely to London, and take care of her every inch of the way, but he'd never forgive her. And why should he? What faith had she ever shown in him? She'd taken all the help he offered, and given nothing in return, but if he were to come to her now, oh, how much she'd give. . . .

She exhaled slowly, and turned to put on her nightgown. Only in her slumbers would she ever be able to surrender her chastity to Lord St. Athan. Tonight she'd had the chance to build upon the new warmth between them, but had thrown it away. There wouldn't be another.

She took the laudanum the doctor had prescribed, and then curled up in the bed, pulling the sheets over her head to hide from the world.

Emily peeped over from on top of the canopy. How sad Lucy was. The little angel was sure it was because of Geoffrey, and wished she could do something to help. But there was nothing. Drawing back, she curled up to make herself comfortable for the night's vigil.

She snuggled on the ancient velvet, and folded her wings. For a while she listened to the sounds of the inn, and the endless drumming of the rain. She didn't mean to fall asleep, but the room was very warm, and the day had been long and arduous, even for an angel. Her eyes closed, and soon she was lost in dreams.

But James was wide awake. He lay full dressed on his bed, willing the minutes away until it was time to commence his plan. He'd heard Lucy's door close, and then Geoffrey's, and knew it wouldn't be long before Lucy succumbed to the laudanum he'd found out about from the same maid who'd given him the spare key. The girl knew about the doctor's prescription because she was the one sent to purchase it from a nearby apothecary.

As his fob watch read midnight, he heard Geoffrey's carriage being brought quietly into the yard below, and he got up to go out to the gallery. He looked over the rail to nod at the waiting postilion, and then went to Lucy's door, which he unlocked very softly indeed.

Emily knew nothing as he stepped silently to the bed and stood looking down at Lucy in her deep, laudanum-induced sleep. Her nightgown had parted slightly to reveal one of her breasts, and anticipation swept carnally through him as he gazed at the inviting curve. He almost stretched his trembling hand out, but then drew it sharply back. All in good time. Soon he would enjoy more than just a breast; he'd have the entire woman!

She didn't stir as he drew the bedclothes back and gathered her carefully into his arms, and Emily slept on as he carried his victim out into the night. But as he began to descend to the yard, the cold air and rain made Lucy stir slightly. Realizing she might come around at any moment, he hurried down the last of the steps.

More rain fell on Lucy's face as he carried her across the yard to the carriage, and suddenly her eyes opened in confusion. Realization dawned as she saw James's grimly determined face, and she began to struggle. "Let me go! Let me go!" she cried, but only the postilion heard, and he'd been paid to turn a blind eye.

James bundled her into the carriage and then leapt in after her, clamping his hand over her mouth as the postilion kicked the team forward. She struggled desperately, but James was far too strong for her. By the light of a lantern he could see how her rain-dampened nightgown clung to her body, and lust rose urgently through him. He wanted to take her right there in the carriage, but somehow he contained himself. All in good time. But at least he'd rob her of some kisses. He pulled her close, and pressed his parted lips over hers.

The carriage drove swiftly on, leaving Auxerre behind and striking along a rain-washed country lane toward a hill, where the isolated church of St. Roch stood among cherry orchards and vineyards.

But James was wrong to think his plan had gone undetected, for something had suddenly jerked Emily into wakefulness. She leaned over the canopy and saw with horror that the bed was empty. Then she realized the door was open, and she flew outside just in time to recognize Geoffrey's carriage leaving. With a gasp she followed and looked inside. The little angel was as frightened as Lucy, whose ashen face and rigid immobility as James kissed her bore witness to her complete dread.

But there was nothing Emily could do, except tell Geoffrey. So she fled desperately back to his room. "Wake up, Geoffrey! Lucy's been taken!"

He sat up with a start. "What in God's name . . . ?"

"James has taken Lucy away in your carriage!" the angel cried.

"He's what? Emily, I told you to guard her!"

Tears filled her eyes and her lips quivered. "I know, but I fell asleep . . . "

He flung the bedclothes back and leapt from the bed to dress. He was stark naked, as always when he slept, but this wasn't the time to be self-conscious. "You say he's taken my carriage?"

"Yes. I was just in time to see it leaving."

"So they've only just gone?"

"Yes."

"Then get after them. I'll have to take a horse from the stables, but I won't know which way to go. I'll have to rely on you for that." He paused as he did up his breeches buttons. "I *can* rely on you, can't I?"

She was defensive. "Yes, of course!"

"Then be off with you, and make *absolutely* certain of their direction before you come back to me," he said, picking up the first of his heavy boots. The moment his toes went right inside, he knew James had stolen the purses. No wonder the blackguard had been able to obtain the use of his carriage!

Emily flew high into the air above Auxerre. She glanced all around, and at last saw the carriage driving swiftly along the country lane. Swooping down to the inn again, she saw Geoffrey about to mount a horse in the stableyard. "I've found them!" she cried.

"Then lead me!" he replied, turning the horse's head and kicking his heels urgently.

Emily flew unerringly through the night, pausing now and then to wait for him to catch up. Soon Auxerre began to slip away behind, and they were on the country road the carriage had taken. The horse's hooves splashed through the deep puddles that had collected in the ruts, and the sound of running water was everywhere from the rivulets that poured from the adjacent orchards and vineyards.

A rambling and dilapidated stone barn loomed out of the darkness, and the road forked in two beside it, one fork leading down toward thick woodland, the other winding up through orchards and vineyards toward the church of St. Roch.

Emily saw the carriage at the church door. "There they are, Geoffrey!" she cried, pointing through the rain.

He urged the horse forward again, knowing a church could only mean forced marriage for an abducted heiress like Lucy.

Thirty-one

Minutes earlier, James had dragged Lucy from the carriage. She was so frightened she couldn't stand, so he had to carry her up the steps and through the richly sculptured doorway. The roar of the rain outside was still audible as his boots rang on the stone flags. At the candlelit altar, the priest waited.

The scent of incense hung in the chill air, and carved saints gazed stonily down from the capitals of columns. There was stained glass in the windows, but the colors were toned to shades of gray against the darkness of the night sky. A Nativity scene had been built by nearby villagers, and on Christmas morning, a real baby would be laid in the crib, but it was empty now. Lucy's terrified glance fell briefly upon it as James hauled her, almost fainting, the final yards to the altar steps.

The priest became uneasy when he saw how unwilling the bride was, and that she wore night clothes instead of a wedding gown, "*Monsieur,* I cannot . . . "

"You can and you will," James interrupted, tossing down a handful of coins. The sound echoed through the shadows.

The priest hesitated, and then nodded.

Lucy looked imploringly at him. "Please, Father! I've been kidnapped! I don't want this man!" she begged, her voice catching with emotion.

The priest shrugged. "Matrimony is a holy estate, *mademoiselle,* and as such will be blessed."

"And you call yourself a man of God?" she cried, trying again to pull free of James.

He tightened his hold. "There's nothing to be gained by putting up a fight, Lucy. You're about to become my wife, and there's nothing you can do about it."

"Never!" She doubled her efforts, but his grip became viselike, and she cried out with pain.

He looked angrily down at her. "You're going to be mine, Lucy, and with you will come your fortune."

"My grandfather will disinherit me!"

"I think not, for you're all he has left. He'll always put his own flesh and blood first now, because he dreads repeating the mistake he made with your father. You'll remain an heiress, and I'll reap the benefit."

"I despise you," she whispered.

"Of what consequence is that? Many a wife loathes her husband, but she must still grace his bed when he so chooses."

"I'll be poor satisfaction, of that you may be sure," she hissed.

"My dear Lucy, whether you fight or just lie there, your body cannot help but satisfy me," he said softly, and then looked at the priest again. "Proceed, Father, for the bride's natural nervousness has been overcome."

Outside, the postilion heard hoofbeats approaching along the lane, and quickly left the carriage to hide behind a low wall. He saw Geoffrey rein in, and ducked low in alarm. *Dieu!* The milord!

Emily preceded Geoffrey into the church, and halted in dismay on seeing the figures by the altar. Almost immediately she realized she'd begun to glow. It was only a soft light, but discernible. Afraid of being seen, she fluttered behind a column and peeped around it to see what was happening. The ceremony hadn't been completed yet, for James was about to take the ring from the Bible the priest held out.

Geoffrey strode in, and the group at the altar whirled about. The ring fell from James's startled fingers and rolled away over the floor as Lucy gave a glad cry.

"Geoffrey!"

The priest pressed nervously back against the altar, but James suddenly pulled out a pistol he'd bought that evening and pressed it to Lucy's temple. "One step more, St. Athan, and I'll see neither of us has her!" he warned.

Geoffrey halted, his eyes flickering toward the pistol and then back to James's face. "I see you put my money to good use, Weybridge," he said scornfully.

"I'm not a fool."

"You are if you imagine you'll get away with this."

James gave a cool laugh. "I'll get away with it, make no mistake of that."

"You'll have to kill me first," Geoffrey replied levelly.

"I intend to."

The priest was alarmed. "Not in the church, *monsieur*, for that is sacrilege!"

Geoffrey was contemptuous. "Is that so, Father? But it is not equally sacrilegious to force a woman into marriage?"

The priest lowered his eyes.

James pushed the pistol tighter to Lucy's temple, and looked at the priest. "Proceed with the ceremony, Father, for now we have a witness to make matters all the more proper!" This last was said with a mocking laugh.

Behind the pillar, Emily quivered with fury, and with fear for her cousin's life. Geoffrey was helpless while the pistol was pointing at Lucy, for the last thing he'd do was risk the trigger's being squeezed. The little angel hovered wretchedly, still trying to keep her low glow hidden from view, but then she paused. Of course! It was forbidden for her to become visible unless it was very important indeed. What could be more important for a guardian angel than to save the person she'd been sent to protect?

She hesitated only a moment, for the priest had retrieved the ring and was resuming the service. Flying swiftly from behind the column, she positioned herself directly above the altar, and as before, her glow became a brilliant light. With her fledgling wings outstretched, she assumed a devotional attitude, her eyes toward the heavens, her little hands clasped in prayer.

She shone with all her little might. Oh, how she shone. She was like a beautiful beacon burning brightly in the darkness, and suddenly she knew she wasn't doing wrong, for other angels were at her side, she could hear them singing. The sweetness of their voices told her He approved, and her light shone even more bravely.

Lucy ceased her futile struggles to stare at the host of angels, and knew without being told that the little one at the front was Emily, for the child with ash-blond hair and green eyes was the very image of herself at that age. "Emily . . . " she whispered, tears of wonder springing to her eyes.

The terrified priest fell to his knees to beg forgiveness for his sins, and James was shocked and dazzled by the unearthly light and voices. Geoffrey seized his chance and lunged forward, snatching the pistol away, but he had no opportunity to level it, for James recovered his wits and fought back. In the ensuing struggle the weapon fell to the floor to lie hidden in the shadows.

Lucy shrank back against a column, terrified that Geoffrey might lose the struggle. As she watched, James suddenly hurled himself forward to butt Geoffrey's stomach with his head. Winded, Geoffrey staggered backward, and James ran like the wind for the door.

Once outside, his first instinct was to take the carriage, but the postilion was nowhere to be seen. Then he spotted Geoffrey's horse, and sprang into the saddle, kicking his heels wildly to urge the animal away just as Geoffrey ran out onto the porch.

In the church, the heavenly vision disappeared, and the only light now came from the altar candles. The priest rose slowly from his knees, crossing himself time and time again as his lips moved in silent prayer.

Geoffrey returned, and watched disdainfully. "A little late, I fancy, Father."

"It is never too late to realize one has gone astray and must return to the fold," the priest replied, turning to him. "I have sinned greatly, and tonight was the peak of my transgression, but from now on I will do the Lord's work as it should be done."

"Nothing will absolve you from the crime you conspired in tonight, Father, and when your allotted span is done, I trust you go to a suitably hot place. Now get out of here, for I think your presence profanes this house of God."

Without another word, the priest obeyed. He paused by Lucy. "Forgive me, *mademoiselle* . . ."

She averted her head, and with a heavy heart he walked on.

Geoffrey wasn't prepared to trust his reformation to the full, and so searched swiftly for the pistol. Then he drew Lucy quickly to her feet. "We must be certain he doesn't make off with the carriage. Priest or not, he's a slippery article, and my postilion is clearly not as loyal as he might be," he said, taking off his coat and putting it around her shoulders before assisting her to the church door.

The postilion had come out of hiding on seeing the priest, but as soon as Geoffrey appeared, he took to his heels, leaping back over the wall and vanishing into the darkness and rain. The priest had ridden from Auxerre, and his horse was tethered at the side of the church. He led it out and mounted, and as he disappeared into the downpour, Geoffrey released Lucy.

"It's all over now; you're safe," he said gently, glancing up as Emily suddenly fluttered excitedly over to him.

"Geoffrey, I am to stay here until dawn because He's pleased with me," she whispered in his ear. "My mother and father are here, and I'll be allowed to play with other little angels just like me! But I'll return to you, for I still have to make sure Lucy reaches England safely, and that we defeat Uncle Robert too!"

Geoffrey had no chance to respond to any of this, for the angel promptly disappeared.

Lucy, who didn't realize her cousin had been close again, looked remorsefully at Geoffrey. "Can you ever forgive me for not believing you?"

He smiled. "Lucy, I hardly believed it myself, so how could I really expect you to?"

"Is Emily here now?"

"She was, but now she's gone. It seems she'll be playing with other little angels tonight. She's delighted, because approval has come from on high. We'll have the pleasure of her company again tomorrow."

"Will I be able to see her?"

"I think not." He explained why, and then smiled. "I know it's a disappointment to you, because you've only seen her tonight, but you may take my word for it that it isn't always convenient to have a small angel constantly popping up at your elbow. There have been occasions when I've been Adam-naked and she's put in an unheralded appearance."

But instead of smiling at his wry remark, Lucy's eyes filled with tears. "You've been dreadfully inconvenienced because of me, haven't you? And all I've done is make your life intolerable!"

"Lucy, if regrets are the order of the day, I have as many as you. For far too long I wasn't exactly Sir Galahad, was I? Anyway, none of all that matters now, for you're safe, and that's what counts." He hesitated then. "Forgive me, but I must ask. Did Weybridge do anything to you? I mean, did he actually . . . ?"

She shook her head, closing her eyes as she remembered. "He kissed me, but that's all," she whispered.

He breathed out with relief, and touched her cheek briefly. "If he'd harmed you . . . " He didn't finish.

She shivered, and he glanced up at the rain. "Come on, I'll get you back to Auxerre." Catching her hand, he led her to the carriage, then he mounted the lead horse and urged the team into action.

The church door stood open behind them, and if they'd glanced back they'd have seen a great light inside. Emily was with the angels, and the joy that filled the building was magnificent to behold.

Thirty-two

But the return journey to Auxerre halted abruptly by the barn at the fork in the lane, because the carriage struck a large stone washed down from an adjacent vineyard. There was a sharp jolt, a cracking sound, and then the vehicle lurched over at an alarming angle.

Geoffrey reined in swiftly as he realized a wheel was damaged. Alighting, he trudged back through the rain and mire, just as Lucy recovered her balance sufficiently to lower the window glass and look out.

He glanced down at the wheel. "We'll go no further on that," he said heavily.

She looked toward the barn. "Can we shelter there until light?" she asked.

"I'll see."

Startled pigeons fluttered away as he entered, and he heard rats, but the air was sweet with the smell of the cherry orchard hay stored at the far end. The roof was crumbling close to the entrance, but was sound further in, where the slope of the land also assisted in keeping everything dry. It wasn't Carlton House, but was decidedly better than the carriage, which was pitched over far too much to be comfortable.

He returned to Lucy. "It will do, come on." He opened the carriage door and reached up to lift her clear of the mud and water. He carried her into the barn and set her down lightly. "Behold, your hostelry for the night, madam."

She smiled in the darkness. "I vow, it's almost Mayfair."

"Would that it were." He glanced back at the carriage. "I'll bring some rugs, and see if I can get into the trunks for some dry clothes."

Before she could say anything more, he'd gone out into the rain again. She shivered as she waited by the entrance. Water dripped through a hole in the roof, and ran freely along a gutter by her feet to join the rivulets in the road. Her flimsy nightgown was damp and now that her fear had died away, she was only too aware of how bitterly cold she was.

After several minutes, Geoffrey splashed back from the carriage, his arms full of rugs and clothes, which he carried to the dry hay at the rear of the barn. Then he turned to her as she joined him. "You'll have to forgive me for rifling your trunk, but it wasn't the time for a painstaking search. I hope I've brought something suitable." He indicated the cashmere shawl, lime woolen chemise gown, gray kid shoes, and white silk stockings he'd found. "There wasn't a cloak or pelisse, at least, not in that particular trunk, but we have the traveling rugs . . . "

"I'm sure it's adequate," she replied, hiding her dismay that he'd only brought what amounted to half the gown! There was an undergown to make it decent, and since she'd never liked the color or style very much in the first place, she hardly ever wore it. Indeed, she didn't know why she hadn't given it away to one of Lady Amelia's maids.

He cleared his throat. "I'll, er, attend to the horses, and leave you to change in privacy," he murmured, and hurried out into the rain again.

She stepped quickly out of the nightgown, and then slipped into the chemise gown. Her teeth chattered all the while, and she felt as if she'd never be warm again as she wrapped it across in front to do up the single button beneath her left breast. It was this totally inadequate fastening which made the undergarment so vital, for she was only too aware of how easily the gown's skirt parted, and how daringly low the bodice was; indeed, the latter barely covered her modesty! Sitting on the hay, she put on the shoes and stockings, and then tied the shawl around her shoulders to cover her breasts, before enveloping herself in a travel rug again.

Geoffrey led the team inside, and tethered them against a dry wall, where they were able to drink from the gutter running toward the barn entrance. He rubbed them hastily down, and then took them several armsful of hay.

She smiled at him. "I vow you'd make an excellent groom, sir."

"I'm a man of many talents."

"I believe you; indeed, I'll believe anything you choose to tell me from now on, but right now it's my belief you should change out of those soaking clothes before you contract a dreadful ague."

Lucy found it impossible to sleep later, when they lay close together in the hay, sharing the rugs and trying to keep warm. They'd chosen a place by the remains of an old stall, where there was a little shelter from the draft of cold air creeping in through the barn entrance.

She was aware of the horses shifting and snorting, of the interminable rain on the roof, of the pigeons fluttering and cooing, and the rats squeaking as they emerged again from the shadows, but most of all she was aware of Geoffrey. If she stretched out a hand, she could touch him . . .

Suddenly a rat scuttered across the hay only inches from her face, and with a gasp of revulsion she sat up, holding the travel rug to her throat.

Geoffrey's eyes flew open. "What is it?" he asked, sitting up as well. His shirt was very white in the darkness, and it was undone to the waist, revealing the hairs on his chest.

"A-a rat."

He smiled, and lay down again. "It won't harm you."

"I know, I-I just can't stand them."

He watched her as she remained warily upright. "Do you intend to try to sleep like that?" he asked then.

She heard the slight humor in his voice, and looked accusingly at him. "I don't think it at all funny, sir."

"Forgive me, it's just . . . Well, it's just much more comfortable lying down," he said, pulling her down much closer to him. "There, with my fearsome presence, no rat will dare approach you."

"You think I'm stupid, don't you? But I've *never* liked rats, or mice, and—"

"I don't think you in the least stupid, Lucy," he interrupted quietly.

Then, in spite of herself, she smiled. "I wonder how many rules we're breaking tonight?"

"Too many to mention, I should imagine, but as we're the only ones to know, and since neither of us is likely to tittle-tattle, I don't intend to give it a second thought."

"Rules can be very tiresome."

He laughed. "True, but the rules in question now are intended to protect the likes of you from the base and unprincipled advances of the likes of me."

"Sir, the only base advance you've made to me was thoroughly deserved on my part. I wasn't prepared at any price to believe what you told me, and I needed teaching a lesson."

He folded his arms behind his head and stared up at the barn roof. "That doesn't excuse me. I shouldn't have done what I did then, or at the dance in Pontarlier."

"Well, I don't remember anything about that, so I can't comment," she remarked dryly.

He leaned up then, searching her face in the darkness. "I found it a most agreeable experience," he said candidly.

She met his eyes. "Why? Because I remind you so much of Constance?" she asked quietly.

"Constance didn't enter into it," he replied.

"Tell me about her."

"When I think back now, there's precious little to tell," he confessed. "My pride smarted a great deal for far too long."

"But you loved her, didn't you?"

He nodded. "For a while, at least. From this distance, though, I don't think my feelings went as deep as I imagined at the time. I'm certainly relieved now that she wasn't free, for she'd be my wife now, and the union would have been disastrous."

"She wasn't free?"

He drew a long breath. "There was a husband of whose existence I knew nothing. It seems the lady was prone to straying from the marital bed. No doubt she'd have strayed from mine too."

"Do you still see her when you look at me?"

"No."

"Are you sure?"

He nodded. "Yes."

She was silent for a moment. "I'm glad you've told me about her."

"Why?"

"Because I understand you now."

He raised an eyebrow. "Do you, indeed? Perhaps that's a dangerous thing, for it doesn't always do to understand someone."

"It's far better than finding them a frustrating puzzle," she countered.

He met her eyes. "Why am I suddenly reminded of the day we visited Chillon?"

"I-I don't know." She had to look away, afraid that even in the darkness he'd see the embarrassed color that flamed into her cheeks.

"What is it? Have I said something?"

"Oh, it's nothing."

"I don't believe you."

Reluctantly she met his eyes again. Was this the moment to throw caution to the winds, and confess to the immense attraction she felt toward him?

He smiled, "Well?"

"It's just . . . Well, I had a dream about Chillon, and us."

"Us?" he repeated softly.

"Yes." Then she was covered in confusion. "Oh, I shouldn't have told you . . . "

He put his hand to her cheek. "Yes, you should, for I doubt if anything you've dreamed about me can compete with what *I've* dreamed about *you*," he said quietly.

Her eyes flew back to him.

His thumb moved softly against her skin. "Dreams so often tell us the truth about ourselves, Lucy."

"I know," she replied honestly. The blood had quickened in her veins, and she was conscious of her heartbeats. She wanted him to take her into his arms. . . .

"What is the truth, Lucy?" he asked softly.

"That I love you," she confessed.

"Oh, Lucy . . . " He bent his head to put his lips over hers.

For a moment she resisted, but only a moment. The rug slipped from her shoulders, and her lips trembled as she met the kiss. His arms enveloped her and he held her close in the darkness. She knew the flimsy knot with which she'd tied her shawl was sliding loose, but she didn't care. The soft cashmere fell to the hay, and the bodice of her gown parted to allow a breast to peep out.

His hand moved to enclose it, cupping its firm warmth and caressing until her nipple pressed eagerly against him. He could feel desire beginning to steal his self-control. There was a raging arousal at his loins, pounding so imperatively through him that it seemed to rule his entire being. He leaned closer, allowing her to feel the throbbing shaft trapped in the tightness of his breeches. If she wanted to stop, he would know. And if she wanted to go on, he would know that too.

Her breath caught with pleasure as she felt his erection. Dizzying sensations warmed her skin. She had to touch him; she had to feel his maleness. . . . Her trembling fingers moved to enclose his hardness through the stuff of his breeches. Her breath caught again, and she raised her parted lips to be kissed again.

He hesitated. "There will be no turning back, Lucy," he whispered.

"Nor do I wish it," she breathed, her fingers tightening urgently around his arousal.

He undid the single button holding her gown, and the soft lime wool parted to reveal her nakedness. He saw how long, pale, and smooth her thighs were, how dark the soft forest of hair at her groin, and how supple her waist. Her breasts were pert and craving, her eyes warm and inviting, and it was she who undid his breeches and loosed the source of the consummation they both yearned for.

His virility sprang against her, pressing to her abdomen as he pulled her into his arms again. Their kisses were hungry and insatiable. Passion carried them both away in a torrent of emotion, and when kisses and caresses could suffice no more, at last he moved fully on top of her. Her thighs parted wantonly and his desire almost exploded with urgency as he pushed into her. There was a little resistance, but then he slid deep into a haven that encased him like warm velvet.

She clung to him as he began to thrust. Tears were wet on her cheeks and waves of delight washed over her. This was paradise. Paradise. Ecstasy swept her away.

He'd never known such gratification before, or such love. He'd taken many women to his bed, but none had meant so much to him as Lucy. Each stroke he made was like the warming of his soul, and when he came, he knew it would be like the first time in his life.

The climax was an experience of shattering delight to them both. Their bodies moved together in complete ecstasy, and there were tears on her cheeks as wave after wave of joy washed through her.

When it was over, she continued to hold him close on top of her, exulting in the knowledge that they were still joined. She could feel him inside her, softer now, but still sweetly tangible.

"I love you so much, Geoffrey," she whispered, her fingers moving tenderly over his back.

"And I love you, Lucy," he replied, kissing her again, and then moving to roll away.

But she still held him. "No, not yet. Please, not yet . . . "

Thirty-three

The rain ceased as dawn broke. Birds began to sing outside, and the pigeons cooed contentedly.

Geoffrey leaned on an elbow to gaze down at Lucy as she slept. How beautiful she was, and how beloved. She'd put the lime chemise gown on again, but it hid very little. He could see her rose-tipped breasts, and the smoothness of her thighs. He pushed a little curl back from her cheek, and she opened her eyes and smiled.

"Good morning," he said softly.

"Good morning," she whispered, reaching up to link her arms around his neck.

But he drew back hesitantly. "There's something I must ask, Lucy."

"Ask?"

"Do you regret last night?"

"Never. Do you?"

"I fear I do."

Dismay widened her eyes. "Please say you don't mean that."

"I won't lie to you, Lucy."

"You think badly of me for letting you . . . ?"

"No, my darling, I think badly of myself for doing it." He stroked her cheek tenderly. "I'm a man of the world; I knew what I was doing last night, but still I did it. God forgive me, I want to do it again now, but to give in to desire doesn't make it right."

"I love you, Geoffrey."

He smiled, bending his head to brush his lips over hers. "And I love you, Lucy, so there's another question I must ask now."

"Another question?"

"Will you marry me?"

She stared at him. "Marry you?" she repeated.

"Make an honest man of me, Lucy, or at least help me live with my conscience."

She lowered her arms. "Why are you asking me, Geoffrey? Is it because you wish me to be your wife, or is it merely to ease your guilt?"

"Can't you see it's both? I shouldn't have made love to you last night; it was wrong, and I knew it. You're young, alone, and vulnerable, and instead of protecting you, I seduced you!" He sat up and ran his fingers through his hair.

She smiled then, reaching out to take his hand and draw the palm to her lips. "But I seduced you too, sir. I don't recall crying out for help, or saying 'No' to anything that happened." She put his hand over one of her breasts. "I wouldn't say 'No' now, either," she whispered.

His fingers closed softly over the breast, cupping it tenderly as he gazed into her eyes. "Say you'll be my wife," he breathed huskily, leaning down so his lips almost brushed hers.

"Do you really want me?"

"More than anything else in the world."

She moved luxuriously against him, her nipple pressing against his palm. "Then I'll marry you, Geoffrey, for I want you more than anything else in the world too."

Their lips seared together again, and the passion that had consumed them through the night returned to rule them again now. Only the pigeons saw them making love in the dawn light.

Afterward, when once again they lay sated in the hay, Geoffrey smiled as he gazed up at the rafters. "How shocked London will be," he murmured.

"Yes, I suppose it will."

"And it will draw certain conclusions."

"Not without some degree of accuracy," she said, turning her head to smile at him.

"But will you mind? That's the question."

"I should, but I won't," she replied honestly. "I'm not ashamed of what we've done here; in fact, it's made me the happiest creature on earth."

"Your grandfather might mind a great deal," he warned.

"Mind that his granddaughter arrives the future Countess of St. Athan? I can't think he'd quarrel with that."

He sat up. "My darling, we've taken risks with nature, the sort of risks that might prove embarrassingly obvious to all." He put a hand gently on her abdomen. "If there are consequences because of what we've done, I want them to occur well within the bounds of propriety."

"What are you saying?"

"That I don't mean you to reach London as my *future* countess,

I want you to actually *be* my countess. We must marry as soon as possible—preferably in Auxerre today—so that not a single night more passes before we're man and wife. Then whatever happens, all will be well." His arm slid around her waist as he kissed her again.

At that moment, Emily flew into the barn. She'd been about to fly back to the Horseshoe in Auxerre, but noticed the carriage in the lane. They were oblivious to her presence as she peeped over the stall behind them, her eyes curious and her wings outstretched.

"Are you and Lucy friends again now, Geoffrey?" she asked suddenly, and with a guilty start he drew away from Lucy.

The little angel fluttered curiously over the stall and sat on the rug next to them. "Why are you here?" she asked.

"The carriage wheel struck a stone," he explained, and then looked quickly at Lucy's startled face. "It's all right, I'm not rambling; it's just that Emily's here."

"Oh!" Lucy sat up quickly, pulling her gown together as best she could, and hoping her heavenly cousin hadn't seen anything too improper. Then she glanced around. "Where is she?"

He sat up and pretended to ruffle the little angel's hair, although of course he couldn't feel her at all. "Right here."

Lucy looked. "Good morning, Emily."

"Good morning, Lucy."

Geoffrey relayed the angel's response.

"I—I wish I could see you, Emily," Lucy said then.

Emily smiled. "I've been told that because I've tried so hard, I can appear to you when we reach London safely. If we go to a church, I'll be allowed to let you see me. And Grandfather, too."

Geoffrey told Lucy what she'd said.

Lucy was delighted. "Oh, I'm so glad."

Emily studied her. "You're ever so different today, Lucy."

Geoffrey didn't say anything.

The angel looked curiously at him. "Why didn't you tell her that?"

Still he didn't respond.

Emily was cross. "Oh, I do wish grown-ups wouldn't have so many secrets! It's not fair!"

"There's one secret I wish to share with you, Emily," he said then, taking Lucy's hand. "Lucy and I are to be married."

Emily was dumbfounded. "Married? But yesterday you weren't even speaking to each other!"

"That was yesterday."

Lucy smiled, for she could guess what the angel had said.

Emily looked at them both. "You really are going to be married? You're not teasing me?"

"I'm not teasing you, Emily. Lucy is going to be the Countess of St. Athan, and the sooner the better. Hopefully today, if I can bring enough pressure to bear on the Auxerre authorities, to say nothing of the church!"

Emily beamed then. "Oh, it's wonderful! Perfect!" she cried, clapping her hands together and dancing all around them with her little wings fluttering.

Geoffrey got up, and helped Lucy to her feet as well. "Before we can do anything, I'm afraid we have to get to Auxerre. I think two of the horses are ridable . . . "

But as he spoke, they heard a cart bumping along the muddy lane. He hurried to the entrance of the barn to see a local farmer driving to market. The man halted, and soon agreed to convey them to Auxerre. He maneuvered his pony and cart past the carriage, and a few minutes later, after Lucy had put on more suitable clothes, she and Geoffrey sat in the back of the little two-wheeled vehicle as it bounced toward the town.

After all the rain, it was good to see a clear sky and sunshine again. The countryside lost its grayness to fill with color once more, and Auxerre sparkled on its hills beside the silver Yonne. The bells of St. Etienne's cathedral echoed across the landscape as the bellringers practiced Christmas carillons, and Geoffrey smiled as he gazed toward the towers of the great church. Where better than a cathedral to make Lucy Trevallion his wife?

When they arrived at the Horseshoe, Lucy was afraid James might still be there, but he'd long gone, after ransacking both their rooms for anything of value. He'd found a little more of Geoffrey's money, but by no means all, for that had been hidden very carefully indeed in the stables, not the inn itself. A wheelwright was despatched to attend to the damaged carriage and bring it safely back, and while Lucy was looked after by the landlady and several of the inn maids, who were appalled to hear what James had tried to do, Geoffrey went to the town hall, where an accommodating official furnished the necessary legal documents. All that remained now, was to persuade the church.

With Emily at his side, he crossed the cathedral square, where the sound of the jubilant bells seemed to shake the cobbles, but as they neared the magnificently decorated doorway, the tips of her wings began to shine, and she drew prudently back.

"I-I'd better not go in," she said wisely.

"Perhaps you're right," he agreed, and went in alone.

Suddenly the carillons ended, and there was virtual silence. Sunlight streamed in through the great rose window, casting spangles of jeweled light over everything. There was no sign of a priest, but then he heard slightly raised voices coming from a side chapel.

After a moment, a rather cross-looking priest emerged, and then halted in surprise on seeing Geoffrey. A quick glance told him the newcomer's nationality. "How may I help you, sir?" he asked in English.

Before Geoffrey could reply, the raised voices became very angry, and the priest smiled apologetically. "You must forgive my fellows, sir, but I fear one of them claims to have seen an angel last night, at the church of St. Roch outside the town."

"A-an angel?" Geoffrey replied lightly.

"Not everyone believes him," the priest explained.

"So it seems."

"Is there anything I can do for you, sir?"

"Yes, you can perform my marriage here today."

The priest stared. "Today? Oh, but that is not possible, sir!"

"I'm sure it is." Geoffrey took out the documents he'd obtained at the town hall, and then glanced meaningfully at a medallion window above the ambulatory. "I see a need for certain repairs, Father, and am more than willing to pay whatever is needed."

The priest hesitated. "You put great temptation my way, sir," he said a little reprovingly.

"If you're tempted, Father, it's because of the great love you have for this magnificent church." Geoffrey placed a plump purse in the man's hand.

The priest smiled wryly. "I had no idea the English had such powers of persuasion, sir. Very well, I will do as you wish. Come to the lady chapel at two o'clock."

The choir sang as Lucy and Geoffrey stood before the priest. She had no fine wedding gown of silver tissue and gauze, no magnificent jewels, and no bridesmaids, but she was a glowing bride, her face radiant with happiness as she made her vows.

Emily watched from an archway high above the nave, keeping out of sight as much as possible so that no one could see her shining light, for Lucy and Geoffrey's wedding mustn't be spoiled by the excitement of *another* "miracle." Tears shone in the little angel's eyes as the ring Geoffrey had purchased only an hour before was slipped on the bride's finger, and Lucy became the Countess of St. Athan.

That night, Emily was forbidden to come into the room at the Horseshoe as Lucy and Geoffrey lay naked between silk sheets that smelled of lavender. He gazed adoringly at his new wife as her ash-blond hair spilled richly over the pillow beside him.

"I can't believe this has happened," he whispered, loving her so much it was like sweet torture deep inside him.

"Nor can I," she whispered back.

"How does it feel to be Lady St. Athan?"

"I'll tell you in the morning," she whispered, wriggling beneath the sheets to kiss his chest, then his waist, then his abdomen, and then . . . Oh, and then . . . Her mouth was soft upon his slumbering virility, moving gently down its length until she reached the tip. As she put her lips around it, it did not slumber for long.

Thirty-four

It was December twenty-first when Geoffrey, Lucy, and Emily set off from Auxerre in the repaired carriage. It seemed impossible now that they could reach London in time for Christmas, but the new postilion was ordered to make haste.

Over the next few days Emily soon became bored. Without the stimulus of having to guard Lucy from the Weybridges, she had as little to divert her as any ordinary child would. It became dull conversing with Lucy through Geoffrey, and the distraction of I-Spy could only endure for so long. She fiddled and sighed, continually inspecting her fledgling wings in the hope they'd grown since last she looked.

At last they reached Normandy, on the last part of their journey to the coast. The countryside was more like England now, and Christmas suddenly seemed much nearer as Lucy saw children gathering mistletoe in an apple orchard.

It was dawn on Christmas Eve itself that they breasted the chalky heights above Dieppe, and saw the sea. The travel-stained carriage drove down into the town, the streets of which ran right to the quay from where the Brighton packet would sail at high tide. The carriage was too big to be stowed in the hold, and so had to be lashed to the deck instead, and while it was being winched aboard, the travelers stole a few minutes to inspect the shops and market on the quay.

There was a great deal of noise. People shouted and laughed, seagulls screamed overhead, and Christmas turkeys and geese added their cries to the general hubbub. There was now no mistaking the imminence of the festive season, it was there in the traditional yule log cakes on a stall, and the carols the women sang as they carried baskets of fish from the returning fleet.

Emily's continuing boredom was only too apparent as she sat sulkily on an upturned basket. Geoffrey left Lucy at a stall to go over to the angel.

"You're behaving very disagreeably, miss."

She lowered her eyes. "I'm sorry, Geoffrey, it's just that I haven't got anything to do."

"I've got something for you to do."

Her eyes brightened.

"You may not like it," he warned, "because it means going ahead of us to London."

"But I don't want to go anywhere without you," she protested.

"I know, but it's really quite important. You see, I'd like to find what your Uncle Robert has been up to. I don't know what I want you to look for exactly, just get the lay of the land, so to speak."

"But you must have some idea what you want me to do."

"No, truly I don't. Just keep your eyes and ears open."

She sighed. "Oh, all right, but how will I find you again?"

He hesitated. "Well, I'd like to drive straight to London when we land, but it's a five or six hour journey, and after traveling overnight this side of the Channel, both Lucy and I will be very tired. I think it's best we spend the night in Brighton and then leave early tomorrow morning. There's only one main road to the capital, so you're bound to see us." He smiled. "After all, you can't fail to recognize the carriage after all this time."

"That's true. I'll go then." She fluttered up to kiss his cheek, and for a moment he was sure he felt her, but then she'd gone.

He turned to find Lucy had come over to join him, and had heard at least some of what he'd said to Emily. "So we're to spend tonight in Brighton, are we?" she asked.

He nodded. "At my sister's house."

Her lips parted. "I-I didn't know you had a sister."

"Only one. Susannah. She's married to Lord Hugh De Carteret, a very close friend indeed of the Prince of Wales, and they have a rather grand residence near the Royal Pavilion on the Steine in Brighton. To be truthful, I don't even know if they'll be at home, for they're usually invited to wherever His Royal Highness happens to be, but even if they're away, we'll be able to use their house."

Lucy lowered her eyes. "Such grand circles," she murmured.

"Not too grand for you," he replied, pressing his lips to her cheek.

She looked at him. "You've got something on your mind, haven't you? Something about Robert?"

He drew a reluctant breath. "Lucy, I don't want to worry you unduly."

"Tell me," she insisted.

"Well, when we reach London, Robert's hardly likely to admit any charges we may lay against him, and we'll have no proof of anything we say. Dorothea is dead, and James has vanished, so we have nothing to support our story that there was a plot on your life. Nothing, that is, except an invisible angel!"

Lucy smiled. "But she *will* be visible, Geoffrey. She's going to appear to Grandfather and me at a church! Grandfather will believe us then," she said, putting her arms around him and resting her head on his shoulder.

He gazed toward the sea, his eyes still serious. "But until that happens, Robert will be a danger. When he realizes you're safe and well—"

A bell rang on board the Brighton packet to warn she was about to sail. Geoffrey caught Lucy's hand, and they hurried on board.

The afternoon sun was beginning to set when the English coast appeared ahead. It was bitterly cold, and the gathering clouds to the east heralded snow. The elegance of fashionable Brighton was perceptible from some distance out as Geoffrey and Lucy stood on the breezy deck. It seemed to take an age for the packet to heave to close to the shore, and when it dropped anchor, the sun had nearly gone. The pilot rowed out, and as some small boats followed to take the passengers ashore, the first snowflakes began to skim through the frozen air. The carriages and other heavy cargo couldn't be taken ashore yet, but would have to wait for flat-topped lighters to sail out on the high tide.

A cloaked man watched from the packet deck as Lucy and Geoffrey climbed down into one of the first boats. It was James Weybridge. He'd waited for their arrival at Dieppe, and had watched them during the crossing. He now knew that Lucy was Geoffrey's wife, and his bitterness was complete. In him, Robert Trevallion still had a willing and cunning accomplice. What Robert offered might not be as fine as the Trevallion fortune itself, but it was better than nothing.

James wanted revenge for the humiliation he'd suffered in France, and was prepared to carry out Robert's wishes to the letter. Lucy might have traveled this far and survived, but she still wouldn't reach London. He'd blotted the heavenly vision from his mind, convincing himself it had been nothing more than a hallucination. Nothing like that could possibly happen again. A chill smile played upon his lips as he glanced at Geoffrey's carriage on the deck nearby. Once it was ashore, there was only one route it would take to London, and somewhere along the way it would fall foul of a highwayman. He intended to see that the ambush that had failed in France, succeeded in England, and that this time Lucy died.

Christmas Eve or not, eager postilions stood for hire on the beach, and Geoffrey selected one who looked as tough as his immense leather boots. A price was agreed upon for the Christmas Day drive to London, and the postilion promised to bring the carriage to De Carteret House on the Steine at dawn. He then departed to the inn he worked out of. James had come ashore while Geoffrey and the postilion haggled a price, and so followed the little man as he left the beach to go to the Three Crowns, a thriving hostelry close to the Steine. Where Lucy and Geoffrey went now was of no consequence, for the postilion would take their carriage to them and then set off for London. All James needed to know was when that journey would commence, the rest was simple.

The joyous atmosphere and excitement of Christmas Eve was even more pervasive here than it had been in Dieppe. Carol singers stood on corners, their faces rosy in the light of lanterns, churches were bright with candles, and shop windows decked with evergreen garlands. Every carriage horse sported a sprig of holly on its bridle, every coachman had a buttonhole of mistletoe, and passing stagecoaches were fully laden with people returning to their families for the season. Villa doors were decorated with red-ribboned holly wreaths, and hardly a window was curtained or shuttered, so that the whole town seemed bright with lights, but James was oblivious to it all as he kept the diminutive postilion in view along the crowded pavements.

He saw him go through the Three Crowns' yard to the kitchens, where the servants were making as much merry as they could on such a busy night. To the playing of a fiddle, a fat coachman was singing "Deck the Halls with Boughs of Holly," and everyone joined in the nonsensical chorus. "Fa la la la la, la la la la!"

Like the guests in the main dining room, they'd enjoyed a fine meal of roast goose with all the trimmings, and the punch bowl gracing their table had already been replenished several times. A fire blazed in the huge hearth, and every seat was occupied by smiling maids and waiters.

The light snow became heavier, and the air and ground were

cold enough for the flakes to begin to settle as James watched the postilion down several cups of punch. When he thought the man might prove sufficiently unguarded, he went into the busy room. No one paid any attention to him as he made his way over to the little man.

"It's Jacko, isn't it?" he said conversationally, taking a cup of punch from a tray on the table.

The postilion looked blankly at him. "No, Harry's the name. Do I know you?"

"You clearly don't remember me. I hired you last summer."

The man shrugged. "I get a lot of fares."

"I was hoping to hire you again. I need to get to London tomorrow."

"I'd like to oblige, but you're too late. I'm already taken, by a lord, no less."

"A lord, eh?"

The postilion nodded. "Lord St. Athan. He and his lady are to leave at first light."

"Ah, well, I'll have to find someone else," James murmured.

"There's Old Sam over there, he'll be glad to—"

"I have someone in mind," James interrupted, and turned to go.

"Oh, right you are then. The compliments of the season to you, sir."

"And to you."

James adjourned to the writing room at the inn to write a very important letter. To Robert Trevallion.

"Brighton, Christmas Eve. Sir. Things have not gone entirely to plan. First, it is my sad duty to tell you that my dear sister Dorothea has drowned in a tragic accident, so now you must rely upon me alone to carry out your wishes. Lucy Trevallion lives, and what's more, is now the Countess of St. Athan, which puts up the price of accomplishing her murder. St. Athan and his new bride will set off for London at dawn, and in the guise of highwayman, I mean to lie in wait at Mary's Cross . . ."

He paused to smile to himself. Mary's Cross was one of the most isolated spots on the London-to-Brighton road. Deep in woodland, it was several miles from the nearest house, and was the frequent haunt of "gentlemen of the road."

He dipped the quill in the ink, and continued to write. " . . . at Mary's Cross, where I will put an end to your niece. If you wish your part in the plot on her life to remain a secret, you had best prepare to pay me much more than at present agreed. Line my pocket sufficiently, and your villainy will be hidden forever. I will call upon you in due course. —J.W."

Quickly he sealed the note, pressed his monogrammed signet ring into the soft wax, and then went out into the yard. It was seven o'clock, and the Sussex Flyer stagecoach was on the point of departure. James slipped the guard some coins to deliver the message to Robert Trevallion, then he strolled away from the inn to find a livery stable at which to hire a good saddle horse. After that he went to procure a *belle de nuit* with whom to share the rest of Christmas Eve. No woman could compensate for Lucy's untasted charms, but she'd serve his purpose.

The Sussex Flyer swept noisily out of the Three Crowns' yard, its horn wavering to the notes of "God Rest Ye Merry, Gentlemen." Fifty-five miles of road lay ahead, hazardous miles in the snow which now fell heavily, but the coach was renowned for its timekeeping. Barring mishaps—or highwaymen—it would reach Blossoms Inn, in the city of London, at half past midnight.

While James followed the postilion from the beach, Geoffrey procured a hackney coach to convey Lucy and himself to De Carteret House. They'd passed James on the way, but hadn't known it was he.

The hackney coach drove quickly through the falling snow toward the Steine, and then past the Prince Regent's brilliantly illuminated residence, the Royal Pavilion. Lanterns adorned every tree in the royal grounds, and were fixed all along the building itself. From the number of lights, and the military band playing seasonal tunes on the front lawns, it was clear the prince was in residence, although the absence of a crush of elegant carriages at the door suggested he was elsewhere on this particular evening.

De Carteret House stood a little further on, its pristine white facade gazing splendidly over the open grassy area that formed the center of the Steine. There were few lights in the windows, and, like the Pavilion, there were no carriages at the door. Geoffrey knew in an instant that his sister and brother-in-law weren't at home, but were probably with the prince, wherever he was.

The hackney coach halted, and Geoffrey climbed swiftly down, leaving Lucy in the carriage as he went to the door, where a large holly wreath shone in the light of an overhead lamp. The sound of the military band by the Pavilion carried clearly on the crisp air. They were playing "Hark! The Herald Angels Sing!" He smiled a little, for closer than that, in the servants' quarters of the house, he could hear some rather raucous singing. "Good King Wenceslaus," if he wasn't mistaken. Dear Lord, if ever a carol lent itself to drunken, tone-deaf bawling, that one did. Clearly, the servants were taking full advantage of their master and mistress's absence. He'd be lucky if they heard him knocking!

He rapped at the door. The light night breeze stirred the ribbons of the holly wreath as the knocks echoed through the house, but the singing continued unabated. He rapped again, more imperatively this time, and the singing stopped in abrupt dismay. He could almost hear the consternation below stairs. Who was it? Had Lord Hugh and Lady Susannah returned early to find their servants in an advanced state of yuletide intoxication?

He heard steps hurrying across the entrance hall, and then a rather disheveled footman opened the door. The man recognized the caller at once. "Lord St. Athan!" he cried disconcertedly, for although it wasn't Lord Hugh and Lady Susannah, her ladyship's brother was the next worst thing!

"The same. How are you, Stowell?" Geoffrey inquired cordially, although the question was somewhat superfluous, given the aroma of hot mince pies and rumfustian wafting from the direction of the kitchens.

"Well, my lord, very well indeed." The footman's face was crimson with flusterment as he belatedly did up the buttons of his coat. He almost gulped with relief when Lanyon, the butler, appeared at his side.

The butler was commendably cool under the circumstances. He bowed low to Geoffrey. "Why, my lord, how very pleasing it is to see you again after all this time."

"Yes, I'll warrant it is, Lanyon," Geoffrey murmured, hiding a smile.

"I fear Lord Hugh and Lady Susannah aren't at home tonight, sir; they have accompanied His Royal Highness to a ball at Arundel castle, and won't be returning until tomorrow afternoon."

"Well, I trust my wife and I are permitted the use of the house until the morning?"

The butler's jaw dropped. "Your-your wife, my lord?"

"That's what I said."

"I, er . . . Yes, of course, my lord. This house is always at your disposal."

Leaving the two servants to glance at each other in astonishment, Geoffrey returned to the hackney coach to assist Lucy down. He smiled and squeezed her fingers reassuringly. "Your first meeting with Susannah and Hugh must wait, for they are in darkest Arundel until some time tomorrow, by which time we'll be well on our way to London. However, the house is ours tonight, although I fear we've ruined the staff's Christmas Eve festivities."

She was nervous as he escorted her up the steps, but she managed a gracious smile as the two servants bowed low. The entrance hall chandeliers were dazzling, and the seasonal aromas from the kitchens vied with the scent of pine from the evergreens decking the walls. A kissing bough was suspended from the center of the ceiling, and it turned slowly in the draft as Stowell closed the door.

Geoffrey halted directly beneath the bough, and smiled into Lucy's eyes as he bent his head to kiss her in front of the servants. Color flushed into her cheeks, and she lowered her eyes as he turned to the butler.

"Let's not beat about the bush, Lanyon. It's clear our arrival has interrupted your, er, revelry, but I assure you my wife and I have no desire to put a damper on the proceedings. All we require is something warming to eat and drink, and the principal guest room to be made ready. After that, your Christmas Eve is your own again, and neither Lord Hugh nor Lady De Carteret will learn of the, er, boisterous goings-on below stairs."

The butler was relieved. "Thank you, my lord. I'll see that a suitable dinner is served immediately."

"In the guest room," Geoffrey said steadily.

"The guest room?" Dinner in a bedroom? The butler was taken back at such a shocking thing.

"That's what I said."

"Whatever you desire, my lord."

"And inform my sister's maid she is to attend Lady St. Athan."

"My lord."

But Lucy put her hand on Geoffrey's arm and shook her head. "It's Christmas Eve, Geoffrey. Leave the maid be; I can attend myself tonight."

Smiling, he looked into her eyes and whispered so only she could hear. "No, madam, *I* will attend you tonight," he promised.

The footman was dispatched to the kitchens to issue orders for dinner above stairs, while the butler relieved the new arrivals of their outer garments and then bore the clothes off to be cleaned of salt from the sea crossing. A moment or so later, two maids and a kitchen boy hurried upstairs with a coal scuttle to tend the guest room fire.

Thirty-five

As Emily reached London, it was still light, and had begun to snow lightly. She flew invisibly along Piccadilly, which was thronged with vehicles and people doing the last of their Christmas shopping. She was excited by so much noise and bustle. Oh, how she loved this time of year!

She slowed to peep in a toy shop window that was so full it seemed it must burst at the seams, and all the dolls, toy soldiers, rocking horses, dolls' houses, and spinning tops tumble out into the street. Her longing gaze was drawn to a dark-haired Parisian doll dressed in rose satin. Emily sighed wistfully. Oh, how she'd have loved such a doll. She'd call her Natalie, or Noelle, because it was Christmas.

With another sigh, the angel glided on, pausing again only when she reached one of London's finest confectionery shops, where there was a mouth-watering array of chocolate and candy. She saw a spun-sugar stocking filled with brightly colored bonbons, holly leaves made of icing, and a large basket of marzipan angels. She pressed her face to the glass, wishing she could sample everything. It would even be worth being sick afterward, she thought, recalling a Christmas when she'd eaten far too many sugar mice.

She continued toward Mayfair, and the sounds of Christmas seemed to accompany her. Hawkers jostled people to buy mistletoe and holly, and children tried to sell simple evergreen wreaths made the night before. There were carol singers on the corner of St. James's Street, a man selling hot mince pies by the gates of Devonshire House, and a group of pretty young actresses shivering in an open barouche as they handed out leaflets about the annual pantomime.

Leaving Piccadilly behind, Emily flew north over Mayfair to Berkeley Square. She paused among the trees in the central garden to gaze across at her grandfather's house, where the windows were decorated with evergreens and the door had a particularly large holly wreath. The door opened suddenly, and Robert emerged, wearing his dark green greatcoat and Hessian boots. He drew on his gloves, tilted his hat at a rakish angle, and then crossed the square, his ivory-handled cane swinging casually to and fro.

Emily drew uneasily back among the trees as he passed. She knew he couldn't harm her now, but she was still afraid of him. As soon as he'd turned the corner into Berkeley Street, she looked at the house again, wondering if her grandfather was in. She fluttered to the drawing room window, which was liberally decked with evergreens, and saw him asleep in his favorite fireside chair. She glided through the glass. It was warm inside, and more greenery was festooned around the walls and mantelpiece.

Edwin had fallen asleep after a good luncheon, followed by two glasses of cognac. There was a knitted shawl around his shoulders, and a tasseled cap on his head, and in his lap lay the miniature of Emily he'd been looking at when he dozed off.

The little angel knelt at his side, her hands and chin on the arm of the chair. "I wish you knew I was here, Grandfather," she said.

He didn't move, except to sigh in his sleep.

Emily gazed fondly at him. "Lucy will be here soon, and so will Geoffrey. You'll like them both, I know you will. I wonder what you'll think of having a countess for a granddaughter?" She lowered her eyes. "Uncle Robert's going to be furious—at least, I hope he is. I hope he's so angry he explodes," she added unangelically.

She knelt there for a little longer. She wasn't sure exactly what Geoffrey wanted her to do. There wasn't anything happening here, and wouldn't be until Uncle Robert returned, which might not be for hours. Maybe she'd be able to tell more when she saw him with Grandfather. In the meantime, she'd have to pass the time somehow.

She stretched and yawned, suddenly feeling very sleepy indeed. Perhaps it was the warmth of the fire after coming so far in the winter air. She rose from her knees, smiling suddenly. She'd sleep in her own bed, but first she'd see if Nettie was still here.

The angel glided down through the house, and heard an attempt at singing as she neared the kitchens. The servants were trying to celebrate Christmas Eve, but their hearts weren't in it, and the carol died raggedly away after one verse. She found them seated around the table, their faces lit by the two-branched candlestick which now replaced the fast-fading light outside. There was a little holly around the fireplace and windows, a bunch of mistletoe hanging from the ceiling, and the cook had made a jug of mulled wine, but there was a glaring absence of any festive spirit.

Nettie wasn't with the others, but was seated alone on the settle by the fire. Her face was sad as she glanced toward the table. "Christmas is horrid this year, isn't it? How can we celebrate anything when poor Miss Emily is hardly cold in her grave?"

"Mr. Robert finds it easy enough," the cook said bluntly, pouring herself some more wine. She was a plump middle-aged woman who shone with health, as befitted a person of her profession.

Everyone shifted uncomfortably, and the butler gave her a warning look. "It's not wise to make such observations, Mrs. Brown."

"Maybe not, Mr. Fairley, but it's only what each and every person here is thinking."

Nettie got up. "Yes, it is. We know Mr. Robert wasn't grief-stricken when Miss Emily died, and I'd lay all my wages that he's hoping there'll be bad news of Miss Lucy as well."

The butler was rattled. "Nettie, you really must not—"

"But it's true, Mr. Fairley," the maid interrupted.

Emily nodded earnestly. "Yes, it is! Oh, how it is!"

Nettie wiped a tear from her eye. "I loved Miss Emily, and I miss her dreadfully. It's just not the same now she's gone, and as for poor Mr. Edwin . . . "

The angel could bear no more. Gliding down to the maid, she pressed a loving kiss to Nettie's unknowing head, and then flew from the kitchens, up through the house to her old bedroom, where she curled up on the coverlet and folded her wings to sleep. The last thing she thought of before drifting off was the beautiful Parisian doll in the toy shop window.

In the drawing room, Edwin began to dream. He was with Emily again. They were building a snowman on the terrace at Trevallion Park. Oh, such a snowman, tall and fat, with coals for eyes and a carrot nose. And then they threw snowballs at their icy creation. Emily squealed with laughter, not seeming to notice the cold. Something puzzled him. He didn't remember the rose satin clothes she was wearing. How very Parisian she looked.

Confusion penetrated his sleep, and he awoke with a start. The dream threaded away, but he could still remember it. He picked up the miniature and pressed it to his trembling lips. "Oh, Emily, my dearest child," he whispered, unable to stem the tears that began to well from his tired eyes.

Then he leaned his head back. How he missed his little granddaughter; her loss filled his heart to bursting. But there was still room to love Lucy as well. Where was she? It was Christmas Eve, and still there wasn't any news.

Emily was awakened at midnight by the joyous pealing of Christmas bells. She fluttered to the window. It was snowing heavily, and everything was white. The bells rang loudly over the capital. What a lovely sound they made, she thought, glancing up at the sky. Somewhere up there, far beyond the earthly world, she knew the angels were singing.

The front door of the house closed, and she glided out onto the landing to look down into the entrance hall. Robert had just come back. His coat and hat were covered with snow as the butler took them, and his boots left wet prints as he ascended the stairs.

Emily wanted to fly away and hide, but something made her stay. She looked at his face, its expression so hard and dissatisfied in repose, and then at his hazel eyes, so bereft of any warmth. She shivered as she felt the draft of his passing, for it was as if he'd brought the ice of the night in with him. She followed him into the drawing room, where her grandfather was reading.

The old man took off his spectacles and turned hopefully as his stepson entered. "Is there any news of Lucy?"

"None at all," Robert replied, going to pour some cognac.

"I'd so hoped to see her for Christmas," Edwin said sorrowfully.

Behind his back, Robert smiled. "You're not going to see her at all, you old fool," he breathed.

Emily looked hatefully at him, but he was oblivious as he picked up his glass and went to sit opposite his stepfather. "Well, I suppose it's time to wish you a happy Christmas, Father," he said, raising his drink.

"I wish you the same, my boy."

"Father . . . "

"Yes?"

"Forgive me for broaching a delicate topic, but the possibility must be accepted that . . . I mean, it has to be faced that Lucy might not complete the journey safely."

Edwin drew back. "Don't suggest such a thing, I beg you."

"But Father, it's been a long time without word. The journey from Switzerland is far from easy; something might have happened to her, and to the Weybridges as well."

Emily scowled. Oh, yes, and you'd know all about things happening to poor Lucy, wouldn't you!

Edwin was distressed. "Please, Robert, I don't wish to discuss such a prospect. I want Lucy to be here so that I may right all the wrongs I did her poor father."

"But, Father—"

"No!" Edwin's tone was unexpectedly strong and there was no mistaking the flash of spirit in his glance.

"I'm sorry, Father, I didn't mean to upset you," Robert said unctuously, but his eyes were as cold as flint.

Edwin quelled his anger. "No, I am the one who should apologize. I know you have my best interests at heart, and that there is some foundation for your anxiety over Lucy. All I can say is that when I have no more reason to hope for her safety, I will honor my promise to you. Then you will become my heir, Robert, but not until then."

Robert fell silent. Damn the old dodderer for his sentimentality. Dear little Lucy should by now have followed her cousin to the grave, but nothing was known for certain. Why in God's name hadn't he heard from Dorothea, or her reprobate brother?

Edwin resumed his reading, and Robert leaned his head back, gazing at the Christmas garlands along the mantelshelf. Emily hesitated. She still wasn't sure whether she'd found out the sort of thing Geoffrey wanted to know. She could report that her grandfather was still waiting for Lucy, hoping to make her his heir, and that Robert was continuing to do all he could to gain the inheritance for himself. In short, everything was the same as it had been when last she'd been in this house. And yet . . . The angel was conscious of a strange sixth sense telling her not to go to Brighton yet. Something important was going to happen, and she should be here to see what it was.

Edwin nodded to sleep over his book, and after several more cognacs, Robert began to snore in his chair. The fire burned low, and time passed slowly, the silence broken hourly by the pealing of the Christmas bells.

Dawn approached, and Emily sat on the windowsill, her arms clasped around her knees, her wings folded neatly. Something made her glance out her window, and she saw a man crossing the snowy square. By the light of a street lamp she saw that he wore the wide-brimmed hat and caped coat of a stagecoachman or guard. He was coming to the house. Her sixth sense surged more strongly, and she knew this was what she'd been waiting for.

The guard from the Sussex Flyer was tired and disgruntled. The journey from Brighton had taken longer than usual because of the snow, and the last thing he'd wanted after that was to trudge four miles across London to deliver a letter. Still, money was money. He strode up to the door, and knocked loudly. The sound thundered through the silent house.

Edwin didn't stir, but Robert sat up sharply. The butler grumbled as he lit a candle and went downstairs in his nightshirt and dressing gown. After a moment he returned, and tapped discreetly on the drawing room door before entering. Edwin still didn't wake up as Robert was given the note James had sent from Brighton.

Emily glided curiously over as the butler withdrew again. Who was the letter from? It must be important to be delivered in the middle of the night. She peered over Robert's shoulder as he broke the seal and began to read. Then her lips parted in dismay. James Weybridge again! And he planned to kill Lucy! Oh, no! She pressed trembling hands to her cheeks, her green eyes round with horror.

Robert's face darkened incredulously as he read. A nerve flickered at his temple, and his furious fingers closed over the note, crushing it into a tight ball. To Dorothea's demise he gave not a second thought, but news of Lucy's survival twisted him with fury. Not only was the creature still alive, but she'd become the Countess of St. Athan! And Weybridge was demanding more to eliminate her! It was blackmail, but he had no option. Lucy had to die, and Weybridge was prepared to do it.

He tossed the letter at the fire and strode from the room. But the letter didn't burn. Instead, it struck the fender and rolled beneath Edwin's chair.

Emily lingered only a moment. It was dawn outside now, and the note said that that was when Lucy and Geoffrey were to leave Brighton. James was going to lie in wait at Mary's Cross, but where was Mary's Cross? If it was near Brighton, she might be too late to warn them. Oh, please don't let that be so! She fled out into the cold Christmas morning air.

Thirty-six

Lucy and Geoffrey had too much on their minds to sleep well at De Carteret House, and had decided to set off for London before dawn. Word was sent to the Three Crowns, and the rather vexed postilion brought the carriage. The snow was six inches deep, but the horses were fresh and pulled the vehicle easily up the long climb out of Brighton toward the Downs.

A lone horseman passed them, but they didn't notice him particularly. He knew them, though, for he recognized the carriage. James had also left Brighton early, just in case something of this kind should happen. For a moment he considered holding them up there and then, but soon changed his mind. It was too open here, with a few houses from where he might be seen. Better to wait until the thick woodland and complete isolation of Mary's Cross. So he urged his horse on.

He seemed to have been riding a long time before he reached the forest ridge, where a sea of pine, birch, and larch stretched away into the grayness of the Christmas dawn. There was no wind at all, and the branches overhanging the crossroad were bowed low beneath their burden of snow. It was believed that the place got its name because a young woman named Mary had hanged herself here after a broken love affair, and was buried beneath the signpost, but the truth was very different. In Saxon times, a cross dedicated to the Virgin Mary had stood where the two ancient roads met. Over the centuries it had fallen down through neglect, and now lay buried and forgotten just beneath the thick undergrowth at the side of the road.

James moved his horse into the concealment of the trees, where he dismounted. After brushing the snow from his hat and shoulders, he examined the pistol he'd purchased in Brighton. It seemed in perfect working order, but one never knew. He fired once into the air. The shot dislodged some snow from a branch, and the report reverberated across the forest. Smiling, he recharged the weapon and put it back in his pocket, then he drank

from a flask of strong liquor, before leaning back against one of
the tree trunks to wait.

He'd only been there five minutes when he was startled to hear
a carriage approaching. They couldn't be here just yet! Then he
realized the sound came from the London direction. It was a
stagecoach, its lamp cutting through the strange half-light of
dawn as the coachman urged his flagging team past. James caught
a glimpse of its name on the red-lacquered door. The Brighton
Flying Machine. It vanished among the trees, making for the Red
Lion, Handcross, and silence returned.

James leaned his head back again, and closed his eyes. His
nerves were at fever pitch now, and he wanted it over and done
with. Come on, damn you.

At last he heard a vehicle approaching from the Brighton direction. At first he couldn't see anything, but then came the flash of
carriage lamps between the trees. He waited, and at last saw the
postilion urging the horses along. It was the fellow from the
Three Crowns! A slow smile of relief spread across James's face.
The waiting was over, and the serious business of highway robbery could commence. Tying a large kerchief over the lower part
of his face, he remounted and took his pistol out in readiness.

In the carriage, Lucy was cozy in the new cloak bought in
Auxerre. Lined with quilted scarlet silk and made of pine-green
wool, it had white fur around the hood and hem. It was very
French, and far grander than any she'd possessed before. Geoffrey had his arm around her as her head rested against his shoulder, and she was thinking about her grandfather. The possibility
of another ambush couldn't have been further from her mind, but
suddenly history seemed to be repeating itself as a shot rang out
and the carriage swerved to a sharp halt.

But this time it was an English voice that rang out harshly into
the darkness. "Stand and deliver! Your money or your life!"

Lucy's breath caught in fear, and Geoffrey gave a low curse,
reaching under the seat for the pistol hidden there.

Lucy's eyes widened. "Oh, do be careful!"

In reply, he took her hand and pressed it briefly to his lips, and
then checked the pistol.

They heard the postilion's frightened tone. "Let us pass, for this
is the king's highway!"

"Hold your tongue!" the highwayman replied.

The postilion knew the voice. " 'Ere, you're the cove what
came to the inn!"

"Silence!" the highwayman shouted, and then turned his attention to the occupants of the carriage. "Get out!"

Geoffrey's eyes hardened to flint, for although the voice was disguised, he recognized it too. "Weybridge!" he breathed incredulously.

Lucy's gaze flew to his face. "Are-are you sure?"

"I'd know him anywhere." Geoffrey cocked the pistol in readiness.

James grew impatient. "Get out now, or I'll kill the postilion!"

Slowly, Geoffrey opened the carriage door and alighted.

James's eyes glittered hatefully, their shine visible in the glow of the carriage lamps. "Both of you," he said, gesturing toward Lucy with the pistol.

She began to obey, but Geoffrey seized the moment, snatching his pistol from his coat, taking swift aim, and firing.

But the shot went an inch or so wide, whining so close past James's head he felt its draft. Fury erupted through him, and he leveled his own weapon at Geoffrey to fire back.

His aim was worse, but luck was on his side. The shot glanced off one of the carriage lamps and plunged into Geoffrey's arm, making him stagger backward and drop his weapon. In a second, James recharged his pistol and directed it toward Lucy. She was at his mercy now; all he had to do was squeeze the trigger, and Lucy, Countess of St. Athan, would be no more.

But help was near. Emily was flying toward Brighton as swiftly as she could. She was approaching Mary's Cross when she heard the first shot echo through the dawn. She halted, turning this way and then that as she tried to tell from which direction the sound had come. The second shot pierced the frozen air, then she saw the crossroad and the carriage lamps. Instinct told her whose carriage it was, and with a dismayed cry she darted down toward the scene. Please don't let Lucy be already dead!

In a blur, she saw her cousin's frightened face, framed with the rich white fur of her new cloak, and Geoffrey leaning weakly against the carriage, his face contorted with pain as he clutched his bleeding arm, but then her attention focused solely upon James as he raised the recharged pistol toward Lucy's heart.

The little angel was desperate, and screamed out to Geoffrey. "Geoffrey, I'm here! I'm here! But I can't do anything!"

His face was ashen, and he was only just clinging to consciousness as the agony from the wound thundered through him like the beating of drums, but he heard her. Hope surged through him as his gaze swung toward the dazzlingly bright child gliding distractedly down from the sky, but he was in too much pain to do anything except call her name. "Emily!"

The single word was all the others heard, and Lucy's frightened eyes fled hopefully to his face. Was the little angel here?

James's attention was momentarily diverted, and in that second the angel flew furiously at his face, but to no avail, for she passed right through him. He felt nothing at all, and her impetus carried her to the far side of the crossroad. Then something miraculous happened, for she halted directly above the buried cross and immediately felt its power sweep over her like a burst of sunlight. She began to glow intensely, her exultant brilliance lighting the darkness like a great flame. Her dazzling golden splendor radiated over the crossroad, filtering between the trees as she was revealed in all her holy glory.

The light was blinding, and James whirled about with a terrified gasp, but the grimmest of smiles played upon Geoffrey's ashen lips. "That's my girl," he whispered, gazing fondly at the brave little angel.

Tears sprang to Lucy's eyes as she stared at her cousin. "Oh, Emily," she breathed.

The stunned postilion could only gape at the apparition. "Oh, my Gawd," he muttered, hastily crossing himself, trying to recall prayers he hadn't uttered for far too long, and at the same time endeavoring to keep control of his suddenly restive team, which shifted nervously.

James was transfixed. It was happening again! Just as at St. Roch's church! His horse began to rear and plunge in fright as both it and its rider felt the angel's intensely disapproving force begin to raise the dread specter of hell and damnation. Abject terror gripped James so completely that he lost balance as his horse plunged again. With a cry he fell to the snow, and the pistol was knocked from his grasp as the horse galloped off into the darkness.

The weapon skimmed to within a few yards of Lucy, and she ran to pick it up. Then she held it in both hands and directed it toward James. "Don't move, or I swear I'll fire," she cried, her voice trembling.

He remained motionless, far more terrified of Emily than any pistol.

Emily was in tears as she shone. She'd saved Lucy again! She'd been all that a guardian angel should, and heavenly approval was all around her. The other angels had come, their voices filling the dawn with sweetness. The beautiful staircase was before her, leading far up into the heavens to the dazzling white light at the top. She could see the wonderful glittering gates, and her parents beckoning. Her task must be complete! She could go to them now!

The angels gathered her in their arms and began to draw her up the staircase. She gazed back at Lucy and smiled, for she knew she'd see her cousin again, and her grandfather, for He had said so. She flew upward with her heavenly companions, and the further they flew, the dimmer their light to those below. Soon they were little more than the glimmer of a distant star, and then that too vanished.

Lucy was suddenly conscious of how grim and cold the dawn was. Emily's departure left an echoing emptiness, through which there suddenly came the rattle of an approaching carriage. She collected her wits. James offered no threat now, for he was still paralyzed with dread, but she kept the pistol upon him anyway. Her anxious glance fled to Geoffrey, and to her dismay she saw he was slipping into unconsciousness.

Alarm electrified her, and she called to the postilion. "I don't care what vehicle it is that's coming—I want you to stop it! We need help!"

The little man scrambled from his horse and ran out into the road, waving his arms desperately. "Stop! Stop, for Christ's s—" He broke off and looked apologetically up at the sky. "Forget I said that," he whispered.

The coachman of the approaching two-horse chaise reined in suspiciously, for Mary's Cross was too notorious to take chances. He reached for the shotgun he always kept handy, but then he saw Lucy and the other carriage. What was it? An accident?

The chaise's single occupant leaned out. He was a young naval officer going home on leave from his frigate in Portsmouth, and his name was Lieutenant, the Honorable Michael Concarn. "What is it, Welch?" he asked.

"I'm not sure, sir. It looks like a carriage mishap."

The postilion ran up to them. "Please help! Lord St. Athan's been shot!"

"Shot? Great God above!" Lieutenant Concarn jumped down and hurried over to Lucy, who had knelt to take Geoffrey's head in her lap as he at last collapsed.

They didn't want to risk James's getting away, and together with the lieutenant's coachman, tied him up with a length of rope from the chaise boot. The prisoner was then bundled unceremoniously into the same boot and left like a trussed chicken among the lieutenant's luggage and the Christmas presents he was taking home to his family.

After a careful examination of Geoffrey's wound, Lieutenant Concarn realized it would only be life-threatening if not properly attended to without further delay. He looked urgently at Lucy. "We must get him to my home; it's only two miles along the road, and as luck would have it, my uncle's spending Christmas there. He's the finest physician in London. Maybe you've heard of him? Sir Stephen Concarn?"

Lucy hadn't, but she managed a rather wobbly smile. "Just save my husband's life," she whispered.

He put a reassuring hand on her arm. "We will, have no fear of that, Lady St. Athan. Leave it all to me. Oh, by the way, I'm Lieutenant Michael Concarn, of His Majesty's frigate *Angel*."

Angel? Lucy wanted to laugh. But instead she burst into tears and hid her face in her hands.

The gates of heaven swung open before Emily, and the wonderful singing seemed to fill her entire being as she glided toward the paradise she'd been so longing for. Her parents and other beloved figures came out to welcome her, stretching forth their hands to draw her inside. The air rang with carols and hosannas, and beyond it all she was sure she could hear the soft sound of a newborn child.

Her little heart surged as she saw the image of the Nativity, with Joseph watching on as the Virgin Mary leaned tenderly over the manger where Baby Jesus lay in the hay. She saw the star of Bethlehem, the three wise men, the shepherds, and all the glory of the first Christmas.

She was filled with awe, for it was so very beautiful, but suddenly she was filled with reluctance to go through the gates. She wanted to see things to their conclusion on earth. It wasn't enough to know she'd see Lucy and her grandfather again; she needed to witness Uncle Robert's downfall. She wouldn't be sure her task was really complete until that happened. And she was anxious about Geoffrey.

The little angel gazed anxiously through the gates. "Please let me go back," she whispered.

She was conscious of an immense sense of understanding coming from the great light beyond the gates, and suddenly she felt herself falling, tumbling wildly through the air, further and further away from the light. Then her wings spread wide, and she began to glide. Something was guiding her through the darkness above the earth. No, it wasn't darkness, for she could see the rays of the sun creeping above the horizon. It was an hour past dawn, and Christmas morning was becoming brighter by the moment.

Her flight halted above a rambling old manor house set in a snowy park. It was a Tudor house, gabled and half-timbered, and to one side of it was a topiary garden that resembled a chess board. The household was still asleep, except for the first servants in the kitchens.

The little angel gazed down in puzzlement. Where was she? She'd never seen this house before. Then she saw two vehicles making their way along the curving drive. One was a chaise, the other Geoffrey's carriage!

Swiftly she swooped down toward the latter, where she found a dismaying scene. Geoffrey was still unconscious. He'd been placed carefully on the seat, with his head on Lucy's lap, but his face was now as white as the snow outside. Lucy was crying softly as she cradled him close, stroking his hair tenderly and willing him to live.

Lieutenant Concarn sat opposite, doing his best to offer what comfort he could, but he was uneasy at the amount of blood Geoffrey was still losing. He didn't know what to do if his uncle had changed his plans about coming to the country for Christmas. Please God, don't let that have happened.

Emily knelt on the carriage floor by Geoffrey. "Geoffrey, wake up, please!" she begged, but his eyes didn't even flicker.

The little angel looked helplessly at Lucy. "Oh, I do wish you could hear me, Lucy."

The vehicles drew to a halt outside the mansion door, and Lieutenant Concarn alighted to arouse the house. Within a minute, all was noise and confusion. Candlelight flickered as people hurried from their beds, and his little brothers and sisters peered curiously down through the bannisters at the top of the stairs to watch, until their nurse shooed them back to their beds, threatening to deny them their Christmas stockings.

To the lieutenant's relief, his uncle had indeed come for Christmas, so Geoffrey was carried up to a guest room, where his wound soon received the proper treatment.

While the lieutenant explained everything he knew to his father, a retired general, Lucy was taken in hand by his mother, plump and fair like her son, and by Sir Stephen's Spanish wife, Lady Concarn. They ushered her into the garlanded drawing room, where a huge yule log glowed in the hearth. There, with a restorative hot posset cup pressed into her hand, she haltingly told them all that had happened, although she prudently refrained from mentioning Emily. It might be Christmas, and the circumstances extenuating, but talk of a little guardian angel was still unlikely to be believed.

In the meantime, the lieutenant and his father had James hauled from the chaise boot and taken to the kitchens, where he confessed everything without prompting. They listened in horror to the tale of Robert Trevallion's wickedness, of attempted murder, death by drowning, dishonor, and covetousness, and the moment he'd finished, a rider was sent to Crawley town to bring the constables. Then James was locked in the buttery with paper, quill, and ink, to write a full account of the horrid tale, and after that to await his fate.

After that, the lieutenant insisted on riding the remaining thirty or so miles to Berkeley Square to inform Edwin what had happened, and to lay charges of conspiracy to murder against Robert Trevallion. He set off on the fastest horse in his father's stables. The sun was bright now, and church bells echoed over the snowy landscape.

Emily wanted to accompany him, but first needed to know that Geoffrey was well. Lucy kept anxious vigil at his bedside, and the little angel knelt to whisper a prayer. "Dear God, *please* make Geoffrey better again. For my sake, and for Lucy's, because we both love him so much." She lowered her hands, and then hastily put them together again. "Amen," she added.

Heartstopping moments passed, but then Geoffrey stirred slightly. His eyes opened and he smiled at his overjoyed wife. "Lucy, my darling . . . " he whispered.

Emily's soft wings fluttered as she rose from her knees. He saw her. "Emily? But I thought . . . "

But she'd gone, vanishing in a twinkling to go after Lieutenant Concarn.

Thirty-seven

The angel left behind a household that, in spite of overnight events, was full of seasonal excitement. The children squealed with delight as they delved into their Christmas stockings, and the indulgent adults looked on, relieved their painstakingly chosen gifts had proved successful. In the kitchens, what seemed to be the largest turkey in the world was being prepared, and an equally enormous plum pudding bubbled in a pan on the open fire.

Geoffrey was weak. Sometimes he was awake, and sometimes he slept, but Lucy remained with him. Occasionally she stood at the window, gazing over the English scene that was so comforting after the hazards of recent weeks.

There was a village adjacent to the manor house, with a parish church that was set among tall elms. Rooks soared noisily around the steeple, at the top of which shone a gilded weathercock. The churchyard was approached through a wicket gate in the topiary garden, and after breakfast, she saw the villagers walking through the snow to attend Christmas morning service. The Concarn family and most of their servants went too, forming an orderly "crocodile" across the formal garden toward the gate.

As the church bell ceased summoning everyone to prayer, and the distant sound of the first carol drifted through the window, Lucy's gaze turned toward the north, where London lay beyond the horizon. What would her grandfather say when Lieutenant Concarn told him what Robert had done? Would he believe his stepson was capable of such villainy? Would he accept the confession of a man like James Weybridge, and the word of a granddaughter he'd never met? Or would he stand by Robert? Oh, she knew Emily wanted to appear to her, and to Edwin, but what if the angel couldn't? What if Robert's infamy could never be proven?

Tears stung her eyes, and she returned to sit at Geoffrey's bedside. He was sleeping, his lashes very dark against his pale cheeks. She wished he were awake, for she needed his strength.

She took her book from the little table by the bed, but not even *La Nouvelle Héloïse* could console her. After staring blindly at the pages for several minutes, she closed it again and reached out to hold Geoffrey's hand.

But in London, before Lieutenant Concarn and his invisible heavenly companion arrived, events were under way that would expose Robert anyway, and it was his own carelessness that was to prove his undoing.

Come rain or shine, high day or holy day, it was his custom to take a daily ride in Hyde Park, and so he went out as usual about half an hour before Lieutenant Concarn and Emily arrived at Berkeley Square.

Below stairs at the house, the servants had drawn lots for the task of tending the fires on Christmas Day, and it was Nettie who proved unlucky. She'd kindled a fresh fire in the drawing room before the servants' breakfast, and afterward went up to put more coal on it. Robert had left on his ride, and Edwin was still in bed, so the room was deserted as she went in.

The scent of Christmas evergreens was strong in the warm air, and as she knelt before the fire, she sat back on her heels for a moment, gazing around the beautiful room. It was then that she noticed something round and white beneath Edwin's chair. Puzzled, she reached down to retrieve it, and saw it was a crumpled piece of paper.

She was about to toss it on the fire, but then hesitated and smoothed it out to see what it was. Mr. Fairley had been teaching her to read, so her eyes widened with shock as she scanned James's hastily written lines.

She got trembling to her feet, her glance flying to the mantelpiece clock. Had the ambush taken place? Was Miss Lucy already dead? She clasped the letter in both hands, uncertain what to do. Mr. Edwin had to be told, but she couldn't do it! Better to go to Mr. Fairley first! Gathering her skirts, she fled from the room.

She brought the kitchens to a standstill, and everyone crowded around the table as the appalled butler read the letter out. There were horrified gasps, and the cook came over so faint she had to be given a sip of brandy. Mr. Robert had had Miss Emily murdered, and then sent two wicked accomplices to Miss Lucy, who might have died this very Christmas morning?

Nettie looked tearfully at the butler. "What shall we do, Mr. Fairley?"

He got up and commenced buttoning his coat. "Mr. Edwin will

have to be told. I will go to him now." He straightened his cravat, placed the note on a silver salver, and carried it up through the house.

His face was grim as he passed Robert's door. If there was any justice in the world, Robert Waverly Trevallion would spend the coming night in a prison cell!

Edwin wasn't asleep, but stood by the window in his dressing gown and tasseled cap. Christmas morning without Lucy made him sad, but he summoned a smile as the butler entered.

"A merry Christmas to you, Fairley."

"And-and to you, sir," the butler replied hesitantly.

Edwin's smile faded. "What is it? Is something wrong?"

"I fear so, sir; indeed, something is gravely wrong. This letter was delivered to Mr. Robert last night." He avoided his employer's eyes as he held out the silver salver.

Edwin glanced at the creased paper, and then looked inquiringly at the butler. "Fairley, it isn't my custom to read Mr. Robert's correspondence."

"No, sir, but you should read this."

"Should?"

"Must, sir."

"You evidently consider it very serious."

"I do, sir."

The old man's stick tapped as he crossed to take the letter. He went to the mantlepiece for his spectacles, but as he prepared to read, Fairley spoke again.

"I think you should sit down to read it, sir."

Edwin looked at him in surprise. "Sit down?"

"Most certainly, sir, for the contents will come as a grave shock to you."

Slowly, Edwin did as the butler advised, and as he scanned the letter, his face grew very pale. "I-I cannot believe it," he whispered.

"I wish it were not so, sir, but it is definitely the note I gave to Mr. Robert; I recognize the writing. I believe he intended to burn it, but instead of falling in the fire, it rolled beneath your chair."

The old man got up a little shakily, and Fairley hurried to assist him, but was waved away. "No, no, I can manage."

"Is there anything you wish me to do, sir?"

"Yes, have my carriage brought to the door as quickly as possible."

"Your carriage, sir?"

"I must find out if anything happened at Mary's Cross. I must know if my, if Lucy . . . " Edwin couldn't finish.

Fairley made so bold as to put a comforting hand on his arm.

At that moment, they heard a horse coming swiftly around the square and clattering to a halt outside. Robert! But then there came a loud hammering at the door, and they looked at each other in surprise. Robert wouldn't knock like that, so who could it be?

Fairley hurried out, and a moment later a very windswept and cold Lieutenant Concarn was admitted, invisibly accompanied by Emily.

The angel fluttered anxiously around her grandfather. "You must believe the lieutenant!" she cried. "Oh, how I wish I could appear to you now, but I've been told it must be in a church, with Lucy there as well. So you *must* believe what you're told now, you simply must!"

Edwin didn't feel the draft of his little granddaughter's wings, or hear her desperate pleas. He received the lieutenant as politely as he could in the drawing room, although after the devastating letter, the last thing he felt like doing was talking to a complete stranger.

But as the lieutenant began his tale, Edwin's eyes lightened with relief. Lucy was well! And not only that, but James Weybridge had been captured and would give evidence against Robert. Edwin showed the lieutenant the incriminating letter, and then the old man's hands clenched into angry fists as he thought of his stepson. How could he ever have been so completely gulled by a creature like Robert Waverly Trevallion?

Another horse halted outside, and this time Robert was heard calling for a groom. Edwin raised his chin proudly, and without a word took his walking stick to go out onto the landing. The lieutenant accompanied him, and so did Emily. The angel was triumphant. This was the moment of Robert's downfall! The moment his sins came home to roost!

But as Robert entered the house, Nettie emerged from the kitchens. Finding herself face to face with the man she now knew to be responsible for killing little Emily, all her rage and anguish spilled out in a single accusing word.

"Murderer!" she cried.

Robert halted, his hazel eyes suddenly very bright and guarded. Then he saw Edwin and the lieutenant on the staircase, and in a second realized it was all up for him. In the space of a heartbeat he'd turned on his heel to run back outside. Lieutenant Concarn gave chase, but Robert was already in the saddle and spurring his horse away. The sound of hoofbeats was lost as London's bells began to peal again.

Nettie looked guiltily at Edwin. "Oh, forgive me, sir, I-I just couldn't help it. You see, I did so love Miss Emily."

He nodded understandingly. "We both did, my dear. Besides, perhaps it's for the best if my black-hearted stepson simply disappears, for I don't think I could endure the horror and scandal of a court case. Nothing can bring Emily back, and in spite of all the efforts of Robert and his accomplices, Miss Lucy is still alive."

Nettie gave a timid smile. "Alive, and a countess," she said.

"Yes, alive, and a countess," he agreed.

It was the late evening of Christmas Day when Edwin's traveling carriage arrived at Concarn Manor. Lieutenant Concarn was with him, and assisted him from the vehicle into the house. Emily, who'd been an invisible passenger, glided inside with them and went straight to Geoffrey's room.

He was propped up on a mound of pillows, and Lucy was with him. Lucy didn't see the angel enter, but as soon as an extra candle flickered into flame on the table next to the bed, Geoffrey knew she was close. Then suddenly she was there, kneeling on the bed beside him.

He smiled fondly. "Hello, Emily."

Lucy straightened. "Emily's here again?"

He nodded. "Where have you been, miss?" he asked the angel.

Emily's eyes shone with happiness. "It's all over at last, Geoffrey. Robert has had to run away because he was found out, and now my grandfather has arrived here to see Lucy. Isn't it wonderful?"

He stared at her. "It-it's *over*?" he repeated.

"Absolutely." She told him everything.

He relayed her words to Lucy, whose immediate smile of relief soon became a little nervous. "My grandfather's here?" she said then.

Emily fluttered up from the bed. "He's longing to see you, Lucy! Tell her, Geoffrey!"

Geoffrey did as he was told, and then looked at his anxious wife. "Go down to him, darling, for he is the reason you've come all this way."

She smoothed her skirts and composed herself before crossing to the door. Emily was going to go with her, but Geoffrey spoke sternly. "Not you, miss, for this is between Lucy and her grandfather. Your moment will come a little later."

Emily pouted. "Oh, but—"

"Do as you're told," he ordered.

The pout intensified, and Geoffrey suddenly began to laugh. "Oh, if only you knew how positively uncherubic you look right now!"

The angel scowled, but then began to laugh too. She flew back to the bed and flung her arms around him. Gently, he returned the embrace, but he couldn't feel anything.

Edwin had been shown into the library. Lieutenant Concarn took Lucy to the door, and left them alone. She hesitated, but at last found the courage to go inside. The room was lit by candles, and the shelves decorated with holly. Firelight flickered warmly, and she saw her grandfather standing before it, his slight figure a mere silhouette against the flames.

"Grandfather?"

"Oh, my dear . . . " He held out his hands, and she ran to him.

He held her tightly. "Lucy, my beloved girl, forgive me for failing your father, and thus failing you."

"I forgive you," she whispered, clinging to him.

They stood holding each other for several minutes, and then she drew slowly back. "Grandfather, there is something I must tell you. It concerns Emily. You see, she hasn't gone yet, not entirely, and tonight I think you and I will see her again."

Thirty-eight

It was just gone midnight when Lucy and her grandfather made their way by lanternlight to the church. The snow was deep all around, but the path had been cleared, and it was a cloudless, moonlit night, with the sound of owls wavering from the yew trees in the churchyard. Thousands of stars glittered in the heavens, and it seemed to Lucy that she could hear distant singing, beautiful singing, sweet and clear.

The church door groaned on its hinges. Edwin's stick tapped and their steps echoed as they walked down the aisle. Moonlight slanted in through the stained glass windows, lying softly over the altar, where a beautiful silver-gilt cross stood among gleaming candlesticks and plate.

Emily had been waiting for them, but now the moment was upon her, the little angel was afraid she might not be able to appear. She desperately wanted her grandfather to see her one more time, and know that she was happy, but it felt as if she wanted it too much.

She watched from the rafters as Lucy placed the lantern on the floor, and then took her grandfather's arm to wait before the altar, but still the angel hesitated.

Suddenly, a gentle, loving voice spoke at her side. "Go down, my darling child, for they will see and hear you."

"Mama?" The little angel's face brightened.

Her mother smiled fondly. "Yes, my dear, I'm here now, we're all here, and soon we'll take you with us."

Emily gazed beyond her and saw the shining host of angels. And she saw the gleaming staircase leading up through the church roof into the sky, where it ended in the blinding white light of the gates.

"Go, my child, for Lucy and your grandfather await," her mother urged, and Emily hesitated no more.

A candle on the altar burst into flame as she flew down and hovered before Lucy and Edwin. The holiness of the cross reached out to her like a helping hand, and she began to glow, at first just faintly, but then in a sunburst of light that seemed to fill the whole church.

The other angels sang, and Edwin gazed enraptured. "Emily," he whispered.

"Oh, Grandfather, I'm so happy you can see me," the little angel answered, tears of happiness on her cheeks.

"I've missed you so much, my dear."

"And I've missed you, but I'm not sad to be going to heaven. Everyone's waiting for me."

"Are you sure you're happy, my dear?" Edwin asked anxiously.

"Oh, yes, for I'll be with Mother and Father again. They'll take care of me." Emily lowered her eyes regretfully. "But I'm the only one you're allowed to see," she explained.

It was already time for her to go. Her mother was calling, and the shining staircase seemed to summon her too. "I have to leave you now, Grandfather."

"But—"

"I must go," she interrupted gently. "But remember that I love you, and that I'm happy now."

"Yes, my dear," he whispered.

The little angel looked at Lucy. "Good-bye, Lucy."

"Good-bye, Emily. And thank you so much."

Emily smiled, and glided away from the altar. The angels guided her gently to the staircase, and the sound of their wonderful singing seemed to reverberate through the night. The light was blindingly beautiful, but as Emily began to ascend the steps, so the light died slowly away. All too soon everything became silent, shadowy, and moonlit again.

But to Emily everything was still dazzlingly bright. She felt the joy and kindness of the other angels, felt the wonder of heaven, and as the gates opened before her, she flew gladly inside. She was a proper angel now; she'd carried out her allotted task, and done the best any little angel could.

In the church, Lucy and Edwin remained before the altar. The lantern, which seemed ineffectual while the angel was there, was now bright again.

Edwin turned to Lucy. "I-I never dreamed I would one day see a miracle, but I have tonight. She really is happy, isn't she?"

"Yes, Grandfather, she is."

"Then so am I."

She smiled and hugged him tightly.

*   *   *

Half an hour later, after seeing her grandfather to his room, Lucy went to Geoffrey. He was waiting, sitting up in the bed in the firelit room. He held out a hand, his fingers closing lovingly over hers.

"Is it done?"

"Yes. Oh, Geoffrey, it was so beautiful."

"Then it's over, my darling. You're safe, you've been united with your grandfather—and you have me."

She smiled. "Yes, I have you."

"Bolt the door and come to bed," he said softly.

She stared. "But, your wounded arm—"

"A man doesn't make love with his arm. So come to bed."

She went to turn the key in the door, and then returned to him, slowly stepping out of her clothes until she was naked. She climbed into the bed, and leaned over to put her lips to the pulse at his throat.

"I love you so much, Geoffrey," she whispered, lowering her lips a little to kiss his chest.

He closed his eyes with pleasure as she lowered her lips still further; then he thought of something and looked swiftly at the unlit candle by the bed, but it didn't flicker into life.

He smiled then, and lay back as Lucy's kisses moved down to that part of his anatomy which was already springing out in urgent readiness. His breath escaped on a long, slow sigh, and his fingers moved luxuriously in her hair as her lips enclosed him.

On Twelfth Night, the sixth of January, a highway robbery and murder were reported in the Bristol newspapers. A lone horseman was set upon at a crossroads outside the city, and when he attempted to escape, he was shot and left for dead. Papers on his body revealed him to be Mr. Robert Waverly Trevallion.

Nine months to the day after Lucy became the Countess of St. Athan, she was brought to bed with the daughter she'd conceived in the Burgundian barn. They called her Emily.